KNIVES
HAVE EDGES
A RINEHART SUSPENSE NOVEL

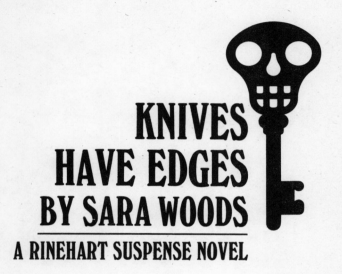

KNIVES HAVE EDGES
BY SARA WOODS

A RINEHART SUSPENSE NOVEL

HOLT, RINEHART AND WINSTON
NEW YORK CHICAGO SAN FRANCISCO

Any work of fiction whose characters were of a uniform
excellence would rightly be condemned—by that fact if by
no other—as being incredibly dull. Therefore no excuse
can be considered necessary for the villainy or folly of the
people in this book. It seems extremely unlikely that any
one of them should resemble a real person alive or dead.
Any such resemblance is completely unintentional and
without malice.

CONTENTS

I cannot tell; things must be as they may: men may sleep, and they may have their throats about them at that time; and, some say, knives have edges.

KING HENRY V, Act II, Sc. i.

FRIDAY, 19th MARCH

1

"What a beautiful word, darling," said Meg Hamilton. "Embracery," she repeated in a thoughtful tone, and gave her companion a speculative look, so that he said hastily:

"It doesn't mean anything like that."

She didn't question his interpretation. "What does it mean then?"

"Attempting to corrupt a juror," said Antony Maitland, as repressively as he could. He was giving her lunch at Astroff's, which is an easy walk from the Law Courts; but the trouble was with Meg, you never knew what she would say next.

"You won't allow me any illusions, will you." She sighed as she spoke and raised her eyes to his reproachfully, so that a solicitor by the name of Watterson who was dining at the next table, and who had himself briefed Maitland on occasion, thought indignantly, if vaguely, that it was a shame to treat the little woman like that. "I was just thinking," said Meg wistfully, "what *fun* you must have."

"I know . . . orgies in the Inner Temple. It's an attractive idea, but I don't think Uncle Nick would stand for it."

"What a shame. But whatever it means," said Meg, suddenly doubling back in her tracks, "it doesn't explain why you're in such a filthy humor."

There was a pause while Maitland considered the fairness of this attack. "Well, if I am," he said after a moment, "it's really no wonder. I mean, there we were, into the home stretch—"

"That doesn't sound a very suitable metaphor, darling."

"If I must be precise, we'd finished with the witnesses; there were just the final speeches to come. And then one of the jurors had to go and tell Halloran that someone had tried to bribe him. And that means—"

"Back to square one," said Meg, putting her elbows on the table and gazing at him soulfully. Antony nodded gloomily.

"It wouldn't be so bad if we could get straight on with it—"

"Why can't you? It's only a matter of empaneling a fresh jury, isn't it?"

Her sudden air of alert intelligence did nothing to placate him. "I dare say you've got ambitions to play Portia, Meg, but must you rehearse the part while I'm eating soup?" he inquired unsympathetically.

"I haven't. I think it's a stupid play. But why can't you get on with your case?" she insisted.

"Halloran wanted an adjournment. I could see his point all right, he's got that fraudulent conversion business coming up next week and it sounds pretty complicated. But it puts my list all to hell."

"What is the trial about anyway?"

"Armed robbery."

"Well . . . not that I want to sound unsympathetic," said Meg, with a sidelong glance at Mr. Watterson, of whose reactions she was perfectly aware, "but I'd have thought if anyone was fed up about the delay it would be the—the defendant."

"Swaine?" (At most, he thought, it meant the postponement of a prison sentence; would his client think that a good thing, or would he rather get it over with?)

"Is that his name? How very lover-like and Arcadian." She sat back to let the waiter take her soup plate, and Antony watched her with the amusement that was never very far below the surface of his thoughts. Meg had really changed very little in the years he had known her: offstage she still wore her dark hair twisted round her head in a long plait; and being small and slightly built she could play the *gamine* as readily as the *grande dame*. The years in the public eye had taught her to hide a forthright nature under a certain amount of affectation, just as she had learned to dress so elegantly that you very rarely noticed what she was wearing. He wondered now what she would have made of Swaine . . . a tough, if ever he'd seen one. But for all her caprice she was a realist, as he knew well enough; he had a suspicion she might prefer the genuine article to the bowdlerized version her imagination had conjured up.

The waiter finished his task and departed. Meg looked down at her plate, and said with appreciation, "Darling, this looks marvelous." Antony picked up his knife and fork and asked idly:

"Why didn't Roger come with you?"

"He had a Luncheon in the City." Her tone was impressive enough to convey a very vivid picture of the Lord Mayor in full regalia, a procession of flunkeys bearing huge salvers, each with its silver cover . . . "So I thought it would be a good chance—" She broke off there and gave him a deprecating look, but her eyes were alight with laughter.

"I might have known you were up to something," said Antony, resigned.

"But, darling, I only want to ask you . . . eat this delicious —this *thing*," Meg encouraged him. "Perhaps you'll feel better then."

"You've taken away my appetite."

"I didn't think anything could. Jenny always says—"

"For that matter, why isn't Jenny here?"

"Because I thought . . . we both thought when I told her . . . that perhaps it would be better if I saw you alone."

"Yes, I see. The presence of my wife, or your husband, would cramp your style, I suppose."

"I don't think that's at all a nice thing to say." Her voice, her whole attitude, were expressive of extreme dejection; which was comic when you remembered that she had made her name, when she first came to London, by a particularly horrifying portrayal of Lady Macbeth.

"It wasn't meant to be," he told her. "I say, Meg, *need* you play to the gallery?"

"That fat man at the next table?" Her interest was revived immediately. "Do you suppose he thinks we're married?"

"He probably knows I am, and he's never met Jenny."

"Do you know him? How awful!" Her contrite air could have done nothing to dispel the illusion which for some reason she seemed bent on conveying. "He probably thinks you beat me."

"If Roger had any sense—"

"Roger thinks I'm perfect," said Meg with dignity. She took a mouthful of fish and chewed it thoughtfully. "At least," she added, her natural honesty getting the better of her, "he says I would be if only I wouldn't make him eat porridge."

"What on earth has your breakfast menu got to do with anything?" asked Antony, exasperated.

"Nothing at all. I never said it did."

"Well, you'd better tell me the worst. Does Roger know . . . whatever it is you want to ask me?"

"Of course he does." She found his eyes fixed on her with an expression that was anything but credulous. "He thinks it's just a nonsense," she admitted.

"And isn't it?"

"Yes, in a way. I don't think Jon has anything to worry about, but it's no good my saying so. If you would just see him—"

"For the love of heaven, start at the beginning. Who is John?"

"Jonathan Kellaway."

"I've heard of him," said Maitland, frowning.

"Yes, of course you have. He's playing Gregory in *A Kind of Praise* at the Buckingham."

"Oh, *that* chap." He thought about it for a moment. "It's a good play."

"It is."

"But that doesn't explain what's wrong with Kellaway. Or why—you'd better answer this first, because it's more important—why it matters?"

"Oh, don't be silly, Antony!" said Meg, stepping for a moment outside the part she had chosen. "Because *he's* good too. Really good."

"You mean, as an actor."

"Of course I do. I don't know anything about his private life."

"Don't you?" said Maitland skeptically.

"Well, only the usual gossip. He's in love with an iceberg, and Ana says—" She stopped short, and if it hadn't been so unlikely he'd have thought the look she darted at him showed a certain amount of embarrassment. He said precisely:

"But it is not, I imagine, about his love affairs that you wish to consult me."

"Darling, you looked *exactly* like Uncle Nick when you said that."

"Never mind! Are you, or are you not going to tell me—?"

"That's why I'm here. I don't think he has a thing to worry about, but he does and it's getting on his nerves. So it's really a good thing about this embracery business, because it means you have a free afternoon." Having said this she went on with her meal, apparently under the impression that no further explanation was necessary. It was touch and go for a moment whether he gave way to his irritation, but then the humor of the situation struck him and he began to laugh.

"All right, Meg. You've had your fun, now tell me—"

"If you think it's fun to have you sitting there, scowling at me like a thundercloud."

"I'm sorry. Anyway, you've had your revenge, because Watterson's opinion of me is dropping by the minute."

"Yes, that's what I thought," said Meg, more cheerfully.

"And whether I shall ever see another brief from his firm—"

"You don't have to worry about that, darling. You're so clever!" Meg told him, with a look of spaniel-like devotion. She placed her knife and fork neatly together, and prepared to become businesslike. "Jon lives in one of those big houses in Gilcliffe Gardens; an apartment, I suppose you'd call it, it isn't self-contained. On Tuesday night there was a fire in the basement where the landlord lives, a man called Dakins."

"I saw that in last night's paper, but it said—"

"They found Mr. Dakins's body in the living-room," said Meg. Unconsciously, perhaps, her voice dropped dramatically, so that the bald statement seemed to take on a significance quite beyond its content. "No one knows how he died."

"Then what has it to do with Kellaway?" asked Antony, declining to be impressed.

"Nothing at all, except that the police questioned him yesterday; and the other tenants too, I suppose. And he's quite convinced they think he did it."

"Did what?"

"Set the place on fire deliberately to burn the body. That would be manslaughter at least, wouldn't it?"

"For heaven's sake . . . don't you know any of the circumstances?"

"Not really."

"Well . . . who questioned him, for instance? One of the Divisional people?"

"He said it was a detective-inspector from Scotland Yard," said Meg, watching his expression. "That makes a difference, doesn't it?"

"It might do," he admitted cautiously. "Do you know who it was?"

"Well, not his *name,* darling." From her tone it seemed she regarded the question as unreasonable. "Jon said he was a very disapproving sort of man."

"Informative!"

"Anyway," said Meg, wisely ignoring the comment, "it means there's something up, doesn't it? I mean, they wouldn't call in Scotland Yard unless they thought there was something wrong."

"Perhaps not. That doesn't mean Kellaway has anything to worry about, unless—"

"I told him that," she interrupted eagerly. "And I told him what I've heard you say: that in the absence of some tangible evidence the police wouldn't start suspecting anyone unless they had a motive. I must say," she added reflectively, "it didn't seem to cheer him much."

"Well, what am I supposed to do about it?"

"I thought—after all, darling, you are rather well known—I thought he'd listen to *you.*"

He was silent for quite a long time before he said, "The thing about motive works both ways, you know." This might have been condemned as rather less than lucid, but Meg seemed to have no difficulty in following his thought.

"I realize that. He might be worried because there was a reason—"

"Or because he really has something to hide. And don't, Meg, don't tell me 'he wouldn't do a thing like that' because

6

for one thing we don't know what—if anything—he's being suspected of."

"Darling, I haven't known you for ten years—"

"Twelve," said Antony.

"Well, twelve, then. I haven't known you so long without learning that's one thing I must *never* say. But I don't know if I made it clear to you,"—she was suddenly in earnest—"Jon's worth helping."

"Because he's a good actor?"

"That's not such a bad reason. But I think—I'm trying to be honest with you, Antony—I think, as far as you ever know about anyone else, as a person too."

"I see. And if this paragon is suffering from nothing more nor less than a guilty conscience?"

"Mightn't he still be worth helping?"

"I suppose . . . but there's nothing I can do, Meg. Damn it all, I don't even know the fellow."

"That doesn't matter. I told him—"

"Does he want my advice?"

"He needs it, darling. Please don't be difficult." She paused, to see how he was taking this appeal, and for the first time began to doubt her ability to persuade him. Maitland was tall, with a manner that inclined to the casual, and dark hair that was just springing up into its normal disorder after being flattened in court under his wig. The humorous look was so much a part of him that she almost took it for granted, but it was absent now, his eyes were serious, even a little worried. "Jon will do what I say because he thinks he ought to be grateful to me," said Meg. "Well, I did suggest him to Ossy for the part—it's a dreadfully difficult one to cast, you know—only, of course, he wouldn't have got it if Ossy hadn't agreed he was suitable. And it's turned out so well; he'd done a lot of good work before, but he hadn't really got a *name*. I can't bear to see everything spoiled just because he's got the jitters . . . and perhaps about nothing at all."

"What does Roger think about it?"

"He said Jon was making a mountain out of a molehill, and I shouldn't bother you when you're busy," said Meg. Her tone made a virtue of her candor.

"Then, don't you think—?"

"No, darling, I don't. I'm not asking much, Antony, it needn't take you half an hour. If he's worried about nothing, tell him so. If not . . . well, you could advise him what he ought to do, couldn't you?"

"If he cares to listen. I don't like it, Meg."

"You weren't always so—so awkward," she told him. "The first time I brought Roger to see you—"

"That was different. You were crying all over the living-room carpet, and I couldn't see any other way of stopping you."

"Of all the revolting, treacherous . . . well, perhaps I did cry a little. If it will help at all, I'll shed a few tears for you now," she added, and the impish note was back in her voice again. "I can when I want, you know."

That was probably all that was needed to complete Watterson's disenchantment, but oddly enough Maitland made no protest. It was obvious that Meg was taking his agreement for granted, and he realized as she spoke that he had already made up his mind. She was, at times, the most maddening of creatures, but she wouldn't make a request like this without good reason. He was inclined to trust her judgment, but she might be wrong about Kellaway; and if she was it would be as well to know it. On the whole, it seemed worth risking a snub.

"You'd better tell him to come and see me in chambers," he said.

"Oh, but . . . that's so impersonal. Besides, he might catch sight of—what's his name?—Uncle Nick's clerk."

"Mallory."

"That's right. He might catch sight of Mr. Mallory and be frightened to death. I know I was the first time."

"I don't think Mallory altogether approves of actresses."

"Well, Jon . . . no, that won't do at all."

"What do you suggest then?"

"He's staying at Taylor's, hardly out of your way. Couldn't you—?"

"Was the house so badly damaged?"

"No, but there was the smell of burning you see." Meg wrin-

8

kled her nose in an expression of distaste. "Jon said he couldn't stand it."

"At least," said Antony, thinking it out, "it would keep me out of Uncle Nick's way for the afternoon."

"What's wrong with Uncle Nick?"

"He's going to the States next week. He doesn't like the idea, and he doesn't like flying."

"Poor darling."

"He is not a darling, poor or otherwise," Maitland corrected her.

"Anyway, if he's feeling cross you'll be much better out of his way."

"So I shall." He resolutely banished the thought of all that might have been achieved if he'd spent this unexpectedly free afternoon in chambers, and smiled at her. "All right, Meg, arrange it as you like."

2

Taylor's Hotel is comfortable, but not in the luxury class, and not quite so conveniently situated as Meg would have led him to suppose. Still, it was not much more than fifteen minutes' walk from the restaurant. Maitland took it briskly—there was a stiff wind that didn't encourage loitering—but he had time to savor his unexpected freedom (the problem of the retrial, which had loomed so large when he left court that morning, was already assuming a less urgent aspect; it could be dealt with when it arose, after all), and to meditate briefly on his own motives in agreeing to Meg's request and the possible difficulties of the coming interview.

Jonathan Kellaway's room on the fourth floor was not very large, and had a complicated view of roofs and chimney pots. He flung the door wide when Maitland knocked, and backed away from it with an inviting gesture.

"It's good of you to come," he said. His voice had a doubtful note, and Antony gave him a grin in which there was a certain amount of fellow feeling.

It was three months since he had seen the play at the Buckingham Theatre, but Kellaway's voice seemed immediately familiar to him; it was deep and very expressive. His features too . . . but there the familiarity ended. Jonathan was a little shorter than he appeared on stage, a thin man, almost startlingly fair and of something over middle height, with elegant, nervous hands and features which, in repose, had a suggestion of the sardonic. He was carelessly and rather shabbily dressed in slacks and a dark green corduroy jacket (the stage-character, on the other hand, had been neat and conventionally attired), but by some trick or other the colored handkerchief which he had knotted at his throat instead of a tie stayed obediently in place through all his gyrations.

There was nothing reposeful about his manner now. Maitland went in and shut the door, but did not attempt to move any farther into the room. "I think I should say, it's good of you to see me; I've only Meg's side of the story—"

Kellaway's relief was as blatant as his doubt had been a moment before; perhaps he found the rather diffident note in his visitor's voice reassuring. Even so, he interrupted challengingly: "I suppose you've come to tell me I've nothing to worry about."

"Not exactly," said Maitland.

He might have saved his breath. The other man went on as if he had not spoken. "How d'you think I can help worrying, things being what they are? There's the police . . . *I* don't know what they're thinking. There's the reporters . . . a damned herd of jackals, if you want my opinion. And Meg, telling me to keep calm." He flung out his hands despairingly. "Calm!" he said.

"I don't think you can talk about a herd of jackals," said Antony in a considering tone. Kellaway looked at him resentfully.

"It's all very well for you, with nothing in the world to do but get up in court and heckle other people."

This didn't seem to Maitland to be quite a fair description of his activities, but he let it pass without comment. "The right person for you to talk to, you know, would be your solicitor."

"Good God, what do you take me for?" Kellaway demanded.

"You've just answered that yourself: a worried man."

"Yes, but . . . my solicitor. It's easy enough to *say*," Jonathan admitted, "and it always sounds so grand. Trust deeds, and title deeds, and family heirlooms, and marriage settlements." His accompanying gesture was extraordinarily evocative, so that Antony could almost imagine cobwebs across the window, a clerk with a quill pen engrossing on heavy parchment, and a pile of black japanned deed boxes in the corner. "I've never had any affairs that needed a solicitor," said Kellaway. "I don't even know one, so far as I remember."

"Well, if you'll tell me what the trouble seems to be, at least I can advise you whether you need one now." They might have been talking, he thought, hiding his amusement, of a pound of tea, or a bottle of cough medicine . . .

"We'd better sit down." Jonathan moved aside so that Maitland could take the chair near the window. For himself, he dragged forward the rather spindly-looking stool from the dressing-table, and sat down with his hands clasped round one knee. "I never thought you'd come," he said, suddenly confidential. "If you did . . . well, never mind that."

"Take your time," Antony told him, making his own translation of an apparently inconsequent remark.

"Didn't Meg tell you—?"

"Nothing of consequence."

"Well, at least . . . about the fire."

"Yes, she told me that."

"And they found Dakins. Of course, he was dead, he'd been pretty badly burned. But then the police . . . they're obviously suspicious."

"Of you?"

"That's what I meant." He had to unclasp his hands again to express his incredulity. "They say it was arson, they've told me that much at least. Someone set the fire, and made no attempt to disguise the fact. As to how Dakins died, if they know they aren't saying."

"Could the fire have killed him?"

"I don't think . . . it was intense, but not very widespread." He hesitated, and then added in a rush, "If someone killed him, and set the place on fire to hide the fact—"

"Is that what the police think?"

11

"They haven't *said* so."

"You'd better start at the beginning and tell me what happened. This was on Tuesday?"

"Wednesday morning, really. Past midnight."

"Was Dakins alone in the house?"

"Yes, he was alone. That's what the police keep on about, you see. Why wasn't I at home?"

"Well, why weren't you?"

"I'd gone for a walk. Look, I went home, there was nothing wrong then. I walked from the tube station, and when I got outside the house I just didn't feel like going in so I went on walking. That was . . . about twelve-thirty, I should think. Someone called the fire brigade at one-fifteen, a neighbor, I expect. The circus was in full swing when I got back."

"What time was that?"

"Two o'clock . . . half past two. I don't remember exactly. After all," he added defensively, "it isn't a crime to go for a walk."

"No," said Maitland. His voice was carefully expressionless. "Have you told the police where you went?"

"So far as I remember. I wasn't *going* anywhere, just walking."

"And is there any confirmation of the time you got back from the theater?"

"None," said Jonathan, and looked suddenly mulish.

"Well, on the face of it you don't need an alibi. Unless . . . had you any reason to want this man Dakins dead?"

"No reason in the world. He was rather a nice little chap, really."

"How long had you known him?"

"I've had his first floor front for five years, on and off."

"What about the other people in the house? Do you think they might have known Dakins well?"

"I've no idea."

"But he had a life of his own, I suppose, besides renting rooms. Friends . . . and perhaps enemies."

For some reason, Kellaway seemed taken aback by this. "I don't know why you should think—"

"Tell me, did the police mention murder?"

12

"No, but it was obvious . . . they wouldn't leave me alone," Kellaway complained.

"Even so, I wonder if you've really anything to worry about."

The gesture that silenced him was imperative. "Suppose someone did kill Dakins."

"Well . . . suppose it. On what you've told me—" He broke off there, got to his feet, and went on rather abruptly. "I'm not asking for your confidence. You may have to put up with a certain amount of inconvenience for a week or two, but when they find you had no reason to want Dakins out of the way the police will lose interest."

Jonathan looked up at him. "You're quite right," he said unexpectedly. "I haven't told you . . . quite everything."

"I see."

"What I *have* told you is true." He got up in his turn and went to the window, and stood looking out. "This isn't anything to do with Dakins really."

"Are you sure you want to tell me?"

"Yes, of course." This was said with a touch of impatience, but then he added, as if it explained everything, "You're not at all what I expected, you know."

For that matter, Maitland thought, neither are you. On the stage, Jonathan Kellaway had impressed him with his capacity for stillness; now, seen at close quarters, he was vividly alive and full of restless energy. "Does that make a difference?" he asked.

"All the difference in the world," Jonathan assured him. "If you're sure you don't mind listening—" There was a rapping on the door, and he broke off and looked at it rather blankly. "Now, who—?"

"Hadn't you better see?"

"Yes, of course." He strode across the room and flung the door open. "Oh . . . Keith!" he said. "Come in." He turned as the newcomer obeyed what sounded to be a somewhat peremptory order. "My cousin, Keith Lindsay. This is Mr. Maitland, Keith. He's a barrister."

Looking from one of them to the other, Antony had the momentary impression that his eyes were playing tricks. Lind-

13

say was as dark as his cousin was fair; otherwise, the physical resemblance between the two men was almost uncanny. There were differences in dress: Keith wore an ordinary lounge suit, not well cut, not very new, but carefully pressed. And here was the stillness that Jonathan so notably lacked. Which was just as well; already the room was beginning to feel crowded, and with two such restless spirits . . .

Lindsay murmured something in response to the introduction. His tone was casual, but his eyes were alert and a little wary. "Does that mean . . . has anything else happened, Jon?" he asked.

"Not really. I was just telling him about Dakins."

"Well . . . I suppose it's as well to get legal advice."

"We were trying to decide," said Antony, in response to a surprisingly helpless look from Jonathan, "whether it would be a good idea for Mr. Kellaway to consult a solicitor. I'm only here as a friend . . . a friend of a friend, really."

"Well, I don't know—" Lindsay had come a little farther into the room now. "I've seen you in court, Mr. Maitland. And I've read about you, of course, from time to time."

"I see." His tone revealed nothing but a polite bewilderment, but Jonathan, watching him, was conscious of a sort of mental retreat. He said quickly:

"Keith's a crime reporter. On the *Courier*."

"I see," said Maitland again. He hadn't liked the reminder of the publicity that had sometimes attended his affairs; and he was also wondering, though rather vaguely, whether this meant that Kellaway counted his cousin among the jackals. "In that case, I imagine, Mr. Lindsay is just as well qualified to advise you—"

"Rather better, just at the moment," said Keith. "That's what I came to tell you, Jon. The police have been talking to Father William."

"Why shouldn't they?"

"They were asking him"—he glanced at Maitland, and then looked back at his cousin again—"they were asking him about Beth."

This didn't mean anything to Antony, of course, but it was obvious that it did to Kellaway. Oddly enough, he made no direct reply, unless his overwrought but strangely ineffectual gesture could be regarded as a comment. Maitland said hopefully, "You want to talk. I'd better be getting along," but both his companions ignored the suggestion. Keith turned and looked at him directly and asked:

"Has Jon told you—?"

"I was going to," Kellaway interrupted. "I haven't had time."

"Well, from what Father William says, the police were taking far too much interest." Lindsay spoke more forcefully now, as though he had made up his mind that perhaps, after all, the stranger might be trusted.

"Who is Father William?" Maitland asked.

"Who—? Oh, he's a jeweler," Keith told him, not very informatively.

"Everyone calls him that," said Jonathan. "And he's more than just a jeweler . . . an artist, really." His hands moved delicately, indicating, perhaps, the intricacy of the work. "My father was his partner, and since he died—" He broke off as there came again a tapping at the door, but this time he turned to open it without any hesitation at all, only a certain impatience. "Old Home Week," he observed as he did so, but the words trailed into silence when he saw the two men on the threshold.

Both were obviously members of the police force, though only the younger of the pair was in uniform. The older man was heavily built, and moved forward with something of the suggestion of an irresistible force, saying as he did so, "Perhaps it would be better if we came in, Mr. Kellaway."

Jonathan backed away reluctantly. "There isn't really room," he said. The detective's eyes went past him then; rested for a moment, indifferently, on Keith's face, and moved on to Antony's.

"My business is with Mr. Kellaway," he pointed out. Evidently he was a man who scorned subtlety.

"What business, Inspector?" said Jon, behind him.

"I should prefer to discuss that in private, sir."

"Yes, but doesn't what I prefer come into it, too? This is my cousin, Keith Lindsay. And—"

The inspector nodded curtly. "I recognize Mr. Maitland. If you wish me to speak plainly—"

"I do." It was an odd thing that now, when for the first time Jonathan showed something approaching calmness, Maitland was aware as he had not been before of the depth of his disquiet.

"In that case I must warn you—" The fears had some substance, then. Antony glanced at Lindsay, whose eyes were fixed somberly on his cousin's face, and turned back to the detective again.

"If that's how it is, Inspector, you must give Mr. Kellaway time to consult a solicitor."

"I imagine he is quite aware of his rights, since he has had the benefit of your advice, Mr. Maitland," said the detective stolidly.

"He'll be given every opportunity." The younger of the two policemen spoke for the first time. "Have to ask you, sir," he added, looking at Kellaway, "to accompany us to the station."

Keith Lindsay said impulsively, "Look here—" And then, rather helplessly, "Are you arresting him?"

Nobody replied to this. Kellaway said, "This business of a solicitor—" His voice was tight now, his hands jammed deep in his pockets as though they might betray him.

"I'll take care of that, Jon," Lindsay told him.

"All right then." He jerked his head in Antony's direction. "*He*'ll know."

Maitland was silent for a moment when they had gone. "Don't you know any solicitors either?" he said at last.

"This would need someone special, wouldn't it? Someone with a criminal practice."

"That would be best."

"Jon said you'd tell me." But for all his apparent compliance, there was an underlying hostility in Lindsay's tone.

"Well, there's Watterson's." Antony's mind escaped, briefly, to the restaurant that lunch time, and Meg sitting opposite him, half mischievous, half in earnest. "They're a big firm, and quite used to this sort of thing." He pulled an old envelope out of his pocket, and sat down at the dressing-table to write. "There's Paul Collingwood, more or less a one-man show, but he's very capable." That took him back a little further, to the adjournment of the court that morning; Collingwood was Swaine's solicitor . . . and the only thing I've got against him is the fact that he's far more handsome than any member of the legal profession has a right to be. And that his managing clerk—what's the fellow's name? Falkner—is a Uriah Heep type, who always gets my back up, one way or another. "Or Armstrong, Horton and Holbrook; if you go to them it would be Geoffrey Horton you want. Any one of those," he said, and drew a line under what he had written. "I hope you can read it."

"I expect I can." Lindsay eyed the scrap of paper a little doubtfully. "I'm grateful," he added formally. Maitland said, with an irritation that surprised him:

"There are plenty of others, you know. You don't have to take anyone on my recommendation."

"It's Jon's affair, after all." His eyes were hard, almost accusing. But then Maitland thought he must have been wrong about that, when Lindsay relaxed and said easily, "In case you really are worried, he'll be all right."

"How do you know that?"

"He always is." But he pretended not to notice his companion's inquiring look; and Maitland went away in an unsatisfied frame of mind.

3

As a general rule, Sir Nicholas Harding's chambers in the Inner Temple were peaceful enough, if only because old Mr. Mallory had a way of dealing firmly with his employer's more spectacular outbursts of temperament. On this particular afternoon, however, Maitland was conscious as soon as he went into the hall of a simmering atmosphere that might, he felt, erupt at any moment into pure frenzy.

He wasn't particularly surprised. Sir Nicholas had agreed in a moment of weakness to address The Palmers' Club in New York, and was now about to redeem his promise. In the meantime, however, he had conceived what his nephew considered an unreasoning dislike for the whole project, over and above his general unwillingness to embark on anything that savored of the unusual.

When Antony went into his room he was engaged in what seemed to be a treasure hunt through the drawers of his desk, but he abandoned this activity with an air of relief in favor of a blow by blow account of the events in court that morning. On the whole Maitland was glad to detach his mind from Jon Kellaway's problems and return to those of his own client and the affair of the incorruptible juror. It was, of course, Mr. Justice Conroy's handling of the matter that interested Sir Nicholas, and he nodded approvingly as the narrative progressed. "Collingwood was furious," Maitland concluded. "And in a way that surprised me, I've always thought him an imperturbable sort of chap. But the next jury will have one hell of a time; being dogged by hordes of policemen, they'll probably bring in a verdict of 'guilty' out of sheer spite. Anyway, it's pretty obvious that whatever was done, our client was in it up to the neck."

A slight spasm, which might have been of pain, contorted Sir Nicholas's features. He was a tall, fair man with an authoritative manner of which he was quite unconscious; good-looking enough to make the word "handsome" reasonably appropriate when it was applied to him by the less restrained members of the journalistic profession; irascible enough to resent the description both bitterly and vocally. But now, in spite of his distress (for he affected an extreme aversion to slang), his protest had an unexpected mildness.

"There's no sense in blaming the man for trying to take a short cut to freedom."

"No, but . . . I'm surprised at Swaine."

Sir Nicholas allowed himself a touch of sarcasm. "An exemplary character, no doubt."

"Well, not exactly. I only meant, he doesn't run with the pack."

"The attempt at bribery was made, however."

"Oh, yes. A man called Bassett. Works for the railway, a ticket clerk, something like that. Come to think of it, he's the one that deserves our sympathy. He was obviously scared stiff."

"Perhaps with reason."

"No, I don't think so. Swaine isn't a bad chap really—"

"I seem to remember," said Sir Nicholas thoughtfully, "something about a gun."

"Yes, but he didn't use it. And he might bash somebody in a temper, but not in cold blood, not for revenge."

"You said he was remanded in custody," his uncle pointed out.

"So he was."

"But you feel his friends are likely to share the—the gentleness of his nature. You may be right," said Sir Nicholas, unconvinced.

"Anyway, the police will take care of Bassett, don't you think?" Antony hesitated, not expecting an answer, wondering whether it would be a good idea to tell Uncle Nick . . . but what was there to tell him about Kellaway, after all? He glanced round the room, noting the evidences of disorder: the contents of the desk strewn haphazard on the hearth-rug; a cupboard door open, and the papers spilling out; the bookshelves even untidier than was normal. "Looking for something?" he asked.

"Isn't that obvious? My passport," said Sir Nicholas in the tone of one who describes an Act of God for which he can be expected to take no responsibility, "has been mislaid."

"Yes, but why look for it in the bookcase?" asked Antony reasonably. "Doesn't Mallory know where it is?" he added in a hurry, as he caught his uncle's eye.

"He says he gave it to me a week ago."

"Then it will be at home." He sounded positive enough, but he only hoped it was true. The prospect of speeding Sir Nicholas on his journey was bad enough; the idea of his being kept in England by a mischance for which he would inevitably blame his nearest and dearest was too horrible to contemplate.

"Do you really think—?"

"I'm sure of it."

"I hope you're right." Sir Nicholas swiveled his chair so that he could regard the chaos on the hearth-rug. "I wonder how on earth all these things got into the desk in the first place," he said, and again his question might have concerned some matter quite beyond his control. "It seems so very unlikely that they will ever go back again."

Antony resigned himself. "Let's try," he suggested. And then, with more interest, "I say, Uncle Nick, here's that proof you swore Bellerby had never sent you with the Cowper brief. . . ."

4

The house in Kempenfeldt Square was quiet when Maitland reached it that evening, and for once Gibbs, a disagreeable old man of venerable appearance who presided over Sir Nicholas's household and performed—when the spirit moved him—the duties of butler, was not hovering in the hall. Antony went upstairs to his own quarters, thankful that his return had gone unnoticed.

His association with Sir Nicholas went back much further than his call to the Bar and entry (after an appropriate interval) into his learned relative's chambers. He had lived with his uncle since he was thirteen, and he and Jenny still had their own flat at the top of the house; a temporary arrangement, hallowed by time, which had started with strict procedural rules, all of which had long since been forgotten.

If the plan had originally been a makeshift one, it was nonetheless comfortable, and perhaps that was Jenny's doing, a reflection of her own serenity. Now, when he went into the living-room it was warm and tranquil, the curtains drawn close against the wind-swept darkness. He went across to the fireplace and stood looking down, with one hand on the mantel. "Do you think we shall survive till next Tuesday?" he said.

Jenny had come in from the kitchen and was pouring sherry. "Is Uncle Nick being tiresome?" she asked. But she knew the answer perfectly well, he didn't have to tell her. "It isn't long now," she added consolingly.

"He's lost his passport, so perhaps he won't go at all," said Antony, declining to be comforted. "He says Mallory has mislaid it, and you can imagine the reaction to that."

"It's in his briefcase," said Jenny, coming back to the fire. He turned his head and regarded her with satisfaction. "I thought you might be early tonight; Meg said you weren't in court."

"I was delayed. Didn't Meg tell you that too?" His tone had only the least touch of sarcasm, for which, perhaps, he might be forgiven. He took his glass and set it down by the clock.

"Yes, but . . . did it take you all the afternoon, Antony?"

"I went back to chambers after I'd talked to Kellaway, and then I stayed on after Uncle Nick left to try to sort out the papers in that breach of contract case Mallory has saddled me with; it's a complicated affair, and I didn't get very far with it."

"Never mind." Jenny sank down onto the sofa with an exaggerated sigh of pleasure. The lamplight tangled strands of gold among her brown curls. "It's Friday," she said.

"So it is."

"Tell me about Jon Kellaway."

"There's nothing to tell you really. The police arrived while I was there, it's up to his solicitor now."

"You mean, he's been arrested?"

"They cautioned him, and they took him to the station. I should think that probably followed."

"I was wondering, Antony . . . did you believe him?"

"I don't even know what he's been charged with, love, so the question doesn't arise. In any case, he didn't tell me . . . we'd better forget it, Jenny, I only went because I wanted to make sure Meg wasn't getting into any mischief."

"I wonder . . . never mind," said Jenny again, putting her head on one side as though that helped her to see her husband in better perspective. "Antony . . . why do you suppose Uncle Nick said he'd go to America?"

"To address The Palmers on the History of English Law. And if you mean, why?" he added, not very lucidly, "because the chap who asked him gave him a damned good dinner first."

"He seems awfully—awfully put out about it."

"That's just the thought of flying. I think he envisaged a nice, leisurely trip, but Mallory tied him up with so much work there wasn't time to go by sea. Anyway, I dare say he'd have been sick. He'll enjoy himself all right once he gets there, though I wouldn't be so sure his audience will get much enlightenment from his discourse."

"Why not?"

"I doubt if he'll get past Edward I," said Antony gloomily. "Last time I looked at his notes he was bogged down in the Welsh marches. But I suppose that doesn't matter, as long as he doesn't start quoting Johnson at them."

"Why shouldn't he?"

" 'I am willing to love all mankind,' " said Antony solemnly, " 'except an American.' And don't tell me he doesn't really think that, love, because you know as well as I do that wouldn't stop him saying it."

Jenny laughed. "Perhaps I'd better hide his passport after all," she suggested.

Two things happened while they were clearing away the dinner things. The phone rang, and Antony went to take the call; as he picked up the receiver someone knocked on the outer door, and he heard Jenny crossing the hall to open it.

"What," said Geoffrey Horton's voice in his ear, "are you up to now?"

There were various responses he might have made, none of them quite satisfactory. "How do you mean?" he inquired cautiously.

"Your friend Kellaway—" Geoffrey began. He sounded a trifle querulous. "Did you tell him to consult me?"

"I gave him your name, among others." For some reason he was surprised by the development, and not altogether pleased, although Geoffrey was a close friend. "What's happened?"

"He's under arrest for the murder of a man called Dakins. I called you as soon as I could get away. He wants to see you," said Horton. He seemed vaguely pleased about this, like a prophet who saw one of his more depressing prognostications being fulfilled.

If Geoffrey had had no dinner, that probably explained why he was feeling out of humor. "Well, but—" said Antony.

"I've fixed it for tomorrow." Horton interrupted him without ceremony. "I'll call for you at ten o'clock."

"You haven't told me—"

"It's a nasty mess, if you want my opinion. But if you've

made up your mind to interfere I suppose it's no use trying to stop you," said Geoffrey unjustly. And suppressed Maitland's protests ruthlessly by saying "Good night" and cutting the connection sharply.

Antony turned from the writing-table to find that Jenny had disappeared with the last of the crockery, and Roger Farrell was settled in the wing chair at the other side of the hearth. He had been too preoccupied to hear the visitor come in, but now he realized that he had been half-expecting him.

"I've just left Meg at the theater, and came to make our apologies," said Roger. He nodded toward the telephone. "Having trouble?" he asked.

"Geoffrey, feeling cross."

"What about?" asked Farrell quickly. Then, "I'm sorry. I only meant . . . not Kellaway?"

"I'm afraid so. He's been arrested." He paused, watching Roger's expression. "I didn't realize . . . is he a particular friend of yours?"

"Good God, no!" He broke off to consider this, and then went on more quietly, "I didn't mean to imply . . . well, I rather like him really; but to do Meg justice, she didn't think it was serious."

"He's been arrested for murder. Are you assuming he's guilty?"

"I don't know anything about it."

"Neither do I," said Maitland.

"What are you going to do?"

"I seem to be committed to seeing him tomorrow. After that, it's Geoffrey's worry; guilty or innocent, I suppose Kellaway will need defending, but not necessarily by me."

"I see."

"What's on your mind, Roger?"

"Meg."

"Very proper."

Farrell smiled at that. He was a stockbroker, and in the two years since his marriage he had taken with surprising mildness to becoming, in the eyes of the theater-going public, "Meg Hamilton's husband," but it was unlikely that anyone who knew him well ever thought of him in this supporting role. He was a sturdily built man, very near Maitland in age, with blue eyes, straight, sandy hair, and a forceful manner. Jenny maintained that he never came into a room without disarranging it completely, and there was some truth in this. "I was only thinking," he said now, slowly. "Knowing Meg, do you really think you'll get out of it so easily?"

"Since you ask me, no." He was still on his feet, and now he moved a little to lean one shoulder against the mantel, and fixed his eyes on a point above Farrell's head. "It's queer, actually, because I've nothing at all to go on. But somehow the case intrigues me. Do you think Meg could give me a bit more on Kellaway's background? It might be a help."

"Come with me when I fetch her," Roger suggested.

"I'll do that." If he was going to add anything, he thought better of it, and then Jenny came back with the coffee.

"I was wondering," she said as she settled herself, "how much longer *Very Tragical Mirth* is going to run."

Roger had taken the tray from her. "I have hopes this summer will kill it," he said, as he set it down and went back to his chair again.

"If it isn't that, it will be another." Antony's tone was casual, but Farrell, who was oddly sensitive to shades of meaning, said quickly:

"I know that. It's just that I never thought it was a very good play."

"It isn't."

"It made quite a hit, you know."

"That was Meg, not the play," said Antony. Jenny was smiling to herself, as though something had amused her.

5

A quarter of an hour after the final curtain Meg was still charged with the energy that had carried her through an exhausting performance. She had emerged triumphant, and with a gasp of relief, from a gown of stiff brocade, and was now enveloped in a wrapper of sorts, that looked more like a dust sheet than anything, and had covered her face with a liberal application of cold cream. Even with these disabilities there was no doubt at all that, as Roger finished his recital, she was registering horror and surprise. Too much surprise, thought Maitland, watching the performance with detached interest, and a good deal too much horror.

"But, darling, I never dreamed . . . I never thought this would happen." And then, almost as urgently, "I wonder if his understudy is any good."

"Good heavens, Meg, anyone would think you'd got money in the play," said Roger, revolted by the irrelevance of this remark. He pushed a box of tissues nearer her hand, and looked at Maitland in rather a helpless way.

"Look here, Meg,"—Antony responded to his cue—"you told me Kellaway was worrying needlessly, and all I had to do was to tell him so."

"But that's true, darling. I *thought* it was true."

"Yes, I dare say. But was it the whole truth?"

"Well, there are always rumors." She was intent on the mirror now, carefully wiping the mask of cream from round her right eye. "You see, darling," she said, very earnestly, "they say he murdered his wife."

"What!"

"Not exactly seriously," Meg assured him. "Nobody really believes it. But it did make me think there might be something to make the police take an interest in him, you see."

"I'm beginning to," said Antony grimly. "Of all the—"

"Don't say it," she begged. "I thought he ought to be—to be represented, and I thought you'd see that he was. But I never dreamed for a moment that they'd arrest him."

"Why didn't you tell me?"

"But, darling, you know . . . one can't help hearing things, but I never repeat gossip."

"Then it's high time you started. You can't leave it there, Meg," he added, seeing her stubborn look. "Forget your principles for a moment, and tell me what you know about Kellaway." His eyes met hers in the mirror and he caught her speculative look. "You've already told me he's a good actor. Go on from there."

"But—"

"When did his wife die?"

25

"Oh, years ago. When he was doing provincial repertory in the north somewhere. I don't really know."

"Did you ever hear her name?"

"Would it be . . . Beth?" said Meg doubtfully. She pushed aside the greasy tissues and reached for cotton wool and an opulent-looking bottle. "I think they brought it in that she killed herself, but for some reason or another there was talk."

"Every year," said Roger, coming back into the conversation with an inconsequent air, "I am increasingly conscious that the world of the theater is a very small one."

"Of course it is, darling," Meg agreed cordially. "But I still don't know anything more about her."

"How did the rumor start?"

"I don't know that either."

"What about the rest of his family then?"

"I don't think he has any."

"A cousin," said Maitland. "Keith Lindsay."

"Cousins aren't family," Meg objected. ("Aren't they?" said Roger under his breath.) "I've heard of him, I think he's a reporter, but I've never met him. And there's somebody Jon calls Father William. I don't think he's a priest, he might be an uncle or something."

Over her head, Roger's eyes met Antony's. "Not really helpful," he said regretfully.

"There are still his friends." He looked down at Meg again. "You said Kellaway was in love with an iceberg," he reminded her.

"Well, he is." She paused, studying her reflection, and then went on argumentatively, as though expecting him to disagree with her, "*I* think that's what she's like, but Ana says I'm wrong."

"Ana," said Roger, "is one half of Ana and Enrique. They dance."

"Even Antony must know that, darling. Geraldine lives with her, so I suppose she ought to know; but I think Ana just can't imagine anybody being cold like that. It isn't really reasonable, you know," she added thoughtfully. "If somebody's in love with you, you either encourage them or—or you don't."

"Geraldine?" said Maitland, declining to be side-tracked.

Meg gave him a reproachful look, but answered readily enough.

"Geraldine Lindsay. I've seen her with Jon once or twice, she's quite beautiful. I think she works in an antique shop, or something."

"Is she a cousin too?"

"I shouldn't think . . . oh, you mean her *name*. I never thought about it before. I suppose she might be." She powdered her face with absent-minded thoroughness and began to pull the pins out of her long hair. "That's all, really, darling. But if you're seeing Jon tomorrow why don't you ask him?"

"I shall."

Roger had been watching his wife go through the familiar routine, but something in Maitland's tone made him look up again and he was surprised to see an appreciative gleam in the other man's eye. "What are you thinking?" he asked.

"Just that I'm beginning to find your friend Kellaway . . . interesting," said Antony slowly. "I wonder how the unfortunate Mr. Dakins comes into the picture, though."

"I don't suppose he does," said Meg with sudden heat. "But, of course, if you're going to take things for granted—"

It took their united efforts to soothe her down again, but she was still a little on her dignity when they left the theater and drove round by Kempenfeldt Square to drop Antony on their way home.

6

It was late by then, and he expected to find Jenny already in bed. Instead, she came into the hall to meet him, and said before he had time to speak, "There's a Mrs. Lindsay here, Antony. She wants to see you."

The living-room door was open behind her. Antony glanced toward it, and then back to Jenny, raising his eyebrows questioningly. She gave a quick nod, and then smiled at him, as though in reassurance. He dropped his overcoat untidily onto a chair and went in.

The woman, who was standing on the hearth-rug, in an attitude that suggested she was nervously prepared for flight,

27

was rather tall, with ash-blonde hair and a pale, clear complexion. Meg had been right in one particular, at least, she was beautiful in the classic way that doesn't leave much room for argument; as for the rest . . .

"Mr. Maitland? I'm Geraldine Lindsay. At this time of night I know it's quite unforgivable—"

"I asked her to stay," said Jenny, cutting short the apology. "Would you like some tea, Antony? I'd better make some fresh." She picked up the teapot and went away with it. Her own cup was empty, balanced precariously on the arm of the sofa; the one by Geraldine's chair seemed to be untouched.

The fire had subsided into an end of evening lethargy. "Don't worry about the time," he said. "Won't you sit down again?"

She went back to the chair, moving with a grace that seemed to him to be unstudied, and seated herself, clasping her hands on her lap. Her eyes met his unsmilingly. "I'd no right to come, but I only just heard, you see . . . about Jon."

He leaned back with one shoulder against the mantel. "I'm afraid I'm not quite clear—"

"Keith told me. He said he met you this afternoon at the hotel. I asked him if you were going to . . . to help us. He said he didn't know."

"Mr. Kellaway has an excellent solicitor. I think you can safely leave things in his hands."

She made an abrupt, almost clumsy gesture, as though of an impatience that was quickly suppressed. "But if the police have made up their minds," she said, "don't you think it may need more than that to prove him innocent?"

He looked away from her then. "Are you so sure of him?" he asked, and was startled by the vehemence of her reply.

"Of course I'm sure!"

"I see. Are you his cousin, Miss Lindsay?"

For some reason she seemed taken aback by the simple question. "In a way, I suppose . . . it's Mrs. Lindsay, Mr. Maitland." He remembered then what Jenny had said. "I was married to Keith, but we were divorced five years ago." She was silent a moment before she went on with determined steadiness, "I think you're wondering why I'm here. I can't give you any other reason than that we're good friends, Jon and I, and I know he wouldn't—"

"What do you know of his relationship with Dakins . . . with the dead man?"

"Nothing. Nothing at all."

"I'm afraid we can't base a defense on your assessment of his character, however well you know him," he told her deliberately, and watched the angry tide of color rise in her cheeks. So she wasn't quite invulnerable. But when she replied her voice showed no sign of emotion.

"That's why I want you to help him," she said seriously, and relaxed a little when she saw him smile.

"Admirably logical," he told her. "Except, of course, that I don't know what I can do, more than anyone else."

Keith Lindsay had said, "I've heard of you." (And what does that mean, except that he knows of my reputation for what Uncle Nick would call "meddling" in things outside the strict sphere of my professional duties?) It was reasonable to suppose that Geraldine knew as much, or why was she here at all? But he was aware of disappointment when she avoided the pitfall, saying only, "I shouldn't have come but I hoped . . . after all, you went to see him this afternoon." He knew then that he would have preferred an excuse for annoyance, however unreasonable; he didn't want to be trapped into sympathy.

"I've promised to see him tomorrow," he said. "After that . . . I don't know."

"But when he left me on Tuesday evening . . . I do assure you, Mr. Maitland, it's quite ridiculous to think he might have been going to commit a murder."

"You saw him on Tuesday?" (Now, why should that surprise him?)

"Didn't he tell you? After the theater, before he went home."

"What time did he leave you?"

"It must have been . . . about ten past twelve."

"You don't sound very sure."

"Well, I'm not." And suddenly, unexpectedly, her mood blazed up into anger. "The police asked me about it, I thought it was just routine. I said, about midnight . . . even that wouldn't have given him much time for what was done."

"How long would it take him to get back to Gilcliffe Gardens?"

"Twenty minutes. Not longer. We worked it out when I knew Jon was worried, but even then I never thought—"

"Of course you didn't. But you changed your mind about the time."

"Yes, I did."

"Why?"

"Because Ana came home at twelve-thirty, I'm sure about that."

"Is Ana sure about it, too?"

"Yes, Mr. Maitland, she is." For a moment he thought she was going to leave it there, but then she added in a small, apologetic voice, "It couldn't have been as much as half an hour after Jon went home."

"What were you doing in the interval? That might help us to fix the time."

"Just sitting and thinking. Wondering." She saw him frown, and added guiltily, "It doesn't help, does it?"

"Let's try it another way. Did Kellaway often visit you after the theater?"

"Quite often. You see, I'd be making some supper for Ana, she hates eating out, so it was quite easy—"

"He had supper with you that night?"

"Yes."

"Did he leave at his usual time?"

"Y-yes."

"Are you sure about that, Mrs. Lindsay?" She hesitated, and he added sharply, "You'll be asked all this at the trial."

"Well . . . usually he'd stay till Ana came home, at least."

"But that night he went earlier. Do you know why?"

She gave a gasp; as though she had dived into deep water and found it unexpectedly cold. "Would it help if I said we'd quarreled?"

"Would it be true?"

"Not exactly." She got up as she spoke, and stood facing him. He saw now that her eyes were an odd, yellowy hazel; he was also conscious, more deeply than before, of her distress. "He asked me to marry him," she said.

"And left early because he didn't like your answer?"

"Yes. He was angry." She looked away from him and added in the same even tone, "I haven't seen him since." He wondered if it was only in his imagination that the words had a desolate ring.

"And yet you want to help him."

"Of course I do!" Her eyes met his again with a kind of frantic appeal. "Don't you see—?" But the emotion died as quickly as it was born. "I'd no right to come, but I thought perhaps if I told you—"

He was occupied with a thought of his own. "You said, *we* worked it out."

"Keith and I. He told me what Jon had said about that night." She hesitated again. "They're more like brothers, really. Keith's parents died, and he was brought up with Jon." But the reserved note was back in her voice again, so that he thought suddenly that perhaps she had never really fallen out of love with Lindsay. "I must go," she said.

"You realize, don't you, that there'll be more questions?" (And why don't I ask them tonight? I was glad enough to find out what Meg knew.)

"Does that mean you're going to do something?" she asked.

"I don't know what it means," he said irritably. "Does it really matter?"

"It might," she said, and gave him a searching look. "It might make all the difference."

"I'll call you a taxi."

"No, don't do that. I'd rather—"

"Then I'll come with you to the bus stop."

But she refused his escort, too, and he found himself unwilling to press the matter. He went downstairs with her, moving stiffly as he so often did when he was tired and more conscious than usual of the pain in his shoulder, and watched her go down the steps and turn left toward Avery Street; and then before he got the door quite shut a figure came out of the shadow of the trees in the center of the square, and crossed the road, and caught up with her on the corner. Maitland paused a moment, half-tempted to pull the door open again to confirm his impression.

But he knew it wasn't really necessary. It had certainly been a man who was waiting there, and he was pretty sure it had been Keith Lindsay.

SATURDAY, 20th MARCH

1

Geoffrey Horton was as good as his word next morning, and they were on their way by five past ten. The solicitor was a few years younger than his companion, red-haired, solidly built, and normally of a cheerful disposition. Today, the most that could be said was that he was less openly grumpy than he had been the night before, but still he had nothing cheerful to say about their prospects. As for Maitland, he was depressed and inclined to be on edge. Lennox Street police station was not perhaps quite so distasteful a setting for the interview as the prison would have been, but still the errand was one that he disliked.

After a while the silence in the car became oppressive. "I'm still in the dark," said Antony. "How did Dakins die?"

"The medical report isn't available yet. To tell you the truth," said Geoffrey, with an air of disapproval, "I don't think they know. But he wasn't burned to death."

"Are they sure it was arson?"

"A sort of funeral pyre." Geoffrey considered the imagery, apparently with satisfaction. "Apart from anything else the doctors may think up, no one's going to believe he did it himself."

"I'll take your word for it. What does Kellaway say?"

Horton did not answer that immediately. It may have been the traffic that demanded his attention, it may have been that he wanted to think out his reply. "Didn't he even tell you how he was going to plead?" Maitland asked, when he felt that the silence had lasted long enough.

"Oh, that! He said he wasn't guilty," said Geoffrey in a level tone that proclaimed his incredulity as clearly as if he had shouted it from the housetops.

"Come now, that's something," said Antony, encouraged. "And it brings us to the point that really interests me. How do the police connect him with Dakins? I know he lodged with him . . . by the way, is there a Mrs. Dakins?"

"He was a widower." He drove in silence for a while, and then went on, "A retired civil servant, he'd been a clerk with the Inland Revenue. You're quite right, he wouldn't have had much in common with Kellaway."

"Then how?"

"I'm coming to that. The police think he was blackmailing him," said Geoffrey, and again risked a sidelong look at his companion.

"Oh," said Maitland blankly. And then, "I ought to have thought of that."

"I don't see why you should."

"Well, you see, there's been some gossip. I got it out of Meg."

"What about?" Horton demanded. And added, glumly, "It only needed that."

"About Mrs. Kellaway's death. And that's *all* I know," he went on, forestalling Geoffrey's further question. "Does it fit in with the police theory, I wonder?"

"Yes, it does. They found some newspaper clippings from the *Penhaven Gazette* in a drawer in Dakins's bedroom. About the inquest."

"Where the hell is Penhaven?"

"In Cumberland."

"Was she murdered?"

"No. At least," said Geoffrey meticulously, "I don't think so. She killed herself, and she left a letter, and the coroner was one of those talkative chaps."

"Are you trying to tell me Kellaway was responsible?" (So this was what Jon had been going to tell him yesterday. A sordid little story, it seemed, but how did it tie in with murder and arson in a London basement flat?)

"It looks that way. But if everybody knows about it, it's hardly a basis for blackmail." Horton was perceptibly cheered by the thought.

"Wait a bit. The theatrical gossip is that he murdered his wife, but Meg says nobody believes it."

"Why repeat it then?"

"For . . . well, for kicks, I suppose. Don't you see, Geoffrey? Something too far-fetched for credence, but titillating; an amusement for an idle hour. And no harm done."

"Slander," said Horton severely.

"I bet I'm right, anyway. No one believed it, or was shocked by the story, except in the lightest, most pleasurable way."

"You seem to know all about it."

"I'm guessing," said Antony, and smiled again, disarmingly; but it was wasted on Geoffrey, who was watching the road. "I don't think you appreciate Kellaway's position: he's just got his first big starring role, and the real story isn't at all amusing. Given to the newspapers, perhaps with a few improvements . . . what was it, anyway? Cruelty? Neglect?"

"I can't remember the exact wording but I can tell you this, Antony, it left a bad taste in my mouth. And the coroner left no doubt at all what he thought." Horton paused, thinking it out. "I see what you mean, of course, but why haven't the papers got hold of it . . . now, when Kellaway has become news?"

"You said the cuttings were from a local newspaper," Maitland reminded him. "I don't suppose the story ever made the national press."

"Then how did Dakins come to have them in his possession?"

"That's just what I'd like to know."

"And Kellaway murdered him to keep him quiet, thus ensuring an even more damaging scandal."

"That's right," agreed Antony readily. "Perhaps he didn't do it."

"You've made up your mind about that, haven't you?" said Geoffrey sourly.

"On the contrary, I haven't the faintest idea."

"Well, it seems to me that once you grant the motive—"

"I don't grant it," said Maitland. "But I don't imagine the prosecution will have any difficulty in persuading the jury of its validity."

"Once you grant the motive," Horton repeated doggedly, "the other things fall into place. Why did he go for a walk, for instance, that night of all others?"

"Love," said Antony. "Hopeless love."

"What do you mean?"

"I have it on the lady's own authority that he proposed to her and was rejected."

"And now you're trying to tell me you're not interested," said Geoffrey in an accusing tone.

"I didn't go to her, she came to me," Antony told him equably. "And don't you think we'd have a much better chance of reaching Lennox Street alive if you kept your eyes on the road instead of glaring at me like that?"

"Of all the aggravating—"

"What else falls into place?"

"Whatever you say, Antony, the fact remains that he did go for a walk, and it could have been because he wanted to give the fire a chance to take hold. The next thing is an empty five-gallon petrol can, alleged to have been stored in the mews garage where he keeps his car, about three minutes' walk from the house. Dakins's body had been soaked in petrol. And finally, a neighbor who was walking his dog saw Kellaway come out of the house 'at about twelve-forty.'"

"I don't like that."

"I thought you wouldn't. He's vague about the exact time," Geoffrey admitted, "but Kellaway has denied he went into the house at all, and even if he changes that story now—"

"Yes, I see. Neat," said Antony admiringly. "When did all that happen . . . his wife's suicide, I mean?"

"August, 1953."

"As long ago as that?" He sounded startled. "They must both have been pretty young."

"She was twenty-six, he was twenty-eight. At least, if the newspaper report was accurate. Which means he's forty now. A long time to wait for success," said Geoffrey, turning into Lennox Street and drawing up outside the police station. "I can imagine a man reacting violently if anything happened to jeopardize it."

"Job had his comforters, too," remarked Antony, getting out

36

and slamming the car door with unnecessary violence. He stood a moment, staring up at the building, a solid structure, a little over-ornate. "Come on, Geoffrey, let's get it over with."

2

A night in custody had done little for Jon Kellaway. He looked haggard and untidy, and he had cut himself shaving. Within the confines of the interview room all his energy seemed to be driven inward, so that he spoke more loudly than was necessary, made wilder gestures. Maitland's expression grew bleaker as their talk went on; if Kellaway was guilty of a singularly cold-blooded crime, that was one thing, but it began to seem more urgent to find out if that was true.

Geoffrey was saying all the right, the conventional things. Antony sat down, and felt in his pockets for the old envelope on which he had already made a few illegible notes, and set it down on the table. When he looked up he found Kellaway's eyes fixed on him, and as though he had only been waiting for the other man's attention Jon said abruptly, interrupting Horton's careful phrases, "Yes, of course. I understand all that. Unless I can make you believe me—"

This was not altogether to Maitland's taste. He said, frowning, "That's an over-simplification really. If I feel I can help, I will; how I go about it is another matter, and depends on what you have to say. And you may have changed your mind about confiding in me."

Jon seemed to be considering that. His eyes were as intent as ever, but after a moment, surprisingly, he smiled. "Have it your own way," he said, and turned his head a little as though to include Geoffrey Horton in what he had to say. "I was going to tell you yesterday why I felt the police might take an interest in me; but I thought then it would only be a—a temporary inconvenience, my real worry was that it might have repercussions."

"Yes?" said Maitland. He shifted his gaze for an instant to Geoffrey, sitting stolidly beside him, and then looked back at the prisoner again. Kellaway had a momentary impression of withdrawal, and raised his voice a little as though it was the only way of making himself heard.

"I just thought it might make them wonder . . . because I was mixed up in two unexplained deaths. But then they'd find out Beth really did commit suicide—she did, you know—and they'd see there couldn't be any connection."

"I'm afraid you're going to have to explain that. About Beth," he added, when Kellaway only stared at him.

"She was my wife." His eyes moved from one of them to the other; perhaps he was wondering whether the statement was sufficient, in any case he made no attempt to amplify it.

"*All* about Beth," said Maitland firmly. And waited again, hopefully, and then asked, "When were you married?"

"In 1946."

There was a pause while Antony worked that out. "You were twenty-one," he said at last, and Kellaway nodded.

"That's right. I didn't come out of the Army until the following year, but I had some leave then, and that's how it happened."

"Had you known her long?"

"A week." He spread his hands in a gesture that seemed designed to demonstrate the adequacy of this period of acquaintance. "She was a pretty little thing, and very gay."

"Were you in love with her?" Unconsciously, Maitland's tone had sharpened. Jon looked at him with vague bewilderment.

"Of course I was. I'm only trying to explain . . . that seemed more important than anything, just then. That we had fun together."

"I see."

"I don't think you do. And it wasn't enough, I can see that now. When I came out of the Army I had this acting thing, and it isn't all that easy to get a start. I suppose I was selfish, I ought to have tried to get what Beth called a proper job; I can see now it must have been hard for her. I mean, my working hours, and never being in one place for long, and not much chance for her to make friends. Somehow she never seemed to cotton on to the theater people."

He broke off there, and seemed to think he had said enough.

Geoffrey glanced at Maitland, and saw that the frown was back between his eyes again. "You were in Penhaven when your wife died," he said.

"We'd been there nearly a year. They had a jolly good repertory for so small a place, and as a matter of fact things seemed easier altogether. I'm trying to say that Beth seemed more content. For one thing, Keith was there, working for the local paper."

"The *Gazette?*" That was Antony, coming out of his abstraction again.

"No, a weekly affair, the *Penhaven and District Advertiser*. He seemed to have more of a knack of getting to know people than I had. That was where—" He broke off, and again his glance flickered from one of his companions to the other. Horton looked impassive, and Maitland seemed to have withdrawn his attention altogether and to be absorbed in a sketch he was making across the corner of his envelope. When the silence had lengthened a little, however, he looked up.

"What were you going to say, Mr. Kellaway?"

"Where Keith got married, if that's what you mean." Jon's reply sounded sulky, almost resentful.

"Mrs. Lindsay was from Penhaven?"

"Yes, her father was a doctor there."

"And you say that having more friends made Beth seem more content?"

"That's what I thought." There was no mistaking it now, his voice had a note of caution. Maitland raised his eyes and asked bluntly:

"Why did she kill herself?"

"I . . . don't know." Jon's hands clenched together suddenly, but his tone remained dry and unemotional.

"You had no reason to suspect that she was contemplating suicide?"

"No reason at all."

"Your own relationship with her was as happy as ever?"

For a little too long the question hung between them, unanswered. "As happy as it had been for years," said Jon at last, evenly. And then he was on his feet with a sudden movement, so that his chair scraped back across the floor. "She was bored

with me," he said. "At least, that's how she acted. I tried . . .
God knows I tried. But it didn't do any good. And I still can't
see why—"

"She left a letter," Maitland reminded him gently.

"Yes, but . . . that's the queerest thing of all." He was leaning forward now, demanding their attention, demanding their
belief. "She said she couldn't bear it any longer . . . I neglected her . . . I was unfaithful to her . . . even, I was cruel.
None of those things was true. And she said she loved me; that
wasn't true either. Not any longer."

"Are you so sure?"

"Of course I'm sure!"

"*None* of those things was true," said Maitland reflectively.

"Well, perhaps . . . that I neglected her. But not . . . not
wantonly. We had to live."

"You have implied, however, that you were not at that time
in love with her."

"No, I—" He straightened himself and added wearily, "In
face of her own indifference . . . but I'm not trying to excuse
myself. I wanted her to be happy, I don't know if you can believe that."

"And the other charges?"

"I've wondered sometimes . . . I was certainly never consciously unkind. And there was no one else, I can't even think
of anyone she might have imagined I cared for." He paused
there, and turned to pull his chair forward again, and sat
down with his elbows on the table. "Nobody thought I was
telling the truth," he said.

"At the inquest, you mean?"

"Yes."

"Did you know what was coming?"

"I'd read the letter, when I found her. I came back from the
theater one night, and she was dead. I knew she'd been to the
doctor, of course, and I knew she said she wasn't sleeping; but
that must have been just an excuse to get hold of the stuff.
She'd taken nearly the whole bottle."

"Yes," said Maitland, too politely. "It must have been a
shock to you." He paused, and then added invitingly, "She'd
left a letter, and you read it."

"Well, of course I did. But it never occurred to me then that the police would take it away with them. I thought it only concerned me."

"If you had realized—?"

"I'd have destroyed it, I suppose."

"And the repercussions you spoke of?"

Jon looked blank for a moment. "Oh . . . yes. I thought the story might become public knowledge once the police started raking things up, and I didn't much like the idea," he admitted.

"Well now, the report of the inquest that appeared in the *Penhaven Gazette* . . . how do you suppose that got into Mr. Dakins's possession?"

"I've no idea."

"Did he ever mention the matter to you?"

"No."

"Or say anything that might have led you to suppose he knew about it?"

"Nothing like that."

"Can't you even hazard a guess as to how the newspaper cutting came into his hands? He didn't find it in your room, for instance?"

"Good Lord, you don't think I'd keep a thing like that!"

"People do the most unlikely things."

"Not as unlikely as that," Kellaway asserted. "I wanted nothing so much as to forget."

"You know the construction the police are placing on their find?"

"They made that abundantly clear."

"But you can't explain it?"

"Well, all I can think is that some friend of Dakins's who lived in the north might have come across the report somehow and known he would be interested. That seems the most likely explanation really."

"Well . . . the least unlikely, perhaps."

"Not that it matters," said Geoffrey Horton, looking up from the notes he was making. "He was in a position to threaten you, and the prosecution can prove it."

"But he never said anything," Kellaway protested.

"Suppose he had," said Maitland. "Would you have minded very much if he'd threatened to make the matter public?"

Jon looked at him blankly, and for a moment Antony thought he was going to take refuge in flat denial. Then Kellaway's hands went out in a gesture that seemed to disclaim all responsibility for what he was going to say. "I'd have done anything in the world to keep it quiet."

"That's what I was afraid of," said Antony heavily.

Kellaway was looking at Geoffrey Horton. "You understand. You've seen the letter, you've seen what the coroner said. I expect he felt he had reason, Beth was so young."

"Yes, I see," said Maitland. Then, *"Anything?"* he repeated.

"Well, I haven't much money. Come to think of it, he must have had a pretty good idea of that; I mean, up to six months ago it wasn't always so easy to find the rent. It wouldn't have been worth his while to blackmail me."

"Would you have killed him?" He added smoothly, as Jon's eyes flew to his face, "If the matter had arisen, of course."

"No, I wouldn't. I didn't mean that." He sounded angry, but then he added in a quieter tone, "I suppose you mean, I ought to be more careful what I say."

"When you get into court you will have to be . . . very careful." He looked down at his envelope, and let the silence lengthen. "So now we come to the question of opportunity."

"But I didn't . . . you do understand, don't you?" Kellaway was suddenly, desperately in earnest. "I didn't kill him," he said.

"We have to consider how we can answer the case for the Crown," Antony explained; but his tone had roughened, and Geoffrey gave him a sidelong, curious glance.

"Yes, I suppose so," Jon agreed without enthusiasm. "But I suppose they're true, the things the police said. And if they are, I don't see how I can answer them."

3

Geoffrey went back to Kempenfeldt Square to lunch, but in spite of Jenny's best endeavors he was still inclined to be truculent when the meal had been cleared away and they settled round the fire. "I don't see what decided you," he said for the fourth time, stirring energetically enough to send his coffee spinning over into the saucer. Jenny passed him the sugar.

"No, I've plenty, thank you."

"You need it," she told him, with a tartness that was unusual in her.

"I . . . yes, I see." He smiled at her reluctantly. "But it's so unreasonable," he complained.

"Why shouldn't I accept the brief?" said Antony. He had taken his favorite position with his back to the fire, and though at first glance he looked solemn enough there was a glimmer of amusement in his eye. "Kellaway wanted me to."

"You know perfectly well what I mean," said Horton.

Maitland sipped his coffee, and took his time about replying. "Our client has told us he is not guilty," he said.

"Well, but you don't have to believe him," said Geoffrey indignantly, and was pleased to see that Antony looked a little taken aback.

"I'm not at all sure that I do . . . altogether. About his wife, now. What do you think of his story there, Geoffrey?"

"I thought perhaps he was telling the truth as he saw it." He made the admission warily. "I expect he led her the hell of a life—these temperamental chaps!—but he probably quite honestly wasn't aware of it."

"I suppose he is temperamental."

"Of course he is!"

"So where you part company with him is on the night of Dakins's death. Is that right?"

"It is."

"Where did he depart from the truth then? No, really, I want to know. He says he got home about twelve-thirty; we've Geraldine Lindsay's evidence in corroboration—"

"Which isn't worth a damn. You said yourself she was uncertain about the time."

"Perhaps we can persuade the jury that they aren't sure either. At least you'll admit they'll be sympathetic towards the picture of Kellaway striding through the streets—"

"On a beastly cold night."

"—wrestling with the pangs of an unrequited passion. Don't be such a wet blanket, Geoffrey. That's perfectly credible."

"If he hadn't already told the police he was thinking about his part in *A Kind of Praise*," said Geoffrey, unconvinced.

"Oh, that! He wasn't even going to mention Geraldine."

"Sheer nobility, I suppose."

"But, of course!" He raised his eyebrows as he spoke, as though surprised that anyone could think of doubting the statement, and in spite of himself Horton laughed.

"All right, I'll give you that. Will you also tell me his denial that he went into the house is convincing, when there's a witness to swear he saw him coming out."

"It will be interesting to see his statement," said Maitland placidly.

"You mean it might not have been Kellaway he saw?"

"Well, I'd like to know just how detailed his story was."

"There's still the can of petrol."

"Yes, and that's a queer thing."

"Not really. Not unless you make up your mind to go dead against the evidence. It was there, it was empty, and it had Kellaway's fingerprints on it."

"But if he hadn't insisted that he left it, full, in the garage . . . doesn't that make you think he may be telling the truth? When a lie would be so easy . . . so convenient."

"He may not have liked to change his first story. If you want to know what I think," said Geoffrey, "he was very concerned to impress *you*."

"Thinking me the more credulous? How right he is."

"Look at it as it stands," Geoffrey urged him, ignoring this. "He doesn't use his car around town, he'd last had it out on Sunday, and the can was full then. The garage is a few minutes' walk from the house, there's no obvious connection between the two. Why should a stranger have gone there for what he wanted?"

"Dakins might have brought the petrol to the house himself, for some reason. Kellaway says he had a key to the garage."

"But why should he have done a thing like that?"

"I don't know," Antony admitted. "I only said, he might."

"If you're not prepared to be reasonable," said Geoffrey, "I'm off!"

"I hate to think I'm driving you away."

"Oh, well, I ought to be going anyway." He relented sufficiently to smile again at Jenny. "I suppose you'll go your own way, Antony, but you're going to find I'm right, you know."

"Who lives may learn," said Maitland lightly. He did not sound at that stage as though the prospect gave him much concern.

4

Jenny did not return to the subject until they came home that evening from the pictures, where they had been edified by a drama that would have put Genghis Khan's activities to shame; and none the better for being played out in a modern setting. After that it was pleasant to turn on the electric fire in the bedroom so that they could have a nightcap there in comfort and relax a little. "After all we've been through," said Antony. But Jenny had already put the rigors of the film behind her.

"Do you really disagree with Geoffrey about Jon Kellaway?" she asked.

"I was telling him the truth, love. I'm not at all sure that I do."

"Yes, but he thought—"

"I'd like to make sure, Jenny."

She was curled up on the rug, with her hands cupped around her glass; and now she raised her eyes and looked at him over the brim, a long, considering look. "You know, I rather wish Meg hadn't asked you."

"I don't suppose she'll be pleased with me if I come to believe he's guilty," Antony agreed. And then the phone rang, and he muttered something under his breath, and put down his tumbler and went into the living-room to quieten it.

It was Paul Collingwood's voice that greeted him, a light, rather pleasant voice that somehow suited its owner very well. Antony had to make an effort to take his mind back to yesterday's case . . . "Maitland? Thank God! I've been trying to get hold of you all the evening."

"Well, I'm here now."

"Yes. Yes, of course. I'm rather upset," said Collingwood, stating the obvious.

"What's happened *now?*"

"That's what I'm trying to tell you. But I have to admit, it is rather unpleasant."

"*What* is?" asked Maitland, at the end of his patience.

"The police have been in touch with me. It's Bassett, you see."

"What about Bassett?" But he was anxious now as he had not been before, and in an odd way Collingwood's words seemed to come as a confirmation of something he had already known, or guessed.

"He killed himself. Somewhere around tea-time, the Inspector told me." Now that the worst had been said, he seemed to find words more readily. "Nasty business," he added, in a tone of regret. "Sent his wife off to see her sister, and cut his throat with one of her kitchen knives."

SUNDAY, 21st MARCH

1

Sunday was quiet until after luncheon, when Geoffrey telephoned. "I've just had a call from a chap called Webster. He says he can give Kellaway an alibi."

"But Kellaway said . . . why didn't he tell us then?"

"God knows." Horton contrived to sound both injured and resigned. "I'm going to see Webster now, in case it seems worth producing him tomorrow. Shall I pick you up?"

"Where does he live?"

"He said he'd meet me at his shop in Bedford Lane. Kellaway and Webster, jewelers," said Geoffrey. "Do you want to come?"

"Father William!" said Antony.

"What—?"

"Keith Lindsay said the police had been asking Father William about Beth. I told you, don't you remember?" He sounded enthusiastic, and Horton's voice became a little more austere.

"I remember, all right. But I don't see anything to get excited about."

"No, really, Geoffrey, this may be interesting. Of course I want to come."

"Then I'll call for you in half an hour."

Antony replaced the receiver, and went into the kitchen to tell Jenny his plans. He found her cutting sandwiches, and ate one absent-mindedly. "But I don't suppose I shall be long," he concluded.

She moved the plate casually out of his reach. "You're pleased about something, Antony. Is it the alibi?"

"I don't even know if it will stand up. I mean, why didn't Kellaway tell us? This chap may have got the facts wrong."

"Then—"

"Oh, just that I'm intrigued, I suppose. Geoffrey's out of temper, I'm not quite sure why. He doesn't seem to like our client."

Jenny considered this. "Perhaps because he's different. He is different, isn't he?"

"Kellaway? Yes. Explosive sort of fellow." He saw her eyes widen, and added in explanation, "Not a bit like he seems on the stage."

"That shouldn't surprise me, should it? I expect it's because he played that part so very well."

"Anyway, you're all right for an hour?"

"I promised to do Uncle Nick's packing for him. That's why I'm doing this now." She waved a buttery knife over the sandwiches.

"Couldn't Mrs. Stokes—?"

"She bullies him so."

"Well, but, so do you."

Jenny looked up at him with her most innocent smile. "Yes, but he doesn't know it," she said.

Today the wind had dropped and a little pale sunshine had struggled through the clouds. Geoffrey's new Humber was clean and shining, and he had obviously taken time to change so that he looked formal and severely professional, though the short drive seemed to have mellowed his mood a little. Antony said, "I don't really do you justice," and stretched his legs and leaned back luxuriously. "If Mr. Webster's at all inclined to be nervous he may not let us in."

It was a narrow little shop, with a grille over the door and a blind pulled down over the glass panel behind it. The window had a slender, jade green vase, and a black velvet cushion displaying a solitary brooch—a spray of flowers and grasses, gold with diamonds and pearls, an unusual and rather beautiful design; there was also a rose, carefully arranged to look as if it had been dropped by a negligent hand. More effective than the usual clutter, thought Antony, studying the arrangement as he waited. What had Kellaway said . . . an artist?

Then the door opened, and there was a little white-haired man peering at them from behind the grille. Perhaps Geoffrey's splendor reassured him, he had produced a key almost before Horton had time to identify himself. "Come in, Mr. Horton. And Mr.—?"

"Maitland," said Antony, following.

"Ah . . . yes. Mr. Maitland." His voice lingered over the name, and just for an instant there was an awareness in the faded blue eyes. But then he was looking up with an air of benevolent simplicity, from one of his visitors to the other. "I am William Webster," he said. "Forgive me a moment while I lock up again, I mustn't encourage thieves, must I? Then if you will come with me."

The shop itself was dim, they followed him down the length of it and came to an open door with light streaming through, into the crowded little office behind. There was a roll-top desk, a Windsor chair with a tattered cushion, and a shabby sofa along one wall to which he waved his guests. The springs had gone long since, and it wasn't exactly comfortable. Antony sat back and prepared to enjoy himself.

Geoffrey, as was fitting, was taking charge of affairs, explaining his companion's presence before he came to his question. "Now, Mr. Webster, you say you can help us."

"Why, yes, of course. The alibi." He produced the word as if he were proud of it. "It's very simple, really. Jon was with me from twelve-twenty that night—that morning, I should say, the morning of the seventeenth—until well after two o'clock." He sat back, and folded his hands across his stomach with a satisfied air. "I think that covers everything, gentlemen. I think it does."

For once in his life Geoffrey seemed at a loss; Webster's bland certainty seemed to dismay him. He said, "Well, but—" and turned to give Maitland a harassed look.

"You see, Mr. Webster, that is not exactly what Mr. Kellaway has told us."

The old man turned to him, and again, for a moment, there was that look of disconcerting intelligence. "It was foolish of him to try to conceal the fact," he said gently. And then, after a pause, "What did he tell you?"

"That he visited Mrs. Lindsay—"

"Yes, she told me that. She lives just about ten minutes'

walk from here," he added casually, and his eyes twinkled with appreciation when Antony laughed.

"I see you've got it all worked out."

"Why, certainly," Webster agreed, without hesitation.

"Well, then, Kellaway says he went straight home, decided at the last minute to go for a walk, and never went into the house at all." He paused invitingly, but Webster seemed to have nothing more to say; he just sat there smiling at them, quietly pleased with himself and the situation. "It might help us to know a little more about his background," said Antony, at last.

"Is that . . . a material point, Mr. Maitland?"

"Let's say, not altogether idle curiosity."

"Then I must do what I can to help you." He glanced at Geoffrey Horton as he spoke. "You are wondering, no doubt, whether I know Jon well enough to lie for him."

This was exactly what Geoffrey had been wondering, and he choked over his disclaimer. Antony said gravely, "That among other things."

"Very well. I've known Jon all his life, his father was my partner. He was killed in one of the incendiary raids, in 1943, when Jon had just been called up into the Army. As for Keith . . . you met Keith Lindsay, Mr. Maitland?"

"I did."

"Keith is a little older, and had already been a medical student for about two years at that time. In a way, I think, Richard Kellaway's death was harder on him than on Jon; but I felt a responsibility for them both, of course." He smiled again at Horton. "Does that answer your question?"

Geoffrey nodded, and looked glum. Antony said quickly, "Why was it harder on Lindsay?"

"Jon has a—a singleness of purpose that is, perhaps, in its way a protection. But it meant a great deal to Keith that he should complete his studies."

"He isn't a doctor, though, is he?"

"No, he never qualified. He left the hospital . . . a year, two years after Richard's death, I can't remember exactly. He told me he had lost interest, but I have wondered since whether the reason may not have been financial." The thought seemed to

50

depress him. "And then he wasn't deferred any longer, and spent several years in the Air Force."

Geoffrey was showing signs of impatience. He threw an exasperated look at his colleague. "To get back to Kellaway, Mr. Webster—"

"He calls you Father William, doesn't he?" said Maitland.

"Oh, yes, indeed. He and Keith, and a good many other people besides. But you wanted to know . . . what did you want to know?"

"Everything," said Antony, simply. And then, relenting, "Well, start with Jon's marriage."

"You're making me go over a great many unhappy things, Mr. Maitland."

"I'm sorry. Was that so unhappy?"

"Well, unfortunate, perhaps." But his smile had come back; he shared it impartially between them. "Beth was a pretty little thing, with very taking ways. But not intelligent. Featherheaded," he went on, making it quite clear.

"Lindsay said the police had been asking you about her. What did you tell them?"

"Yes, the police." His smile faded, and for a moment the blue eyes were cold, not kindly any longer. "What could I tell them, except where she died, and when? They could easily find out the rest." He broke off there, but finding Maitland's eyes fixed on him questioningly he added, "That she loved Jon, and he had ceased to care for her."

"Is that how it was?"

"I'm afraid so, Mr. Maitland. But you must make allowances for the artistic temperament, and for his natural preoccupation . . . the necessity to make his way."

"I seem to have led you away from the point, sir. Which is not what I think of Kellaway, but what we can make the jury believe."

"But surely now, when I am willing to swear . . . aren't you forgetting that?"

"There are two points, Mr. Webster: why didn't Kellaway tell us himself? And who is the second witness?"

"Yes, I was afraid we should get to that," said Father William, drawing his depression about him like a cloak. But this time Maitland was sure it was for effect only, that the air of amusement lingered. "You see, the man who was with me that night when Jon called . . . his name is Michael O'Keefe, and I believe him to be a burglar."

"Is he, though?"

"I should have said, he has been convicted on several occasions of that offense."

"And when you are asked, in court, why he was visiting you . . . at midnight—?"

"A kindly thought on his part, Mr. Maitland. Wednesday was St. Patrick's day, you know. He brought me some shamrock."

"I don't have to ask you if you can produce what he gave you. I'm sure you can."

"Certainly." He was bubbling over with gaiety again. "A little wilted, it is true, but I have it safe." He turned to Geoffrey as he spoke. "Well, Mr. Horton, will you need me tomorrow?"

"I should prefer to reserve our defense."

"I see. You don't believe me."

"I think," said Geoffrey carefully, "that your evidence will have more effect at the trial."

"But Jon's story of his movements . . . his quite erroneous account."

"He won't be called, either." He hesitated. "Do I understand you, Mr. Webster? Kellaway knows O'Keefe's occupation."

"Of course he does. I imagine he felt Michael would not be the best of witnesses,"—his eyes flickered to meet Antony's for a moment—"in spite of the fact that I have been trying to help him to go straight."

"Well, I wish myself he was more impressive. However, I'll have to see him."

"I'll write down his address. But I'm sorry to think . . . how long will it be before the trial, Mr. Horton? I'm afraid Jon won't take kindly to prison life."

"It won't come on until the Easter term, anyway. The end of April, perhaps later than that."

"Oh, dear, I hoped something could have been done immediately. Still, if you think it is the best thing."

"I do," said Geoffrey firmly. He was carefully not looking at Maitland. The old man pulled a pad toward him, and began to write. Antony said into the silence:

"One other thing, Mr. Webster—"

"Yes?" He wrote a beautiful, copperplate hand; it seemed to take all his attention.

"You know Mrs. Lindsay?"

"Naturally." He finished his note and blotted it carefully. "She works for me here."

"I didn't know."

"How should you?" He wasn't amused now, his eyes were shrewd but not unfriendly. "You are finding the relationship a little confusing, no doubt?"

"Well—"

"Geraldine is Keith's wife, you know. They were married in 1953."

"I understood—"

"Yes, there was a divorce, seven years later. I regretted it very much, and Keith was naturally anxious about her future. She came to me as a temporary expedient, and has been here ever since." He paused, contemplating an arrangement that seemed to give him pleasure. "Do you know her, Mr. Maitland? She has beautiful hands."

Comment on that point didn't seem to come within his province. "Isn't it ever awkward? I mean, with your being so close to Lindsay."

"Why should it be? There was no animosity about their divorce. Perhaps I shouldn't say this to a lawyer, but I believe these things can be arranged," said Father William with an air of innocence that was blatantly insincere.

"And now Kellaway—"

"I don't know anything about that."

"No, of course not. I'm a bit muddled," Antony apologized.

"Are you?" asked Webster, benevolent, but definitely skeptical.

"You see, when it was a matter of explaining why he was walking about the streets instead of going home to bed—"

53

"I don't think I do see, quite."

"Hopeless love!" said Geoffrey scathingly.

Maitland looked dejected. "Yes, I was wrong about that." He got up as he spoke. "You've been very kind, Mr. Webster. Mr. Horton will be in touch, of course, but if I should want to see you again—?"

"You will find me here. I have a kitchenette, and a room I use as a bed-sitting-room," he explained. "My needs are really very simple."

"What a very convenient arrangement," said Antony vaguely. The old man got to his feet.

"Believe me, Mr. Maitland, I shall look forward to furthering our acquaintance," he said. And turned to Geoffrey with a quite unnecessary query as to whether his handwriting was legible.

Back in the car, Maitland looked at Horton and allowed himself to grin. "What do you make of that?"

Geoffrey snorted. "Pack of lies!" he said, and set the Humber in motion with a good deal less than his usual smoothness.

"All of it?" said Antony.

His air of detached interest seemed only to infuriate his companion still further. "How should I know? But I suppose I meant the alibi really."

"Well, if you aren't calling him tomorrow, we'll stick to our arrangement about the preliminary hearing. You'll be having a word with Kellaway first?"

"Of course."

"And what about Father William? Will you call him when the trial comes on?"

"What else can I do? He'll never admit in so many words that he made it up. The thing is, what kind of a showing will he make?"

"Excellent, I should think." If Maitland was still amused he was hiding the fact. "He wouldn't see the necessity for playing the hypocrite with us, but he's quite capable of hoodwinking a jury, I should say."

"I'm glad you think so. Not that I'd call him tomorrow in any case, I want to hear the other evidence first, and then I'll have to see what Mr. O'Keefe has to say for himself."

"It could be true, you know," said Antony in an encouraging tone.

"All this nonsense about shamrock?"

"That Jon Kellaway felt he would be even more deeply compromised in the eyes of the police if he admitted where he had been. Though, of course, he may not know—"

"For heaven's sake, stop being cryptic," snapped Geoffrey, as the sentence trailed into silence. "What may he not know?"

"That Father William is a buyer . . . a receiver of stolen goods. Surely you appreciate the significance of his nickname; you don't make the most of your opportunities, Geoffrey. Or are all your clients innocent?"

"Well, of course, it's obvious," said Horton, who realized now that it should have been. "But at least the jury won't know anything about that."

"No," said Maitland thoughtfully.

"What's wrong now?"

"I was just wondering why he'd come up with this story—"

"A moment ago you were telling me it might be true."

"Well, so it might." He was still reflective, but apparently unabashed by his own inconsistency. "But if it isn't . . . did he invent it to help Jon Kellaway, or to spite the police?"

On the whole, Geoffrey found this irrelevant. "What I'd like to know is, why are you so interested in this chap Lindsay?"

"You haven't seen him, have you?"

"What's that got to do with it?"

"If you had you'd realize . . . except for his coloring, he might be Kellaway's twin."

"So that's why you were so fascinated by the neighbor's evidence. You think it might have been Lindsay he saw coming away from the front door."

"It's a possibility. I must find an opportunity of asking him where he was that night."

"Even if he was in Gilcliffe Gardens he may not be too keen on admitting it."

"That's true." They were halted by a traffic light, and he seemed to Geoffrey to be studying the creation in the dress shop on the corner with an undue degree of attention.

"There's the further possibility, you know, that Lindsay might have had a key; or Dakins could have let him in."

"That seems to be going a bit fast, Antony, even for you."

"Somebody knew about the jerrican in Kellaway's garage."

"Wouldn't it be easier to believe that Kellaway himself—"

"Easier, yes." The car moved on in the thin stream of the Sunday traffic. "The only thing about that is . . . suppose it isn't true." Whatever pleasure he had taken in their expedition seemed to have disappeared now; he sounded subdued, uneasy. Geoffrey said in a bracing tone:

"Anyway, there's no need for you to concern yourself any further. Father William has the matter well in hand."

Maitland did not reply. When they stopped again and Horton was able to glance at his passenger, he thought that the other man had an uncomfortably stubborn look. It seemed doubtful whether Antony had even heard the attempt at reassurance.

2

Sir Nicholas and Jenny were having tea when Maitland reached home. "It seems you were wrong," Sir Nicholas greeted him, "in thinking that unfortunate juryman was safe."

"I didn't know you'd heard about that, Uncle Nick," said Antony, helping himself to buttered toast and putting his plate on the mantelpiece for safety. He had a pretty good idea that Jenny wouldn't have mentioned Bassett's death. "It wasn't in the papers surely?"

"If you'd troubled to read the Stop Press . . . and if you didn't, how did you know what had happened?"

"Collingwood telephoned, late last night." He frowned at the recollection. "The police say it was suicide. What did the paper say?"

"*Found dead at his home.*" Sir Nicholas considered the statement for a moment. "In the circumstances, do you think it is likely that he killed himself?"

"It isn't easy to cut a man's throat for him without leaving any other signs of violence," said Antony. He spoke absently, and ignored the slightly acid flavor of his uncle's murmured,

"I suppose I can take your word for that."

"Anyway, Bassett's death doesn't concern me—thank goodness!—except that I'm sorry it happened, of course." He passed his uncle the plate with what remained of the toast, and replenished his own with three sandwiches and a slice of cake. "I'm more bothered about Jonathan Kellaway." Sir Nicholas raised his eyebrows inquiringly. "If you read the paper carefully enough to notice a Stop Press, you couldn't possibly have missed that."

"I never read headlines," said Sir Nicholas austerely.

"Jonathan Kellaway, the actor. Murder. Arson." Maitland spaced out his words, and watched the older man hopefully for some sign of dawning intelligence.

"Oh, that! You didn't tell me."

"There hasn't really been time. Did you see *A Kind of Praise*, Uncle Nick?"

"Was that Kellaway?" He sounded more interested now. "A quite outstanding performance."

"Yes, wasn't it? Geoffrey thinks he's guilty," he added, and passed Jenny his empty cup. "I'm not so sure. Anyway, he seems to have an alibi."

"Then isn't Geoffrey being a trifle unreasonable?"

"Not really." He did not elaborate, but he was aware that Sir Nicholas's look had become more intent.

"Are you getting ideas about this case, Antony?"

"It's a bit early . . . oh, well, yes, I suppose I am." He bit into a sandwich, and glanced at his uncle, half-amused, half-apologetic. "Kellaway's past is shady, and his friends seem a disreputable lot, but I can't help feeling—"

"Not again!" said Sir Nicholas in an overwrought way.

"It's all quite straightforward . . . I told you," Antony assured him. But he had already said too much. He set himself to endure, with what patience he could muster, a cross-examination that would certainly have occasioned comment in court, even if directed at the most hostile of witnesses.

Jenny finished her tea, and sat quietly listening. She thought it was perhaps a good thing if Antony was beginning to believe in Jonathan Kellaway, but later, when they were alone together, she didn't bring up the subject again, but told him instead about the difficulties of packing into a small suitcase all the things Uncle Nick thought necessary for a week's sojourn in the wilds of the United States.

"Why worry?" said Antony, relaxed now, and ready to be diverted. Jenny looked at him reproachfully.

"You know he'll go mad if they try to charge him excess baggage."

"Well, are you sure they won't?"

"Oh, yes, I weighed the case on the bathroom scales." She stretched, and gave him a sleepy smile. "And I brought it upstairs with me, it's in the hall cupboard; so he can't put anything else in. And he can't go taking everything out, either, to see if I've remembered to pack his evening studs," she added, with simple satisfaction. "It would have been quite fatal to leave him alone with it, of course."

MONDAY, 22nd MARCH

1

Paul Collingwood seemed to have recovered his composure; in fact, looking at him, Maitland found it hard to believe that he had ever lost it. The solicitor was a big man, with blond hair cut short enough to be tidy in spite of a strenuous tendency to wave, features of classical regularity, and a hearty manner. Beside him, his clerk looked insignificant . . . almost insignificant. Falkner was undersized, and sharp-featured; and would have been very like a fox-terrier if only he had displayed any of the little dog's aggressiveness, instead of the faintly obsequious manner that was always an irritation. He had a slight limp, no more than a dragging of one foot really, that never seemed to hinder his progress in the slightest.

"Ah, Maitland, good morning." Collingwood contrived to sound as though this was the one thing needed to make his day. "You know Falkner—no, don't go, Albert!—we were just discussing the effect all this will have on Swaine's affairs."

Definitely, the solicitor was in form again. He offered a chair with a wide and hospitable gesture, and Maitland sat down. Falkner was holding out a cigarette-box. "There was quite a piece in the paper about the Kellaway case this morning," he said, turning his head to include his employer in what he was saying, "and I thought to myself, that's just the sort of thing to interest Mr. Maitland." He snapped the box shut and put it back on the desk, and stood looking at Antony expectantly. "Am I right, sir?"

"Near enough."

"I didn't see any mention of Mr. Maitland's name, Albert." Collingwood was leaning back, tipping his chair dangerously but with the most complete unconcern.

"No, sir, you wouldn't. Not in *your* paper," said Falkner.

Paradoxically, his tone was so deferential as to be almost condescending. "The *Courier,* now . . . an informed guess, they said. But you see they weren't so far wrong."

"I see." Paul Collingwood's eyes met Antony's, an amused look, not altogether without malice. "What it is to have a reputation," he sympathized.

There didn't seem to be much to say to that. Maitland smiled, and let the silence lengthen before he asked, "You've seen Swaine?"

The front legs of Collingwood's chair came to the floor with a crash, and his hand went out to the cigarette-box. "Yes, of course. Yesterday. Thank you, Albert." (Trust Falkner to be ready with a light.) "I'll give you three guesses what he said."

"I suppose . . . that he didn't know anything about the bribery." In contrast to the solicitor's heartiness, the diffidence of Maitland's tone was very marked.

"Got it in one!" said Collingwood. "Or about the threats, of course. Well, what could he say?"

The question, it was to be hoped, was rhetorical. Antony was occupied with a thought of his own. "It isn't his kind of thing," he said tentatively.

"Oh, but my dear fellow . . . who else would it benefit?"

"I don't know."

"Neither do I."

"Have you heard from the police again?"

"No, except that the inquest's on Wednesday. Which doesn't really concern us, does it?"

"The papers are still being cautious . . . still suggesting suicide. At least, mine was." He glanced inquiringly at Falkner as he spoke.

"Oh, but surely, Mr. Maitland, there's no question of anything else."

"You could tell the fellow was upset." Collingwood was smoking, as he did everything else, with an air of single-minded energy. "Some people, the slightest thing sets them off. Besides, it's one thing to threaten . . . why should anyone want to kill him?"

Antony shrugged. *"Pour encourager les autres,"* he suggested;

and added, as he caught Falkner's eye, "Anyway, in this case even the *Courier* has no special knowledge."

"They didn't say anything, Mr. Maitland." (But, of course, they wouldn't. The "special knowledge" of Jon Kellaway's affairs was Lindsay's, obviously. Bassett's death was something else again.)

"Thank goodness Halloran insisted on a postponement," said Collingwood. "At least it gives us time for the talk to settle down. What do you think of Swaine's chances then?"

"He may as well plead guilty and have done with it," said Antony pessimistically, "for all the chance he's got. Not that he had much anyway."

"Well, he's sticking to his guns, I'll say that for him. But, Maitland, what you said just now . . . do you really think Bassett was murdered?"

"No, but . . . oh, I don't know. I don't think I meant anything really." Two pairs of eyes were fixed on him reproachfully; or was there not a hint of speculation in Collingwood's gaze, and something else—a sort of knowing look—in Falkner's? Then Collingwood said:

"If you're busy we'd better get on with it, hadn't we?"

"Then we can forget about it until the case is called again," said Maitland with relief.

2

It was nearly noon when he got back to chambers and found Sir Nicholas's clerk lying in wait for him. "A Detective-Inspector Watson is waiting to see you, Mr. Maitland." Old Mr. Mallory wasn't quite such a snob as Gibbs, but he had a naturally regal attitude that could be daunting on occasion. Antony stopped in his tracks, and said "Oh?" and frowned as he tried to place the name; but at the same time he was conscious of a certain amount of sympathy with the unknown visitor, who had probably found himself heavily outclassed.

"I informed him that the time of your return was uncertain," said Mr. Mallory in his stately way; the faintest emphasis served as a reminder that this was not a desirable state of affairs. "However, he was rather . . . insistent"—he lowered his voice as he spoke, as one deploring a social solecism, and allowed his eyes to turn expressively toward the closed door of Sir Nicholas's room—"so I took the liberty of allowing him to wait for you."

"Yes, of course," said Antony vaguely; he couldn't remember an Inspector Watson, but he must be a gentleman of a certain force of character to have so far prevailed on Mallory. "Is he—?"

"In your room, Mr. Maitland."

"All right, thank you."

He had changed his office three years ago, and the present one was certainly an improvement, though still a trifle cramped for space, being long and narrow, with a glass-fronted bookcase taking up the whole of the wall opposite the desk. There was just one window, and Jenny had said at the time that the room was too dark altogether and it might be a good idea if she came in one weekend and cheered it up by painting the walls primrose; an idea she had abandoned with reluctance in face of Sir Nicholas's absolute veto, though she thought it unreasonable of him still to object when she offered to substitute apricot as a suitable alternative. Now, with a gentle drizzle falling outside, it would in any case have seemed gloomy, and the light was still further obscured by a thickset man who stood with his hands behind his back looking down into the court. He turned when he heard the door open, and something about his figure and the way he moved seemed familiar; then he shifted his position a little so that the light fell on his features, and recognition came on the instant, even before he said, "Good morning, Mr. Maitland," and the slightly husky voice was familiar too. Not Watson at all . . .

"Sergeant Watkins," said Antony. And then, "No, Mallory said 'Inspector,' didn't he? Congratulations."

"Thank you, sir." Maitland could see the detective clearly now; he hadn't changed at all. There were the mild brown eyes and the five o'clock shadow; and the blue serge suit was shiny enough to be the one he had been wearing when last they met. How long ago was it? Four years, or five?

"It's a long time since we saw each other," said Watkins, echoing the thought. "I've made a move since then, there was an opening came up in the C.I.D. Well, I'm not one to let an opportunity go by."

"No, of course. What can I do for you, Inspector?" He moved to his own place behind the desk. Watkins sat down, too, choosing unerringly the most comfortable of the other chairs, and immediately looked at home: leaning back and stretching his legs, and giving a sigh that seemed to indicate a fair degree of contentment.

"If I'm causing you any inconvenience, I'm sorry for it," he said with obvious insincerity. "It's about a man called Bassett."

"Is it, indeed?"

"You'll have heard what happened."

"Collingwood told me. And, of course, the papers this morning—" Watkins was looking at him with a half-smile. Maitland broke off, and added more sharply. "They said he killed himself; at least, they implied it. Isn't that true?"

"I can't say it isn't," said the inspector, "and I can't say it is. The doctors, you know . . . they will take their time."

"I see." He paused, and added, frowning, "Could it have been done by someone else, without leaving traces?"

Watkins ignored the query. "Just now, it's the other business that's worrying us. Bribery and corruption," he said, and seemed to be savoring the phrase. "I used to read about that in the history books at school, and think it was something that happened in 'those days.' Not that I'd ever come up against it myself."

"Come now, Inspector, don't tell me you were ever as innocent as that."

"I've a credulous nature, Mr. Maitland. Seeing a thing in print, like that—"

"You must have found life in the police force disillusioning," said Antony, amused.

"Well, I'm not denying there's some as do. Superintendent Briggs now—Chief-Superintendent, I *should* say—he was all for getting you to come along to Central, but I talked him out of that. No good putting your back up at this stage, now was there?" Watkins said blandly.

Maitland's reaction to this artless question was completely

automatic, and could have been predicted with a fair degree of accuracy by anyone who knew him well. "Now, what in h-hell's name does B-Briggs want with me?"

"There are a few questions, Mr. Maitland. To ask for an explanation, you might say."

"I don't understand you, I'm afraid." He managed to keep his voice level, to control the betraying stammer. It was ridiculous, he knew, that the mere mention of Briggs's name . . . but he'd disliked the fellow since the first day they met, and the superintendent in his turn—and just as instinctively—had distrusted him; nothing that had happened since had caused either of them to modify an opinion which had now reached the proportions almost of an article of faith. Even so, he didn't quite see . . .

"Now, you know, Mr. Maitland, you know as well as I do: once an allegation has been made it's got to be investigated."

"Just a minute, Inspector. Does this concern my client? Because if so—"

"Only indirectly. I thought I'd made that clear." The brown eyes were friendly and innocent; he was apparently unaware of Maitland's simmering fury. "Bassett had a friend, a neighbor called Hudson. And Hudson has made a statement." At this point he seemed to notice for the first time the open cigarette-box which Antony had pushed toward him invitingly. There was a pause while he helped himself, and lit up, and inhaled with an air of conscious enjoyment. "The statement *does* concern you," he said.

"In w-what way?"

"This man Hudson, now. He's a greengrocer, has a little shop just round the corner from where Bassett lived. He says Bassett went in to buy his vegetables as usual on Saturday morning—and that's true, because one of our men was keeping an eye on him, you know—and he left Mrs. Hudson looking after the customers and took Bassett through into the room at the back for a cup of coffee. Well, of course, he was curious, all the neighbors were. And Bassett seemed nervous and upset."

"*That* doesn't surprise me," said Maitland.

"No." Watkins was thoughtful. "Someone had done a proper job of scaring him."

"But you'd talked to Bassett before this . . . someone from the police had, anyway."

"Immediately after the court adjourned on Friday. But he didn't tell us much more than he said in the witness-box: a man had come to see him the night before, he'd just got home and was having his tea. This man had offered him money to hold out for an acquittal, and you know perfectly well, Mr. Maitland, if one man's determined it can go a long way with the rest. Or, at worst, you'll get a disagreement. And when Bassett demurred he told him—in some detail, I gather—just what would happen to him if he didn't agree."

"Yes, he said all that in court. But wasn't he asked anything about the man who threatened him . . . what he looked like, for instance?"

"Oh, he gave us a description. 'There was nothing about him really, a middling sort of chap,' " quoted Watkins scornfully. "When pressed, he added that the man was short, and slightly built, and had dark, rather oily hair."

"Difficult for you," said Maitland, with a polite lack of sympathy.

"Well, now, Hudson says Bassett was too scared when he talked to us to make a proper statement. Stands to reason, if he'd told us all this on Friday we'd have been here before now."

"*Here?*" said Antony. And then, "All what?"

"As it was the weekend, at Kempenfeldt Square, I suppose," Watkins conceded. "As for what Hudson told us, I'm coming to that." His pause might have been because he was choosing his words, or it might have been for emphasis. "You're not going to like this, Mr. Maitland."

"I dare say I shan't, but hadn't you better tell me?"

"He says Bassett told him that you were behind the attempted bribery," said Watkins. He made the statement almost casually, but his eyes were watchful.

There was a stillness about Maitland now. "You're q-quite right, Inspector. I *don't* like it much. But the assertion worries me less than the f-fact that it's brought you here. You can't possibly think—"

"I can see I shall have to do some explaining myself," said Watkins tolerantly.

"It might be as well."

"No one's likely to say you approached Bassett yourself. The description doesn't fit," he admitted, with a conscious generosity that raised Antony's hackles again. "But Bassett said—to Hudson, you know—that he recognized the man who came to see him."

"Well, in that case—"

"He didn't know his name." If Watkins was disappointed by this negative reaction he didn't show it. "Nor yet who he was—"

"Now, look here!"

"—but he'd seen the chap talking to you one evening, at the corner of Middle Temple Lane. He said it was a conversation, two people talking who knew each other well; not just someone asking the way. But when he mentioned your name that evening, the visitor tried to make out he'd never heard of you, and that made Bassett suspicious, because of course if he was at all interested in Swaine's affairs he must know who his counsel was. So he said right out to the chap that he'd have to trust him a bit more if he wanted his help, and after a bit he admitted that you'd sent him. He said Bassett had better not repeat that, or there'd be trouble; and no one would believe him anyway."

"I should have thought that last remark was true, at least. A story at third—no, fourth hand. You can't really expect me to take it seriously," said Maitland contemptuously.

"Not if that was all."

There was something about the quiet way in which this was said that brought Maitland up short, jarring him out of whatever confidence he might still have been feeling. "What else?" he asked.

"Well, you see, Bassett said: how did he know the chap was being straight with him now? I'm still quoting Hudson. And that was when the other man said to him 'He has the reputation of always winning his cases; have you ever wondered how that was managed?' And, you know, Mr. Maitland, I've heard that said myself."

For the moment Antony had no thoughts to spare for the absurdity of the statement. "You know better than that, Inspector."

"Maybe. But it's a queer thing for a man like Hudson to have invented. Or Bassett either. However, I'm bound to say the next point is more significant . . . or might be, to someone with a suspicious nature."

"You haven't finished, then?"

"Not quite, Mr. Maitland. Just one more thing. This chap —the man who visited Bassett—went on to coach him in all the things he should say when the jury were arguing the case. Proper convincing he was, according to Hudson; might even have convinced Bassett, if he hadn't had his own reasons by now for believing Swaine was guilty. Just like a lawyer . . . that's what Hudson said."

"All the same—"

"His story is suspect, naturally."

"But not by you," said Maitland quickly.

"Well, you know, I was never one to believe the worst. Not without proof. Superintendent Briggs now . . . there's a man that knows his own mind," said Watkins in an admiring tone.

"Which is just another way of saying he's a pig-headed old bastard," Antony agreed. "You don't have to tell me what *he* thinks, though I can't recall that he's ever accused me of this particular misdemeanor before. But you know perfectly well this story doesn't mean a thing. There isn't even anything to explain."

"Not a word of truth in it," echoed Watkins, unimpressed. "Still, if you could tell us who Bassett saw you talking to at the corner of Middle Temple Lane, it might be a bit of a help."

"Which evening?"

Watkins shrugged. "After the trial started, anyhow."

"Not that it matters, because I'm pretty sure I didn't stop to speak to anyone on the way back to chambers, while Swaine's trial was on. That's pure invention, like all the rest."

"The question is, then, who's lying: Bassett, or Hudson, or the unidentified go-between . . . or you?"

"You'll have to make up your own m-mind about that, Inspector. There's no corroboration of Hudson's story—"

"The only man who could have confirmed it being dead."

"Oh, for h-heaven's sake! You'll be saying next I k-killed him."

"Now, you know, Mr. Maitland, I wouldn't do a thing like that. Not but what I wouldn't like you to tell me what you were doing with yourself last Saturday. For the record, you might say. Routine."

Antony got up and went to the window and back again with long, impatient strides. "Yes, I know the jargon," he said, and halted by the desk and looked down at Watkins with an angry glint in his eyes. "You should have got here earlier, Inspector. From what Collingwood told me I've a pretty good idea when Bassett died."

"I'm not trying to trap you, Mr. Maitland."

"What makes you think he didn't kill himself, anyway?"

Watkins considered. "I could tell you I'm not here to answer questions," he said.

"And I could tell you to g-go to the d-devil," retorted Antony, and flung himself down in his chair again. "He was under police protection, wasn't he? How could anyone have killed him?"

"If you'll tell me what I want to know, Mr. Maitland, I might consider giving you some information . . . on an exchange basis, you might say."

"Have I any choice?"

"I'm sure I needn't explain the position to *you*, sir," said Watkins with unimpaired good humor.

"No, of course. All p-perfectly p-proper. I wonder," said Antony savagely, "what ingenious persuasions you'd think up if I d-declined to co-operate."

"I'm afraid you've got some very cynical ideas in your head," said Watkins. The idea seemed to sadden him. "Now, I'm a simple sort of chap, and it seems to me—"

"Tea-time," said Maitland, interrupting this renewed self-analysis without ceremony. "What does that mean on a Saturday? Five o'clock?"

"Thereabouts."

"And the papers said he lived at . . . Barnet, was it?"

"Not very far from High Barnet station."

"Well, I was at home until four o'clock . . . Geoffrey Horton was with us until about three, you can check that if you like. And I expect Gibbs saw me go out."

"Did Mrs. Maitland go with you?"

"No. I was going to chambers to pick up some papers." He spoke stiffly, but for the moment he seemed to be trying to hide his resentment. "The wind had dropped by then, so I walked both ways."

"And how long did this expedition take you?"

"I got home just before six." He saw a calculating look in Watkins's eye, and added angrily, "You're right, of course, it needn't have taken so long. We were going to the cinema, so we'd arranged to have a snack about six. I wasn't in a hurry, and I came home through the park."

Inspector Watkins still seemed to be engaged in mental arithmetic. He said, after a moment, "It's not too difficult to get from High Barnet to Charing Cross." His tone was thoughtful, with no trace of apology, but suddenly Maitland laughed, and sounded for the first time genuinely amused.

"All right, Inspector. It's your turn now. What makes you think Bassett didn't cut his own throat? The medical evidence?"

"I doubt if we'll get anything definite from the doctors. What they say rather tends to suggest that he did." The brown eyes rested speculatively on Maitland's face. "You've pointed out the difficulty a man would have in doing a job like that without leaving traces; you haven't mentioned the fact that *you* would have found it almost impossible."

That brought Antony to his feet and back he went to the window again. "Q-quite impossible, if you w-wish to be accurate," he said, looking out. Watkins did not reply, but waited placidly while the silence grew between them. When Maitland turned at last he was still flushed, but his voice was controlled, even a little hard. "If you knew that . . . did you want to make a fool of me?"

"I might ask you the same thing," the detective pointed out. "That arm of yours—"

"It's nothing to do with you," said Antony furiously. Watkins seemed to be eyeing him as if he were a specimen on a slide, and it didn't help at all to know that his own reaction was unreasonable. "Why should I care if you go haring off down a blind alley?"

The other man seemed to be giving this his serious consideration. "It might amuse you," he said at length. "Or you might find it convenient. But the medical evidence isn't quite the whole story, Mr. Maitland. There was the telephone call, for one thing."

"What telephone call?"

"The message from Mrs. Bassett's sister, asking her to go over to Belsize Park right away."

"Thus giving Bassett the opportunity—"

"Wait a bit, wait a bit, Mr. Maitland. There *was* a phone call, Mrs. Bassett agrees to that. And Bassett took it, and said it was a neighbor phoning for her sister, who'd had a fall. But when she got there, the sister was perfectly well, and surprised to see her."

"So there are two possibilities," said Antony, his interest caught and his anger dying. "Someone wanted her out of the way; or Bassett himself used the call as an excuse to invent a story to get her off the premises."

"That's right." Watkins nodded his approval. "And, however it was, he escorted her to the station; and the man who was guarding him went along to see fair play."

"You think someone got into the house while they were gone?"

"It's a possibility, at least."

"But what about getting out again? Wasn't there a man at the back too?"

"No, there wasn't." Later, Antony was to remember Watkins's fondness for giving information, though always with some reason of his own. "The houses in Westmead Road back on to the railway cutting. They're semi-detached, with the kitchen door at the side, and just a slip of a yard behind where the dustbins are. Then there's a wall, and a ten-foot drop to the tracks."

"Wait a bit! How was Bassett found?"

"Mrs. Bassett tried to phone him when she got to her sister's, and the chap outside got worried when he heard it ringing, on and on. He knew Bassett was inside, you see, and it didn't seem natural."

"Well, if you ask me, everything you've told me so far could equally well fit suicide as murder," Antony told him. "I mean, someone *could* have got in while the watchdog was trailing along to the station, and *could* have left along the railway line. But unless the medical evidence backs you up—"

"My other point is an intangible," said Watkins, with a rueful look. "It rests on Bassett's character."

"The D.P.P. would never stand for that."

"No." The inspector sighed, this time as if all the sorrows of the world were crowding in upon him. "Bassett, you see, was a religious sort of chap. Wouldn't have reckoned much to the idea of killing himself, from what they tell me."

"Yes, but look here . . . it wasn't a reasonable thing to do anyway."

"Illogical," Watkins agreed.

"Well, then, if 'the balance of his mind was disturbed'—"

"I've often wondered exactly what that meant," said Watkins, in a ruminative tone. "But it's no use arguing, it isn't a point that can be proved either way. It's just that a cleverer chap than me might find it . . . suggestive."

"Yet his first instinct when this man approached him was to agree with what was proposed."

"It wasn't the money, he said, it was the threats that were used. But when he'd had time to think it over he got in touch with Mr. Halloran. It was late by then."

"If Mrs. Bassett was present at the interview," said Antony, following his own train of thought, "she could give you a pretty good idea whether or not Hudson was telling the truth."

"The visitor said it was business, so Bassett took him into the front room. His wife stayed in the warm kitchen, like a sensible woman."

"Did she even see the man?"

"Yes, for a moment. She couldn't describe him very well, and she doesn't think she'd know him again."

"But Bassett didn't tell her this story . . . of course he didn't, or you'd have brought that up by now."

"Don't you think perhaps we've got enough to be going on with. You say you can't help us to identify the intermediary—"

"For that matter, you've only Hudson's word he was an intermediary."

"You're right there, but can you give me one good reason why Hudson should have been lying?"

"A dozen, I dare say, if I gave my mind to it." (But he was giving his mind to it now, for the first time; and he began to see—though without any lessening of resentment—that perhaps Watkins's attitude wasn't so unreasonable after all.)

"Well, perhaps you could," said the inspector indulgently. "I never was one for having much imagination myself." The cigarette had burned down almost to his fingers; he gave it a regretful look and reached forward to stub it out in the ashtray. "But still, we shall be looking for the man—"

"I shan't lead you to him, Inspector."

"No, but we're hoping that he might lead us back to his principal," said Watkins. His look was frankly appraising. "You seem upset, Mr. Maitland," he added; and now he sounded concerned.

"Well, you know, I'm not particularly keen on being disbarred; I'm not even particularly keen on going to prison. Odd, isn't it?"

"But since you tell me there's no word of truth in the story, what can you possibly have to worry about?"

"If someone's trying deliberately to incriminate me—" He broke off with a helpless gesture.

"Do you really think that's likely?" There was no skepticism in Watkins's tone, nothing but a sort of mild interest in what the other man was saying.

"No, I don't. But I can't make sense of it any other way." Antony watched the detective get to his feet, and roused himself to follow suit. But he was still thoughtful when he pushed open the door of his uncle's room a few minutes later.

"Are you coming to lunch, sir?"

"I was waiting for you." Sir Nicholas took off his glasses,

and got up in his leisurely way. "Who is this Inspector Watson? I thought he was never going."

"You remember Sergeant Watkins?"

"Very well."

"He's been promoted, and transferred to the C.I.D." He hesitated an instant too long to be completely natural. "He works under Superintendent Briggs now . . . Chief-Superintendent, I *should* say," he added, unconscious that he was mimicking the inflection his visitor had used.

For the first time Sir Nicholas looked at his nephew closely. "Is that why you look like a cat with its fur rubbed the wrong way?" he asked.

"I—" said Antony, and stopped. He had just realized that his own view of what had happened might not be shared with complete sympathy by his uncle. "I lost my temper," he confessed.

"It is hardly necessary to tell me *that*," said Sir Nicholas coldly. "But you might care to tell me why."

"It's this Swaine business. It seems to be Briggs's case, and I suppose I should have realized . . . he's believed the worst of me often enough in the past, and sometimes I don't think he's ever been altogether convinced he was wrong."

"Let me understand you, Antony. Has some accusation been made?"

"No—not exactly. A man called Hudson has made a statement to the police, saying that Bassett believed I was behind the attempt to bribe him. I was asked for an explanation. That's all."

"But—"

"I know. It's too stupid, there's no kind of proof. All the same, they seem to be taking it seriously."

"Why?"

"Because . . . oh, various reasons." He paused a moment, and then plunged into an account of his talk with Inspector Watkins. Sir Nicholas's expression grew bleak as he listened. "There's no action they can take, of course," Antony concluded. "But I can't say I like the position much, even as it stands."

"I suppose we should have anticipated something like this,

in view of Briggs's attitude in the past. Which could have probably been avoided," said Sir Nicholas in a considering way, "if you had ever displayed the slightest discretion in your dealings with him." He paused, watching his nephew's expression, and then went on more gently, "Shall I postpone my trip?"

"You can't, Uncle Nick. What would you tell them?"

Sir Nicholas grimaced. "Not the truth, certainly."

"No, really, sir, it would be much better for you to go."

"The question is, what are you proposing to do in my absence?"

"I've got my hands pretty full with the Kellaway brief."

"Yes, but about this juror, Bassett?"

"It does seem," said Antony evasively, "that he may not have killed himself after all."

"It would be most unwise for you to concern yourself in any way with the affair."

"I suppose it would." He wasn't quite sure whether Sir Nicholas would think this reply satisfactory, and added in a hurry, "Watkins had the cheek to question me about my movements, and then point out I couldn't have done it anyway." He paused, and a startled look crept into his eyes. "I suppose he really believes that."

"Whether he believes it or not, it could be readily demonstrated." He came round the desk as he spoke, and Antony turned to take his uncle's overcoat from the peg near the door. "It occurs to me," said Sir Nicholas shrugging his way into it, "that I have always considered Watkins to be well disposed towards you."

"Well, whether he is or not, he certainly enjoys stirring the pot to see what comes to the surface," said Antony. It was only later that it occurred to him that if his uncle hadn't been seriously worried his story would hardly have been received with such an unexpected degree of forbearance. And when it did occur to him, he found no comfort in the thought.

3

For all his protestations to Sir Nicholas, the Kellaway case wasn't really on Maitland's mind just then, and it is doubtful whether he would have thought of it again so soon if Geoffrey Horton had not arrived in his office at the same time as the afternoon tea and biscuits. "We're going to have trouble with Kellaway," Geoffrey warned, helping himself to a custard cream. "For one thing, he can't seem to make up his mind where he was that night. For another—" He broke off, his eyes on Maitland's face. "It'll keep," he said.

Antony pushed away the papers on which he had been working, and transferred a Marie biscuit from the plate to his saucer. "No, tell me." For all his good intentions, he sounded resigned rather than interested. "Did they ask for an adjournment?"

"No, they produced some dribs and drabs of evidence. And they called the neighbor . . . the one who saw Kellaway leaving the house." Antony sat up suddenly and picked up his pencil, and a distinct note of satisfaction appeared in Horton's voice as he went on. "He said there was a light over the front door, and Kellaway's hair is so fair you couldn't possibly mistake it."

"Oh, I see." Maitland looked up with a rather rueful smile. "I thought I had a good idea, that's all." He drew a line carefully through the few words he had written, and went back to his tea again. The Marie biscuit had become warm and soggy. "Tell me, Geoffrey, did the prosecution give any indication of the line they're going to follow . . . ?"

4

The second reminder of Jon Kellaway's affairs came much later, when the telephone bell roused him from his first sleep. Jenny never woke up for anything, not unless you really worked at it, so it was no use hoping she'd answer it. He went himself at last, resentfully; and took up the receiver and snapped "Hallo" as discouragingly as he could.

For a moment there was a dead silence at the other end of the line, so that he wondered whether the caller had given up just before he arrived. But it wasn't the dialing tone he could hear, there was someone there all right. . . .

"*Señor* Maitland? *Quisiera*—" The speaker caught herself up on the word. "May I speak to *Señor* Maitland, please?"

Curiosity got the better of his irritation. He said, "Speaking," and then, encouragingly, "*Quién habla, por favor?*"

"I am Ana." There was an innocent arrogance about the announcement that amused him. "Of you Margarita has told me, and also Geraldine. Is it correct, then, that I telephone you?"

"Can I help you?"

There was a pause while she considered that, and evidently she took the question literally for she said at last, decidedly, "No," and "*Gracias*" followed very much as an afterthought. "But Geraldine you must help," she added firmly. "Because, though she is so foolish, I do not at all wish her to die."

"I . . . did you say die, *señorita?*"

"Do I not speak clearly?" Her calm tone reproved his emotion.

"Where is Mrs. Lindsay?"

"Why, here, in her bed. And now all is well . . . she will be well tomorrow, the doctor says. And he says it is all *accidente*, but this I do not believe. She is so unhappy, *señor*."

"What has happened?"

"But I am telling you. An overdose of the drug she takes for sleeping; this I might do, because I am scatterbrain"—she paused over the word, as if it gave her some satisfaction, and he had time to think that she didn't sound it—"but Geraldine is so careful. So how do I know she will not do it again?"

The question seemed unanswerable, he responded with one of his own. "Have you told the doctor what you suspect?"

"He is a man, *señor. Estúpido*," said Ana emphatically.

For that matter, he wasn't feeling exactly bright himself. "What can I do?" he asked; and hoped he didn't sound as helpless as he felt.

"If you will talk to her . . . tomorrow when she is better."

"What good will that do?"

"You can tell her that all will be well. With Jon," she added kindly, obviously thinking him incapable of working this out for himself.

"But I don't know—"

"From what Margarita has told me, *señor,* I did not think you would be so unkind," said Ana severely.

"I . . . oh, all right then, I'll come."

"That is better." She gave him the address and he wrote it down without further protest. "It is convenient for the theater, you see, and for Geraldine for the shop. Very well, *señor,* I shall sleep now."

"But are you sure—"

"Geraldine will sleep too," she assured him. "And she will not make another mistake, because I have taken the tablets away. Tonight there is no need to concern yourself, and tomorrow you will see her."

It didn't seem any good trying to explain that he had very little of comfort to offer. It didn't even seem worthwhile asking any more questions, he was pretty sure she wouldn't answer them. "Tomorrow," he echoed.

"Muy bien," said Ana briskly. "At eleven o'clock, *señor.*" She evidently took his agreement for granted, for she added *"Buenas noches"* and rang off without further ado. But Antony sat looking at the telephone for several minutes before he realized how cold he was getting and went back to bed.

He noticed as he did so that it was already four o'clock, much later than he had thought. Jenny turned over and mumbled something, and he tucked the blanket round her shoulder in an absent-minded way. "At least," he said aloud as he switched out the light again, "she didn't try anything so messy as cutting her throat." But that just showed how much the other affair was on his mind; the logical comparison was with Beth Kellaway's suicide. And Beth had taken an overdose of sedative, too.

TUESDAY, 23rd MARCH

1

After that there was no question of going into chambers next morning, but even old Mr. Mallory at his most tyrannical wouldn't expect anyone who had been through the ordeal of seeing Sir Nicholas off on a journey to do any work for the rest of the day. His "But, Mr. Maitland—" when Antony phoned him was the merest formality; his heart wasn't in it.

The task of getting Sir Nicholas to the airport was actually Jenny's; Antony went no farther than the front door, and watched the Jaguar slide smoothly from the curb, and wondered as he turned away whether the return journey would be accomplished quite so sedately. He went upstairs again to fortify himself with another cup of coffee, ignoring Gibbs who had popped up at the back of the hall like a disagreeable genie for no other purpose, it seemed, than to demonstrate his own superior devotion to duty.

The coffee was still hot, and Antony drank it slowly, carrying the cup over to the window and looking down into the square, and thinking that Uncle Nick was right, he should concentrate on Jon Kellaway's affairs. (If this was a rather free translation of what Sir Nicholas had said, at least he might have approved the decision.) Watkins's visit had been an unpleasant reminder that his dealings with the police in the past had not been wholly free from dissension, but it would be foolish to regard it in any more serious light.

It was precisely two minutes to eleven when he arrived at Maddox Court and pushed open one of the heavy plate glass doors. The array of plants in the lobby didn't surprise him, you could see them from the street, but the décor and furnishings were luxurious beyond expectation. He seemed to remember having read somewhere that Ana and Enrique com-

manded a fabulous salary, which was just as well because it
hardly seemed likely that Father William paid Geraldine
enough to enable her to meet even half the rent of the smallest
apartment.

When Ana opened the door to him it at once became evident that the flat she rented was by no means the least com-
modious. The vestibule was not very large, but a wide archway
gave an impression of spaciousness, and the room beyond,
though rather low-ceilinged, seemed almost too big for comfort. He stood a moment, looking round him, and perhaps,
after all, his first impression had been mistaken: the chairs and
the one sofa were so obviously designed for relaxation. On the
other hand, the senses were stimulated by a spectacular use of
color.

"But, come in, *Señor* Maitland," Ana demanded.

And again, studying her, he met the unexpected. The theater lights had been kind to her, he thought, and the vivid col-
ors of her costume, and the swift movement of the dance. Now
he saw a tall woman with an oval face a little sallow without
make-up, and black, straight hair tied back carelessly with a
brown ribbon. Her long housecoat was brown too, though with
some gold embroidery at the neckline. Her eyes met his
gravely, and he thought she was pleased that he had kept his
promise; but it would be a relief if she smiled at him, even the
half-smile she had worn on the stage.

"How is Mrs. Lindsay this morning?" he asked.

"She is well. But we must not be speaking here, or she will
think we make a plot together. Or perhaps that I am telling
you—" She turned as she spoke and made for a door at the
other side of the room, and she never completed her sentence.
But at the time he hardly noticed the omission because she
moved with a grace that compelled attention. . . .

"No hay prisa," said Ana, reprovingly, from the doorway.

"I'm sorry."

She smiled at him then, though rather, he thought, as a gov-
erness might have done, commending her charge's good manners, and led the way across a narrow passage to a room where
venetian blinds were lowered against the morning sun.

"Here is *Señor* Maitland, Geraldine. He has come to see you, so we must have light, a little." She went to the window as she spoke, raising the blind a few inches and pulling the right-hand curtain so that the head of the bed was still in shadow. And now he could see the room, though dimly; a cool, impersonal place with none of the brightness they had left behind. He wondered whether Geraldine had chosen the decorations herself, or whether Ana, with unusual perception, had chosen them for her.

He had thought Geraldine Lindsay pale when he saw her on Friday evening, now her pallor was frightening and he glanced anxiously at Ana, expecting that she would notice it too. But she had gone to the bed and was plumping up the pillows as composedly as if her proper place was the sickroom, as though she had never heard and responded to the wild beat of flamenco. . . .

"I shall leave you to talk," she said. And set a chair, and patted it invitingly, and was gone.

Geraldine said, "Good morning, Mr. Maitland," and gave him a wan smile which at once roused his admiration and made him wish he were anywhere else in the world. "Ana must have phoned you. It was kind of you to come."

"I don't know . . . are you feeling well enough for visitors?"

"Oh, yes, I'm very well." She sounded tired and her movements were languid, but there was no weakness in her voice. "Please sit down." Against the green counterpane her hands looked very white and slender.

Now why, in heaven's name, had he let himself in for this? He took the chair and said, feeling his way, "I was sorry to hear you'd been ill," and was surprised to see her smiling again.

"Ana thinks . . . one is never in any doubt what Ana thinks," said Geraldine. "I suppose she told you, she thinks I tried to kill myself."

"She said you had some sleeping stuff . . . you'd taken too much."

"Then she was being unexpectedly tactful." The air of amusement still seemed to cling around her. But that was one thing explained: Geraldine was here because there was a real tie of affection between the two women, perhaps all the stronger because they were so unlike. And Ana must understand her friend far better than he could do, so maybe after all . . .

"You say she thinks . . . is she wrong then?" he asked bluntly.

"Quite wrong."

"What happened?"

"I don't know. I remember waking up, and thinking I hadn't taken the tablets, and somehow it seemed awfully important that I should have them. I suppose I must have taken a second dose." She paused, thinking it out. "Ana would say, subconsciously I *wanted* to. But I don't think I did."

"I'm glad of that."

"It wouldn't help anything, would it? Are things hopeless . . . for Jon?"

The question startled him, perhaps because his mind had been occupied with Bassett, and Swaine, and Paul Collingwood's unexpected agitation . . . his own affairs, in fact, not Jon Kellaway's at all. "Of course not," he said, and thought the denial sounded unconvincing. "Didn't Mr. Webster tell you they were together that night?"

"Father William?" She was frowning now. "But that can't be true, Mr. Maitland."

"Why not?"

"He'd have told me."

She hadn't seen Kellaway, she must mean the old man. "He may feel the fewer people know the better."

"But . . . doesn't this make everything all right?"

"I don't know." (So much easier to lie to her. Why did he feel he had to explain?) "There's a conflict of evidence—"

"The man who said he saw Jon in Gilcliffe Gardens." She saw his questioning look and added quickly, "Keith told me that."

Lindsay, of course, would have attended the magistrate's court hearing. "Did he also tell you that the man described his cousin very exactly?"

"Yes, he said that. I see what you mean, Mr. Maitland, it isn't quite so simple, is it?"

"But not hopeless."

"No. But I wish—"

She was silent for so long that he ventured to prompt her. "What do you wish, Mrs. Lindsay?"

"That I felt differently . . . about Jon."

"I see."

"I don't suppose you do. You see, I do love him . . . in a way."

"Like a cousin, perhaps."

She hadn't been looking at him, but now she raised her eyes quickly to meet his. "Not at all like a cousin," she said steadily; and for the first time color flooded her face.

"I see," he said again. And again it was untrue. "Mr. Webster should make a good witness," he added, with studied irrelevance.

"Yes, but . . . won't they ask him how well he knows Jon?"

"I expect they will."

"And think he's lying. They're bound to think that, aren't they?"

He did not answer her directly. "Is that what you think?" And when she did not reply, "Is he so fond of Kellaway?"

"I don't know," she said hesitantly. And suddenly it seemed important that he should find out.

"Try to tell me," he urged.

"If it were Keith I could answer quite easily. I always think Father William feels responsible for Jon in some way." She paused again, her eyes searching his face. "That isn't what you wanted to hear, is it?"

"Then we must end on a note of mutual dissatisfaction," he said lightly, and got to his feet. There was a hint of exhaustion in her voice, he thought he had stayed too long; but that was why she had spoken so frankly—wasn't it?—because she was too tired to worry about her replies. It wasn't nice, what they did to you after an overdose. "I haven't helped you either, have I?" he asked.

"But you are trying to help Jon?"

The answer was obviously of some concern to her. "So far as I am able," he said, and thought with a little stab of bitterness that it was exactly true, but still evasive. "May I see you again when you're feeling stronger?"

"Any time. I shall be up tomorrow."

"Don't rush it," he said. "Don't worry." And what was the use of that?

Ana was waiting for him in the big living-room, sitting erect in a high-backed chair that was upholstered in some loose-woven, tawny-orange material. She came to her feet as he entered and signified by an imperious gesture that she wished him to close the door; when he had done so and come a little way into the room she gave him a piercing look and asked suspiciously, "You have not upset her?"

If this seemed unreasonable to Maitland he made no sign, but his expression relaxed a little. "No," he said. And then, offering the statement as corroborative evidence, "She's talking about getting up."

"*Qué bien!*" Ana nodded approvingly.

"She says—"

"I know what she says," she told him flatly.

"You don't believe her?"

"Do you, *señor?*"

"I don't think," he said, hedging, "I am as qualified to judge as you. I mean, I hardly know Mrs. Lindsay."

"What did you tell her then? How long will Jon be in prison?"

"*Señorita . . . lo ignoro por completo.*"

If he had hoped to disarm his companion, he was to be disappointed. Ana followed him without comment into her own tongue, spread her hands and said passionately, "But that is your affair, *señor*. To set him free."

"It isn't quite so easy," Antony said, translating Geraldine's phrase, and thinking how apt it was.

"Then what is a lawyer for?"

He made no attempt to answer that. "You know Jon Kellaway?"

"Of course I do."

"Do you think he would kill a man?"

Ana was frowning at him. "If he had cause, *señor.*"

"And this man, Dakins—" For some reason they were back in English now; he thought he would keep it that way, it seemed to generate less excitement.

"Of him, I know nothing. But do not think that I am blaming Jon. It is all the fault of being repressed," said Ana positively. "I tell Geraldine—"

"You mean, she wouldn't have him, so he got it out of his system by setting fire to his landlord?"

"*Es un asunto serio,*" she told him stiffly, but after a moment she smiled. "*Señor,* you are clever. That is exactly what I meant."

"But still you think he should go free?"

"Yes, of course," she said again, and seemed surprised by his stupidity. "I do not wish that Geraldine shall be unhappy."

Antony was looking past her at the window, with its bright, modern curtains framing nothing more exciting than the grimy brick wall at the other side of the street. "Is she in love with him?" he asked; and noted with a renewal of amusement, which he was careful this time not to display, that she found nothing strange about the query.

"Is it not obvious, *señor?*"

"What about Keith Lindsay?"

"He has been her husband. That is always a bond."

"Yes, I suppose it might be." His tone was serious, but not quite serious enough. Ana darted a fiery glance at him.

"Perhaps it is his fault, that people now think her cold. One would not wish, after all, to be married to a wolf." For a moment her expression startled him. It was a reminder that in a dancer as successful as Ana there must also be something of the actor, but there was something else besides, something he could only half recall . . .

"One wouldn't . . . would one?" he said helplessly. This time the look she gave him was the more familiar, scornful one; with an undercurrent, perhaps, of that charity which is due to the feeble-minded.

"I do not wish to say any more," she said, and immediately went on to contradict the assertion. "He is not, I think, a man for one woman; but for one woman, perhaps, over all."

"Did Mrs. Lindsay divorce her husband? I mean, was she the—the injured party?"

"I believe so, *señor.* This is before I am in England, and Geraldine does not speak of it, but he has told me 'she does not understand.' "

The picture that conjured up was irresistible. "Did he—did he make a pass at you, *señorita?*"

Her cold look seemed to deplore the crudity of the question. "I tell you only so that you will, perhaps, understand Geraldine a little. She has been—"

"Disillusioned," he suggested when she paused. Ana accepted the word graciously, inclining her head.

"So now she sees that life is not always simple. But sometimes, *señor,* I think it is more than that. She is attracted; there is, after all, a great likeness between these two who are cousins. But she is cautious, too, and sometimes I think she is frightened."

"Of Jon?"

"Who else? He is a man who gets his own way, that one."

"Then I don't quite see why you're so worried to get her paired off with him."

Ana shrugged. "It may not work. *Es muy posible.* But she will not be happy until she has tried."

"So you think she took an overdose of whatever-it-was last night, and if you hadn't found her . . . how did that happen, *señorita?*"

"I have supper with Enrique. Geraldine has a headache, and will go to bed early, she says. What should I do then, but go to her room when I return? She is flushed, *señor,* and breathing heavily; and I see the bottle of tablets, open, and the glass of water, nearly empty. And she will not wake."

"How many tablets had she taken? She told me—"

"That I do not know. The doctor said it might be true, that she had taken, twice, the biggest dose allowed. But the doctor —pouf!" said Ana, despairing to find a more adequate comment. "He says it is an accident. He does not know her heart."

"But wouldn't she have taken more than that . . . enough to make sure—?"

"*Señor,* you are asking me to make a—a divining," said Ana, severe again. "If the doctor who ordered the medicine knew his business, two doses should certainly have been enough."

This seemed to Maitland rather a peculiar point of view,

but it wasn't much good arguing. "Is there anything I can do?"

"You ask me that, and Jon is still in prison!"

"I meant—"

"No, all is well." She relented sufficiently to smile at him again. "*Señor* Webster will come tonight when I go to the theater. He is kind, do you not think? And in the meantime, I am a good nurse."

He said, on an impulse, "Could any stranger have been here while you were out last night?" and saw her puzzled look.

"I should have known, be sure of that. And I do not know why you should ask me."

For that matter, he didn't know himself. The doctor was right, or Ana was; or perhaps there was some truth in both their assertions. "I must be going now," he said, and turned toward the door. But when he looked round again she hadn't moved from where she was standing, and he saw her face stripped of all its assurance. "Don't be afraid, *señorita. Todo se arreglará.*"

"*Así lo espero,*" said Ana, and shrugged, and was her brisk self again. "*Adios, señor. Muchas gracias.*"

It did not seem to Maitland, as he waited for the lift to take him down to the street again, that he had given her much cause for gratitude.

2

From Maddox Court, he went straight to Geoffrey Horton's office, but if he expected any solace from that quarter he was destined to be disappointed. "Irrelevant," said Geoffrey, when he heard what had happened to Geraldine Lindsay. And then, "Some of these women have no sense."

"I'm inclined to believe her," said Antony mildly. "At least when she says she didn't mean it."

Horton's expression seemed to indicate that his friend's credulity caused him no surprise. "It makes no odds anyway," he said.

"She's unhappy, and Kellaway's under arrest."

"There's nothing you can do about it," said Geoffrey reasonably. "Not yet, anyway."

"I suppose not." Maitland cleared a space at the corner of the desk, and sat down, swinging his leg. "Have you seen O'Keefe?"

Geoffrey was too accustomed to this casual treatment to bother to protest. "I have. Yesterday evening."

"Such devotion to duty!"

"It had to be done," said Geoffrey crossly; which was unreasonable, because the comment only underlined a fact he had intended to convey. "He's a smooth character, quite capable of holding his own."

"Father William chooses his associates well." He paused, staring across the room with a rather vacant expression, and then turned his head to look down at Horton again. "You don't think it will serve?"

"It might," said Geoffrey grudgingly. "But . . . no . . . I don't think it will," he added, as censoriously as if it were all Maitland's fault. "It isn't them I distrust, so much as our client."

"No, I gathered that." He paused, and began to fiddle absent-mindedly with the knobs on the desk calendar. "Will you put someone on to finding out about Dakins's past?" he said.

"What about it?"

"I want to know if he and Jon Kellaway had any common acquaintance."

"Very well." Horton put out a hand, and removed the calendar well out of Maitland's reach. "You may wish it was June, 1972, Antony, but I've rather a lot to do before then."

"I'm sorry. Tell me then, was there anything else to be learned from the hearing? The cause of death, now—"

"The medical evidence was still inconclusive. They say there was a lot of blood."

"He'd been killed where he was found then?"

"It seems so. After all, if you're going to set fire to a body, why move it?"

"Why, indeed? But had he been stabbed, or shot—"

"Not shot, anyway. They'd have found the bullet by now."

"Still, the blood might be a point in our client's favor. Did the neighbor—what is the man's name, anyway?"

"Butler."

"Did Butler say if Kellaway was carrying anything?"

"He's quite sure he wasn't."

"Well, then! What happened to his bloodstained clothes? We'd have heard about it if they'd been found in the house."

"I'm afraid that doesn't help."

"No, of course . . . the funeral pyre. Damn!"

"You're beginning to appreciate the difficulties," said Geoffrey. The idea seemed to give him some satisfaction, his mood was mellowing as Maitland's grew more despondent. "I'll tell you the rest of it over lunch," he offered.

Antony slid off the desk. "I'm not at all sure I want to discuss a bloody, charred corpse while I eat," he protested, "even if you are paying for the meal." But Geoffrey ignored this as a further irrelevance.

Outside, it was beginning to rain.

3

They talked, in fact, of everything under the sun except Jon Kellaway's affairs; and except for the subject that kept intruding itself on Antony's thoughts . . . the bribing of Bassett. There was nothing to be gained by dwelling on that . . . not even sympathy, he suspected, though in that he was less than fair.

Afterward he walked back to chambers, and did his best to concentrate on the problems involved in the breach of contract case, which might possibly be reached, or so Mallory told him, before the end of the week. In this he was so far successful that he didn't notice Keith Lindsay until he had almost passed him, and then only because he heard his name spoken. He turned then, and saw Lindsay coming from the shelter of a doorway. "They said you'd be back, Mr. Maitland, but I thought I'd rather wait for you out here."

As it was raining steadily, this seemed an odd preference. "You'd better come in now, anyway," said Maitland, and led the way across the court and up the stairs to Sir Nicholas's chambers. If Lindsay really wanted to talk, he had no choice but to follow; and sure enough there he was when Antony paused in the hall to remove his wet raincoat. He did this a little awkwardly, and was annoyed when he found Keith's eyes fixed on him in an appraising stare.

His room seemed gloomier than ever today. He turned on the desk light, to make it more cheerful, and waited until Lindsay had seated himself and lighted a cigarette, and then still waited. After a while Keith said uneasily, "I went to the magistrate's court yesterday."

"I rather thought you would." He paused, and then added with a diffident air that went oddly with the bluntness of the words, "In what capacity are you here, Mr. Lindsay? I can't talk to the Press, you know."

"I'm worried about Jon."

"I see." He picked up a pencil, and began to scribble idly on the blotter. "The day they arrested him you told me he'd be all right."

"Yes, well, it's a habit of his. And he would have been, wouldn't he? Father William came along with an alibi. But now there's what that man Butler says about seeing Jon. I don't like the sound of it."

"You think the jury will believe him, rather than Mr. Webster?"

"Don't you?"

"I haven't the faintest idea." He sat back a little to observe his sketch, and wondered vaguely for a moment why the figure he had drawn should have been standing on its head. He abandoned it and, thinking of Ana, drew instead a wolf with a bushy tail.

"With all the rest of it—" said Keith impatiently.

"Yes, that's rather the point, isn't it?" He raised his head, and his eyes met Lindsay's with sudden alertness. "Who has a grudge against Jonathan Kellaway?" he asked.

"I don't understand you, I'm afraid."

"Surely you've considered the point. Or don't you believe your cousin's story?"

Maitland was reminded again of Keith Lindsay's capacity

for stillness. "I don't think Jon killed Dakins," he said carefully.

"The rest of the police case might be explained away, with some hope at least of being believed. The newspaper cuttings that will be held to show motive are another matter. It seems unlikely that their presence among Dakins's belongings can be accounted for by coincidence."

Lindsay was frowning. "Therefore, if Jon is innocent, someone planted them. But couldn't that have been . . . well, self-preservation on the murderer's part?"

"Someone who knew the details of Mrs. Kellaway's death," Maitland insisted, and laid his pencil down carefully across the corner of the blotting-pad.

"But there's no one—"

"We don't yet know of anyone. Mr. Webster, for instance, had no known connection with Dakins—"

"Aren't you going a little far?"

"I'm going even further in a moment," Maitland assured him. "You, of course, must have been well acquainted with the circumstances—"

"I thought we should come to that."

"—but you didn't know Dakins. Or did you?"

"I've seen him to pass the time of day, of course. Jon had lived in Gilcliffe Gardens a long time." .

"That hardly answers my purpose," said Maitland regretfully. "There remains . . . Mrs. Lindsay."

Keith's stillness was somehow as eloquent as another man's protest might have been. "You can't really believe that."

"I don't believe anything," said Antony; a rather sweeping assertion, but true enough as far as the matter under discussion was concerned. "And speaking of Beth Kellaway, I was rather surprised to find that the prosecution aren't calling you."

"Why should they?"

"They have an excellent excuse to go into the circumstances of her death, in the course of establishing motive. The police have talked to you, of course?"

"Yes, but I don't think they know I was ever in Penhaven. They didn't ask me, and I didn't go out of my way to tell them."

90

"Good. Now, I know Mr. Horton means to get in touch with you, but as you're here . . . if you were asked in court about your cousin's relationship with his wife, what would you say? You'd be on oath, remember."

"Would it be answer enough to say I hope I shan't be asked that?"

"I'd prefer you to spell it out for me." He paused, and did not go on until it became obvious that Lindsay had nothing to say. "You remember she left a letter?"

"Yes."

"She said Kellaway neglected her. Was that true?"

"They didn't see much of each other, those last months. I suppose," said Keith reluctantly, "it was all his fault."

"And that he was unfaithful to her."

"I don't know . . . I don't *know* about that."

"And cruel."

"That might mean anything."

"So it might. But in spite of all this, she also said she loved him."

"I think . . . I'm afraid . . . that was true."

"So the coroner's remarks were fair enough, on the whole? I don't think we shall be calling you, Mr. Lindsay."

"Thank God for that, anyway!"

"Yes, I suppose you would find it distressing. Did you know Mrs. Lindsay has been ill?"

For a moment Keith sat staring at him; perhaps he was trying to relate the question to what had gone before. "Father William told me," he said at last. "I suppose that's why . . . I suppose you think she tried to kill herself."

"Don't you?"

"I don't know."

"Would you say she was fond of Kellaway?"

"She isn't in love with him, if that's what you mean."

"I see."

"I wonder if you do," said Lindsay. "You could take my word for it, as a matter of fact. I know her rather well."

"I'm sure you do," said Maitland cordially. There had been a bitterness in the other man's tone, but now Lindsay gave a reluctant laugh. "We were married for nearly seven years," he said.

"And are still good friends."

"Why not?"

"I just wondered." Maitland sounded vague. "Mr. Lindsay . . . what did you make of the medical evidence?"

"I don't think anyone could have made much of it. But why ask me?"

"I thought perhaps you wouldn't be quite a layman in these matters."

"I suppose Father William told you that. You seem very interested in my affairs, Mr. Maitland."

"Well, you see, until I heard how precise Mr. Butler's description of your cousin had been—"

"You thought it might have been me!"

"The idea occurred to me. The likeness is really very marked."

"So I've been told." Oddly enough, this plain speaking seemed to have a soothing effect on Lindsay. He sat back in his chair and said, with much less tension in his voice, "I suppose I must be grateful that Jon's so fair, otherwise Father William might be having to find an alibi for me, too."

"That brings me to the other question I wanted to ask you." Antony picked up his pencil again, but this time his scribbling led to nothing more interesting than a series of geometric designs. "When we met before you told me that Kellaway usually fell on his feet—"

"Did I say that?"

"You implied it. And I've been wondering, you see . . . how much has Mr. Webster had to do with that?"

"Father William's done a lot for him . . . for us both," Keith corrected himself. "But Jon's always had the luck."

"Including what happened at Penhaven?"

"Once the inquest was over . . . he wasn't in love with Beth by then, you know."

"You mean, he was glad of his freedom. But now—"

"You *are* worried about him." Lindsay sat back and gave his companion a quizzical look. "Do you realize that's the nearest you've come to a positive statement the whole time I've been here?"

"Well, you know," said Maitland apologetically, "I don't quite see how you can divorce the reporter from the anxious relative. Not altogether."

"So it's no good my asking you—"

"None whatever."

"Then I'll be getting along." He didn't sound resentful, but really it was impossible to tell. Lindsay got up, started toward the door, hesitated, and came back to stand by the desk again. "How did you know Geraldine was ill?"

"Ana told me."

"Did she say . . . Father William said she was better."

"She is." He got up himself, and added on an impulse as he met Lindsay's eye, "Don't worry. I saw her for a moment, and she's perfectly well now. Only rather tired."

"You saw her!"

"Ana hoped I could reassure her—"

"About Jon." He stood a moment, considering this, and then made for the door again and this time reached it. "I hope you managed to set her mind at rest," he said, pausing for a moment with his hand on the knob. "It's more than you've done for me."

He wrenched the door open then and went out, slamming it behind him.

4

After that Maitland worked steadily, and by the time he went home was hopeful that he had made some sense of the breach of contract papers. There was plenty of news to exchange with Jenny, and they were still talking after dinner when there was a knock on the outer door, and immediately someone pushed it open.

Roger Farrell was already in the hall when Antony got there. "Have you seen the evening paper?" he inquired abruptly.

"Yes, why?"

"This is a late edition of the *Chronicle*. I just picked it up. I thought you ought to know—"

Antony took the paper that was being held out to him, and moved a little until he was under the light, which wasn't designed for reading. The front page headline was unhappily all too familiar, and so was the story under it that began, *Fighting has broken out . . .* but at the left hand side of the page, in smaller print that still leaped to the eye, was something of more immediate concern. BRIBERY CASE—IMPORTANT NEW EVIDENCE. And below that, *A statement has been made by a friend of the dead juror . . .*

He raised his eyes briefly to meet Farrell's. "Read it," said Roger grimly.

. . . which, it is understood, has thrown new light on this tragic affair. Yesterday a member of the legal profession who is connected with the case was interviewed by the police; they are said to have believed he could assist them in their inquiries . . . He glanced quickly down the rest of the column . . . *not yet known . . . Mr. Hudson's statement . . . afraid of consequences . . . police protection.* A story on the face of it as innocuous as a fairy tale, and in the column beside it a picture of himself, a little blurred but easily identifiable, even without the caption which gave his name and added for good measure: *COUNSEL FOR THE DEFENSE in what has come to be known as the bribery case.* The implication was as obvious as a slap in the face, and a good deal more shocking.

Antony stood staring down at the paper, and after a moment Roger reached out a hand and took it from him. "Of course, it doesn't actually say it was you the police questioned—"

"No names, nothing so vulgar. But enough innuendo to sink a battleship," said Antony gloomily. He turned his head, though he wasn't conscious of having heard any movement, and saw Jenny standing in the doorway. "You'd better look at this, love. I can't pretend to like it, but it doesn't do to take these things too seriously."

Roger gave her the paper. After a moment he said unhappily, "I don't understand."

"Of course you don't. I'll tell you in a moment." Antony was watching Jenny as she read. "I suppose Hudson talked out of turn, but I don't quite see—" He let the sentence trail into inconclusive silence.

Jenny looked up. "I don't like it either," she said. Her voice trembled a little on the words.

"What are you going to do?" Roger demanded.

"I can't take them to court, if that's what you mean. It would only turn out that the story really referred to the editor's grandfather, who lives in retirement at Chipping Norton. Besides, so far as it goes, it's true." He took Jenny's arm and began to urge her gently toward the living-room. "Roger wants a drink," he said, "and I *need* one."

After that he went through it all again, everything Watkins had said. "But when I thought about it afterwards there didn't seem to be much I could do about it, and this doesn't really alter the situation."

"If someone's trying to frame you"—Roger's glance shifted momentarily to Jenny's face, but she was sitting quietly, staring into the fire—"this might be the second move in the game."

"I wonder." Antony was silent for a while. "I suppose you mean, I can't just leave it there," he said at last, and paused again before he added, "I'm afraid I agree with you."

"So?"

"Find out who tried to bribe Bassett . . . find out where the slander started . . . find out who was responsible for Bassett's death. Simplicity itself!" he said, and spread his hands in an extravagant gesture.

"That sounds very fine." Roger ignored the hint of mockery in Maitland's tone. "The thing is, can I help?"

There was a silence while Antony sat staring at him. Then he got up restlessly, but either of his companions could have told, from the way he moved, that his shoulder was giving him pain. "I don't quite see—"

"You may need a witness. If you want to see Hudson, for instance."

"Yes, of course." His tone was lighter now, but he still had his intent look. "Tomorrow?" he said.

"Whenever you say." Farrell leaned forward to stub out his

cigarette. "There's one thing I've been wondering though."

"What's that?"

"Has it occurred to you that all this happened after it was known you were taking an interest in Kellaway's defense?"

WEDNESDAY, 24th MARCH

1

Roger's idea kept going through Antony's mind all night, making his sleep spasmodic and his waking periods an agony of indecision. At three o'clock he thought there might be something in it; at four-thirty he was convinced it was all nonsense. Neither conclusion comforted him at all.

Roger had promised to clear the decks for action by midday, and the picture of him sweeping through the office like a whirlwind—which would certainly ruffle his partner's feelings if not his person—enlivened the breakfast-table considerably, so that Antony was able to conceal his anxiety well enough. He had a feeling—unreasonable after so many years of examination and cross-examination in open court—that he might manage Hudson better alone; but the wisdom of Roger's suggestion was undeniable.

He took a cab, because he wanted to get to chambers early, and then changed his mind half-way and directed the driver to Bucklersbury instead. When he climbed the stairs to Paul Collingwood's office he found that the solicitor hadn't yet arrived, so he asked instead for the managing clerk. Falkner was in his own room, perusing the morning's mail, but he received the visitor with an enthusiasm which rather put Antony off because it couldn't possibly be genuine at that time of day.

The room somehow just missed being comfortable, or was that merely a reflection of his own state of mind? "I was hoping to see Mr. Collingwood," said Maitland, seating himself, "but perhaps you'll give him a message."

Falkner went back to his chair. "Of course. Of course. I shall be only too glad." His eyes were bright and speculative. "You aren't going to the inquest then, Mr. Maitland?"

"Inquest?"

"On poor Bassett's death."

"But we decided—didn't we?—that it was no concern of ours."

"Oh, to be sure. I thought perhaps you might have changed your mind."

"No," said Antony, and smiled. He was perfectly well aware that Falkner would have liked to add, "after what the papers said last night," and wondered briefly whether there was anybody at all connected with the legal community who hadn't seen the report and drawn his own conclusions.

The smile was evidently not a success, Falkner looked almost nervous. "I only thought—"

"Never mind. I want to see Swaine."

"But, Mr. Maitland, it will be at least two weeks before the trial comes on again; it may even be postponed until the next session."

"I know all that."

Perhaps it was the hardness of his tone that sparked Falkner to a show of firmness. "I assure you, Mr. Collingwood questioned him very closely."

On the whole, Maitland thought this unlikely. "Even so—" he began, and was interrupted by the arrival of Paul Collingwood, who flung open the door and came in breezily. His greeting was effusive enough to set the seal on Antony's depression by convincing him that it was a cover for embarrassment.

"Here's Mr. Maitland wanting to talk to Swaine," said Falkner. With the arrival of his employer his manner had reverted to normal. "I was telling him—"

"Yes, well, never mind that. Come into my room a moment, will you, Maitland?"

Antony was on his feet. "There's no need for me to disturb you. If you could just arrange an interview—" But Collingwood was waiting for him with inexorable good humor; there was nothing for it but to follow him, to take the chair he offered, to wait while he settled himself, straightened his blotter, took pen and pencil from his breast pocket . . .

"So you want to see Swaine?"

"I seem to have been saying very little else for the last quarter of an hour," said Maitland with sudden tartness. Collingwood's answering smile only added to his irritation.

"I don't think he'll tell you, you know."

"Tell me what?"

"Who he employed in this bribery business. That's what you're after, isn't it?"

"And how the bargain was struck, how payment was to be made. Everything."

"I asked him all that myself, as a matter of form." Collingwood's gaze was direct, too direct. "Equally as a matter of form, he denied any knowledge of what had been going on. I'm not at all sure that I want him to be pressed about it."

"I see. Prejudicial." He hesitated, and then added unemotionally, "Did you see yesterday's *Evening Chronicle*?" Collingwood gave an abrupt nod. "Then you know I shall be sending back the brief. It was good of you not to remind me of the necessity."

"My dear fellow!"

"So if an interview could be arranged, *not* as his counsel,"— this time there seemed to be some genuine amusement behind his smile—"I'll guarantee not to tell you anything he may tell me."

"I can see it's important to you, of course."

"You could hardly fail to do so," said Maitland dryly.

"Very well." Collingwood seemed to make up his mind. "I'll phone you."

Antony went away before he could change his mind.

2

Old Mr. Mallory must have heard him come in, for he appeared in Maitland's room not two minutes after he had got there, closed the door firmly, and proceeded, first, to voice his disquiet, and secondly to ask a number of surprisingly pertinent questions. Antony supposed wearily that an acquaintance which dated from his own schooldays was enough to justify his uncle's clerk in bullying him; in any case, there was nothing he could do about it.

One way and another it was nearly eleven o'clock before he

could make the call he had in mind, and then he found—as he should have remembered—that Bruce Halloran was in court.

His coffee arrived as he put down the receiver, and with the door open he became aware that a hush had fallen over the place . . . the sort of atmosphere occasionally engendered by Sir Nicholas's moods, but which he could never before recall being a tribute to one of his own. When he was still at the junior bar one of his clients—a pickpocket—had confided his troubles as a wartime evacuee. "No fish and chips, that was bad enough. But the worst thing of all was the 'orrible 'ush," he had said, and for the first time Maitland knew how he felt. "For God's sake, Willett, bang the door as you go out . . . sing 'Rule Britannia' . . . drop the Law Reports out of the window on somebody's head." But Willett only smiled in an understanding way that sharpened his annoyance, and as the door closed behind him the phone rang: Chief-Inspector Sykes was here and would appreciate the favor of a few words.

"Send him in," said Antony, and hoped his tone did not reflect his lack of enthusiasm. He'd had about as much of the C.I.D. as he could take . . . "And ask Willett for some more coffee, will you?"

It was characteristic of the chief-inspector that he should come in, after a brief delay, carrying his own cup. "I hope they gave you enough sugar," said Maitland, when greetings had been exchanged; and Sykes smiled in his sedate way and said:

"I saw to that," and began to stir the liquid with a gentle, persistent motion. He was a square-built, fresh-faced man, with a comfortable look about him, as of a farmer, perhaps, who had put through a good deal at that day's market. After a moment, "I saw in the paper that Sir Nicholas has gone to the United States," he said. "I hope Mrs. Maitland is well."

Antony was pondering the reason for the visit. He knew the other man too well to be at all deceived by this leisurely approach; Sykes had a strong sense of propriety, and a genuine affection for Jenny, too. He was saying now: "I'd have come round home to see you, this being strictly unofficial. But then I thought I might upset her."

The movement of the coffee-spoon seemed to have a mesmeric effect. Surely even Sykes's customary five lumps of sugar would be dissolved by now. "Whereas this way you'll only have shocked Mallory," said Antony, and raised his eyes at last to the detective's face. "What do you want with me, Chief-Inspector . . . unofficially?"

"A word of advice, Mr. Maitland, which I hope you won't take amiss." He stopped stirring, and put the spoon down carefully in his saucer. Antony gave him his sudden smile.

"Who knows, I may even be grateful?"

"As to that," said Sykes, who had known him for a good many years, "I'm not counting on it." It was not in his nature to show embarrassment, but he was picking his words with care. "It's about this bribery business, you see, and Bassett's death."

"Did you know, I thought it might be? Are you working on that case too?"

"No, but I've seen the reports; including the one of Inspector Watkins's talk with you, Mr. Maitland. And last night's papers, which I expect you've seen yourself."

"Tell me something, Chief-Inspector . . . was that report inspired by the police?"

"It was not. Someone put the reporters on to Hudson, from what I hear. And I'll tell you straight, they won't be content with hints for very long." He paused invitingly, but Antony was silent. "It all adds up to trouble," said Sykes, "but you don't need me to tell you that. Now, you've done me a favor or two in the past, Mr. Maitland. I wouldn't like to see you let things get out of hand."

"I don't quite see what I'm supposed to do about it."

"You might try being a bit frank with us for a change," said Sykes bluntly.

There was a pause while Antony considered this. "Isn't that where we c-came in, Chief-Inspector?"

"Sometimes I've wondered where you've got your knowledge," Sykes admitted. "And sometimes it's been quite clear you knew more than you were telling. This time it's obvious—"

"You'd b-better explain that, d-don't you think?"

"If we assume your innocence, Mr. Maitland—and I can't see why that should annoy you—we are left with the probability that someone is trying to discredit you. I can't think of any better reason than that you've got some special knowledge that they don't want to be spread abroad."

"Yes, I see. The only trouble is, I haven't." He thought as he spoke of Roger's theory, but Sykes would only laugh at that. Or would he? He was still hesitating when the detective went on earnestly:

"I do urge you, Mr. Maitland, to reconsider that statement. That isn't to say that I believe you have any guilty knowledge—"

"Kind of you!" Antony told him. But there was no mistaking Sykes's sincerity, and after a moment he went on more quietly. "No . . . I mean that. Briggs, I gather, isn't inclined to be quite so forbearing, but I suppose I shouldn't be surprised. He's always thought I'd go to any lengths to get a verdict."

"The chief-superintendent is a man of very strong opinions," said Sykes carefully. And added simply, "That's why I came."

"Well, I'm sorry I lost my temper."

"I can understand that you're very worried about all this."

The remark was rather too pointed for comfort. Antony counted slowly up to ten; conversation with Sykes gave you time for that sort of exercise. "Will you tell me something, Chief-Inspector? Do the police think Bassett was murdered?"

"Unofficially, Mr. Maitland . . . yes. Officially, it would be difficult to prove, except by showing system. And that might be the most difficult thing of all."

"You mean, there have been other cases?"

"There have been other cases of suicide among men who had recently been on jury duty," said Sykes in his precise way.

"By the same means?"

"Each one had cut his throat. There was a particularly macabre touch about Bassett's death," he added thoughtfully. "The knife he used—or seemed to have used—was part of a set his wife got free with coupons from some washing powder or other." He stopped, and sat looking at his companion with a benevolent expression.

"You can't leave it there," Maitland protested. "How often

has this happened? When? Where? What sort of cases were involved, and how did the verdicts go?"

"Now then!" said Sykes.

"And who noticed the points of similarity?"

"As to that, it seemed to me when I read about Bassett that I'd seen something like it before. So I began to poke about a bit, but I've no means of saying I've got a full picture yet."

"Still, you can answer my other questions, as far as you've gone."

"I've reviewed three cases: one in London, that was the one I remembered; one following Lewes Assizes; one Exeter. The earliest was four years ago. In each instance the defendant was found guilty and got a stiff sentence."

"Was there anything to connect the men—the defendants—except that they were clients of the same agency?"

"Well now, Mr. Maitland, I haven't got as far as that. They *may* have been, but you must remember they were all convicted."

"And one of the jury cut his throat soon afterwards." His own words to Collingwood came into his mind. "Just plain revenge, or was it as a warning?"

"That we don't know. There'd been no hint of attempted corruption in any of these cases, you see. But I'll tell you something one of the defendants had in common with your Mr. Swaine,"—perhaps Antony was wrong in thinking that Sykes hesitated before he went on—"he had the same solicitor."

"Collingwood? That doesn't mean anything. His practice is mainly criminal."

"So it is," agreed the chief-inspector, at his most placid.

"If Bassett had refused outright," said Maitland, already forgetting what Sykes had said in his interest in the next point, "would he have been given the chance of talking to Halloran? Poor chap, I wonder if he knew how brave he was being." He paused, thinking of the scene in court the week before, and shivered as though the warm room had grown suddenly chilly. "I think he knew," he said.

"Yes, I dare say." Sykes sounded as stolid as ever, but there was a speculative gleam in his eye. Antony looked at him and through him unseeingly.

"If one man is responsible—"

"Or one man and his accomplices," Sykes supplied.

"—*this* time, something seems to have gone wrong with his timing. He's getting careless. Or getting a taste for blood," he added soberly. "Which might amount to the same thing."

"And somehow," said the chief-inspector, dragging him back again from the realms of speculation, "you've got in his way."

Antony made up his mind. "Could it be over some other case?"

"Are you trying to pull the wool over my eyes, Mr. Maitland?"

He was too interested in the conversation to be annoyed by this further evidence of distrust. "Not at the moment. I was thinking of Jonathan Kellaway."

"That brings me to something else I wanted to say," Sykes told him. "You've been consulting Father William, I hear."

"How did you know?"

"Things get about," said the detective, vague in his turn. "But I wonder if you're altogether wise—"

"Now what are you implying?" But it was obvious enough. The police had got wind of the alibi, and were wondering if he'd had a hand in arranging it. "Look here, has the old boy ever been inside?"

"Not yet," said Sykes. There may have been a touch of regret in his tone. "But you're evading the issue, Mr. Maitland. It's Bassett I came here to talk about."

"I've nothing to tell you about that." He sounded tired now, and discouraged. Sykes got to his feet.

"Then I'd best be getting along. If you should change your mind—" he added, and shook his head sadly when Antony did not reply. "Make no mistake about it, Mr. Maitland. Whether your knowledge of this affair is innocent or guilty, you're riding for a fall."

When he had gone Antony looked down with distaste at his coffee, untouched, and covered with a wrinkled skin. Sykes's cup was empty. After a moment he pushed his own away, and put his left elbow on the desk, and rested his head

on his hand. His thoughts were chaotic, and all of them unpleasant.

He sat like that for what seemed to be a very long time.

3

By some means or other, Roger Farrell managed to find a
parking spot in the city each morning, but he had declined to
give it up on the chance of there being another near Astroff's.
Maitland, therefore, joined him for lunch, and while they were
waiting for cheese and biscuits he went out and tried to phone
Halloran, but again without success. And again he didn't
know whether he was glad or sorry. The conversation might so
easily prove difficult. He was rather silent during the drive to
Barnet, though he roused himself once to say unkindly, "It
would have been quicker by tube." Roger only grinned at
that, but not—thank heaven!—at all sympathetically, and
continued to guide the Jensen through the afternoon traffic
with imperturbable skill.

When they turned into Westmead Road Antony sat forward, looking at the numbers. "That's where Bassett lived," he
said after a moment. The blinds were drawn, and there was no
sign of life. "I wish we could, in decency, talk to Mrs. Bassett,"
he added in a discontented tone.

"Talking to Hudson is going to be difficult enough," Roger
reminded him. "That looks like the shop on the next corner."

"It is the shop. I wonder if it's early closing day."

"It doesn't matter, if they live there."

"He might still be celebrating after the inquest. If that's the
right word," he added doubtfully. "I wonder how good a
friend of Bassett's he really was."

According to Mr. Hudson, a very good friend indeed. He received them with surprising readiness, called on Ma to come
and take over, and led them into an untidy little room behind
the shop. The fresh smell of vegetables and cut flowers was the
most pleasant thing about it. Hudson's lugubrious look was
not attractive, but still might be genuine enough.

"So you're Mr. Maitland," he said. The curiosity in his eyes
was unpleasant. "Sit down . . . you and your friend." (Roger
prepared to efface himself, which he did with surprising ease

for so positive a personality.) "I wasn't *expecting* to see you," Hudson added, as though it were a reproach.

"I'm hoping you'll give me an account of what Mr. Bassett told you," said Antony briskly, and saw without surprise that Hudson's eyes shifted away from his own. The greengrocer was a long, rather limp figure of a man, and if he had worn his Sunday-best for the inquest he had discarded it now in favor of a white overall that equally with its wearer looked in need of starch. And he was embarrassed, but there could be more than one reason for that.

"You weren't at the inquest, Mr. Maitland?" he said, temporizing.

"I was not."

"I gave my evidence there . . . well, they didn't want details. Your name wasn't mentioned, sir."

"But you did mention it to the police."

"As was my duty, Mr. Maitland. Repeating what was told me, *without* prejudice, and not to say I believed it."

"Then there's no harm in repeating it again, to me."

"Not the least in the world. So long as you understand, sir, I take no responsibility—"

"I realize the position, Mr. Hudson." It went against the grain to say it. "I want your help."

"Then I'll tell you, and willingly." (And that was the queer thing, he *was* willing to talk.) "What do you want to know?"

"How long have you known Mr. Bassett?"

"Oh, for years and years." His tone seemed to stretch the time out to infinity. "We were good friends."

"On visiting terms?"

"Yes."

"Was he in the habit of confiding in you? Had he ever done so before?"

"Perhaps before there'd been nothing to tell." He thought for a moment. "Still, I wasn't surprised when he did."

"Then perhaps you will tell me—in his own words as far as you remember them—exactly what was said."

"I can try," said Hudson obligingly. "Bert, he said to me, I've been foolish; there's things I did ought to have told the police. And then he said, that man who came to see me, I got a thing or two out of him."

"Did he describe the man?"

"Only to say he wasn't much to look at. But he said he'd seen him before, talking to you; he said it looked as if you knew each other. And then the man said, first off, he'd never heard of you, but after a bit he changed that and made out you were the one who sent him."

"And Bassett believed him?"

"He did in the end, along of what the chap told him about how to go on, you see. Had it all off pat, legal-like, Bassett said it fair made his head swim. And he'd heard of you, you see, Bassett had; and this would be one way to win cases, wouldn't it? You can't deny that."

Antony glanced at Roger Farrell. "I can't deny it," he said, and turned back to Hudson. "Did you discuss this at all with your friend . . . give him any advice?"

"I said he should tell the police," said Hudson virtuously.

"Did you think he would?"

"Well, you see, Mr. Maitland, he was in a bad state. Jumpy. I thought perhaps if he calmed down a bit, *then* he'd tell them."

"You didn't feel it was your duty—?"

"And break a confidence, sir? You can't have thought what it would mean."

Antony smiled for the first time. "A shocking suggestion," he agreed. "Would you be equally shocked if I asked if you foresaw his suicide?"

"Did he kill himself, Mr. Maitland? That wasn't what the coroner's jury said."

"What!" He saw Hudson bridle at the sharpness of his tone, and added with deliberate calmness, "What was the verdict?"

"To put it plainly, sir, they said his throat had been cut, but there was no evidence to say who done it."

"I see," said Maitland, and looked at Farrell again. Roger's attention was fixed on Hudson, he had a cold, almost a calculating look. "Have you seen Mrs. Bassett? What does she think about it?"

"I'm sure I couldn't take it on myself to say." But he

changed his mind and added, not quite so smugly, "She doesn't think he was lying about the message from her sister."

"So someone deliberately . . . yes, I see." He got up as he spoke, and Roger followed his example. "One last thing, Mr. Hudson. Did you tell the Press what Bassett had said to you?"

"Well, I didn't. Not that I see what harm it would have done."

"Don't you?" A certain skepticism had crept into his tone. "You say I wasn't named at the inquest; but the *Evening Chronicle*—and probably some of the other papers as well—implied a connection between Bassett and me."

For a moment when the visitors rose, Hudson had been all smiles. Now his eyes were shifty again. "I can't help you there, Mr. Maitland. I didn't tell them, that's all I know."

"Didn't you?" The incredulity was very marked now.

"It isn't a nice thing to call a man a liar in his own house," said Hudson, offended.

"You may be telling the truth about this for all I know . . . or care. But who paid you to give that story to the police?"

"I don't understand you."

"If I thought you invented it yourself—"

Hudson took a step backward. "I assure you, Mr. Maitland . . . you asked me to tell you what Bassett had said," he added with nervous desperation, "and that I've done." Roger came up to Antony's elbow, and the greengrocer went back again until he was brought up short by the table. "Barring what Mrs. Bassett had to say about the man—"

"I thought she couldn't describe him."

"She couldn't either."

"Then what in hell's name do you mean?"

"He—he limped."

"Heaven and earth!" said Maitland blankly, and closed his mouth with a snap, as though he had just realized the indiscretion of whatever he had been about to add. Hudson said eagerly:

"Just dragged his foot a little, that's all."

"I see." The tableau held for a moment longer and then Maitland said shortly, "So far as you have tried to help me, I'm grateful," and turned on his heel.

Outside in the street again he took a deep breath. "I wonder if the police are really giving Hudson protection, as the papers suggested."

"If they are, your visit must have made them think," Farrell said dryly.

"So it must. What fun." Antony was not amused. "He was scared, wasn't he. I expect that's why he told us . . . I mean, I think he was telling the truth about that, don't you?"

"You recognized the description," said Roger impatiently.

"It fits. Oh, Lord, it fits. The thing is, I don't quite know what to do about it."

"If you're under the impression that you've explained anything—"

"Haven't I?" He looked vague for a moment. "Albert Falkner drags his left foot slightly when he walks," he said at last in an expressionless voice.

"Yes, but who is Falkner?"

"Paul Collingwood's managing clerk. And Collingwood is Swaine's solicitor."

4

"I still say," maintained Roger stubbornly, nearly half an hour later, "that you should tell Watkins all this."

"Come to think of it, he must know already. But it wouldn't mean anything to him, of course. I doubt if he's ever seen Falkner, Collingwood always goes into court himself."

"Why not give him the benefit of your knowledge then?"

"I don't ever remember talking to Falkner at the corner of Middle Temple Lane," said Antony in a worried way, "but it's quite a likely sort of thing to have happened. Suppose I forgot."

"What of it?"

"It could mean that Hudson was telling the truth."

"And Bassett too, I suppose. Falkner trumped up this story when he was questioned—"

"Don't you see, Roger, if the police question him he'll tell the same tale again?"

Farrell looked doubtful. "Then what are you going to do?"

"Talk to him," said Maitland in a hard voice.

"To Falkner?"

"I think he might be prevailed upon to tell me who his principal is."

"And if he doesn't?"

"Then I must find out for myself." He hesitated. "I didn't tell you, Sykes came to see me," he said, and plunged into the story of the other jurors who had died. "It looks as though one man was behind it all . . . don't you think?"

"You've been talking about Falkner's principal, but how do you know—?"

"I decline to accept our Albert as a mastermind," said Maitland firmly. "Now I come to think of it, Sykes mentioned that Collingwood was the solicitor in one of the other cases, but that isn't even a coincidence if Falkner was involved. In fact, it might explain why Collingwood was so uncommonly upset about Bassett's death."

"What sort of a fellow is he?"

"Extrovert type. A bit overpoweringly friendly."

"Has he any reason to dislike you?"

"Well, I've lost a case or two for him, but it can't be that because he keeps on sending me briefs."

"Be serious for a minute."

"I am." Antony sounded hurt. "But the idea of Collingwood nursing a grudge until he got the chance to frame me—"

"It might not be as silly as it sounds."

"No." He sounded depressed, and Roger's severity relaxed in a grin.

"There are times when you'd madden a saint, but I didn't mean that."

"What about your idea that it was because of my interest in Kellaway that all this started?"

"It was only an idea."

"I know, but I've been thinking about it. Suppose the two cases were—were completely interlocked?"

"How could they be?"

"I don't know. I offered the idea to Sykes, but he wasn't having any. But *if* they are, there is a sort of pattern. Because I think there's an attempt to frame Jon Kellaway . . . and now it seems someone is playing the same game with me. And there is one person connected with Kellaway whom the suggestion of organized bribery would fit like a glove."

"I suppose you mean this chap you call Father William. Look here, Antony, did Sykes tell you outright that he is a fence?"

"If you really want me to be accurate, I should say that I implied it and he implied his agreement." He turned to look at Farrell, and saw him frown. "Not good enough?" For the first time a trace of amusement crept into his voice. "Uncle Nick doesn't like my guesses either, but he's three thousand miles away."

"Why should Father William frame Jon, and then give him an alibi?"

"We don't know yet that the alibi will stand up. And you must remember that in giving it he made it clear that O'Keefe will swear to *his* whereabouts, whether anyone believes Kellaway was also there or not."

"That's a bit devious, isn't it?"

"Father William is devious. But there's another possibility—" He paused, and stared out at the row of shops they were passing and the crowded pavement, and did not see them. "Meg wouldn't like this one," he said.

"That Jon really is guilty? In that case, of course, there's no connection at all."

"Oh, but it fits very well. Suppose Father William has been bribing jurors. Then, for whatever reason, Dakins had to be killed—"

"Wait a bit! What reason?"

"Well, most likely, I think, because he'd discovered something about the racket. This *will* upset Meg; I'm afraid in that case we must postulate that Jon Kellaway was a party to whatever was going on. And—it does fit, Roger, rather nicely —Jon didn't know about the newspaper cuttings, or he'd have moved them. His arrest was unforeseen, hence the alibi, and he didn't want my help, but I expect he thought it would seem suspicious to refuse it—"

"And Father William decided it would be safest to get you out of the way, so he arranged to fix you through an operation

111

on which he was already embarked," said Roger, and broke off, looking appalled. "I don't know what you're sounding so pleased about. It does fit, but I don't like it at all."

"It's a working hypothesis," said Antony submissively.

"Yes, but there's one thing. It doesn't explain why the body was burned. It couldn't have been to prevent identification; I mean, in Dakins's own flat."

"You do have the most damnable habit of finding fault. Still, nothing explains the bonfire, so I don't see much point in worrying about it." He glanced sideways at his companion again and said tentatively, "You do see, don't you, why I want to talk to Father William?"

5

A telephone call established that William Webster would again be spending the evening at Ana's flat. "From seven o'clock on, Mr. Maitland. I'm sure she will have no objection to your visiting me there." He sounded as benevolent as ever, perhaps even pleased at the prospect of some distraction from his vigil.

"About nine," said Antony, and rang off a little more abruptly than good manners might have dictated. Somehow, Father William's blandness was an irritation; what chance was there of getting a straight story out of anyone as slippery as that?

The phone rang twice before they had finished dinner. The first time it was Paul Collingwood. "Friday at ten-thirty," he said. "Will that do?"

"Unless I'm in court. I don't think I shall be. I'm very grateful."

"Think nothing of it." Collingwood's tone was as hearty as ever. With his talk with Roger in mind and a sudden, reprehensible desire to shake his confidence Maitland said:

"I want a word with Falkner some time. Shall I find his address in the phone book?"

"With . . . Albert? What on earth for?" The tone was as sharp a contrast to his previous one as Antony could have wished, but already he was regretting the impulse that had led to the disclosure. It might not be wise. . . .

"This and that," he said vaguely. "I expect he'll tell you." He replaced the receiver gently, cutting off Collingwood's protests, and almost immediately the bell rang again. He thought for a moment it was the solicitor calling back, but he wouldn't have had time to re-dial the number.

This time it was a well-known voice; Bruce Halloran was one of Sir Nicholas's closest friends. "Maitland?" The barest pause for Antony to identify himself. "Does last night's paper mean what it seems to mean?"

"In a way."

"I see." The cautious reply had obviously conveyed a good deal more than he would have wished; Antony reminded himself that Bruce Halloran knew him very well indeed. "I didn't see the report till midnight, and I've been in court all day—"

"I know, I've been trying to phone you." He could see Jenny looking at him inquiringly; even in the courtroom Halloran's voice often seemed over-loud, now it could be heard clearly right across the room, though probably the words were indistinguishable.

"As soon as Harding goes away—" he was saying, bitterly. "But that's beside the point. You'd better tell me."

"There's nothing to tell." But, of course, there was. By the time Halloran had finished, Antony—who hated explanations, especially when he was making them—was beginning to stutter, and was not much comforted when the other man said briskly:

"Then the police have nothing definite against you?"

"D-don't you think it's b-bad enough as it is?"

"And today you went to see this man Hudson."

"How the d-devil do you know that?"

"This evening's *Chronicle*. It may be in the other papers, as far as I know, though I doubt if there's been time. A picture of you leaving the shop," Halloran explained.

"But, I didn't—"

"No reason why you should have noticed the photographer. Now, you'll take my advice, Maitland, leave well alone. Give things a chance to die down."

"I—"

"Harding is staying at the Waldorf Astoria, isn't he?"

"I s-suppose you mean you'll t-tell him," said Antony, angry again.

"Unless you give me your word not to talk to anyone else concerned with the case. Except the police, of course," he amended.

"If I meet Collingwood in the street I'm to cut him, I suppose."

"You know perfectly well what I mean," said Halloran coldly.

"Blackmail."

"It's for your own good."

"It only n-needed that!" Halloran started to expostulate, but he went on quickly, "All right then, I promise. Will that content you?"

"It will. And if it wasn't that you wanted my advice," said Halloran, who never forgot a point, "why were you trying to call me?"

"To ask you what Bassett said."

"No more than I told the court."

"Nothing that would give us a clue?"

"For the last time, Maitland, leave it!"

"I'm sorry. I was forgetting," said Antony sarcastically, "that you come under the terms of the interdict yourself. We'd better ring off, hadn't we, before you accuse me of breaking my word?"

He hadn't realized until then that Halloran's temper, too, had been held in check, though rather more successfully than his own. "You always were a fool, Maitland," he said now, and slammed down the receiver.

Antony replaced his own more slowly, and stood a moment rubbing his ear before he went back to the table. "That was Halloran," he said unnecessarily.

"I could hear him," said Jenny. "What did he make you promise?"

"Not to meddle any further with the Bassett affair. I don't want Uncle Nick round my neck, love," he added, almost as though she had raised an objection.

"You won't be seeing Mr. Falkner, then?"

"No." He smiled at her, but vaguely. "There is nothing, however, to prevent me from proceeding as planned with my inquiries into Dakins's death."

6

Roger came in for coffee before they set off for Maddox Court. "We may as well walk," said Antony, when they set out; but after all they took the car and were lucky to find a parking place not too far down the street. "Do you know Geraldine Lindsay at all?" Maitland asked, as they waited for the lift.

"I've seen her around. I think someone introduced us once, but we've never done more than scream at each other politely for a few minutes at parties." Roger glanced sideways at his companion. "This idea of Meg's is all nonsense, you know."

"Which one?"

"That Geraldine is cold. And if you want my opinion—which I dare say you don't—she's in love with Jon."

"There are degrees of affection, wouldn't you say?"

"To be more precise, then: I'd say she hasn't gone overboard yet, but she's all ready to do so."

"As good as Aunt Ethel's *Answers to Correspondents* in the *Courier*," said Antony admiringly. He did not speak again until they were in the lift and the doors had shut behind them. "Can you be in love with two people at once?"

"I've never tried. I know what Aunt Ethel would say, though." The door slid open as they reached the fourth floor, and he put his finger on the STOP button, holding the lift motionless. "Why is it important?"

"I don't know. I just feel it is." He was staring straight in front of him, down the length of the empty corridor. "Ana doesn't like Kellaway," he added. "And there's always the question, what really happened to his wife?"

"*She* didn't cut her throat," said Roger.

"No, but . . . come along. Perhaps Father William can tell us."

Mr. Webster seemed pleased to see them. Mrs. Lindsay was

much better, he said, in reply to Antony's inquiries; she had been up for a little while during the day, but now was in bed again and he hoped she was asleep. "An anxious business," he said. "A mistake that could have had quite tragic results."

"You don't agree with Ana, then . . . about what happened?"

"Miss Ana is too severe." This was said with a sigh, but somehow there remained the familiar undercurrent of gaiety. "I am to give you a drink and ask you not to smoke, if you please. Will that be a hardship? The chairs are more comfortable than they look. Now, Mr. Maitland," he went on when they were all settled, "I suppose it is about my evidence. Mr. Farrell is, no doubt, an associate of yours."

A useful, all-embracing word. "That's right," Antony told him. "Mr. Horton has your statement by now, I take it. I'm trying to range a little farther afield."

"I shall never understand the law," said Father William. "I should have thought my testimony was sufficient." It was impossible to believe him insincere . . . equally impossible to credit him with quite so much simplicity.

"Unfortunately the prosecution will also offer evidence of Mr. Kellaway's whereabouts at the material time."

"That makes it difficult, doesn't it?" said the old man with a sad, saintly smile. "How can I help you?"

"Can you tell me anything about Beth Kellaway?"

Father William looked at him in silence for a moment. "Beyond what I told you the other day—"

"About her family, for instance. Is Kellaway still in touch with them?"

"I think she had a brother. I never heard of anybody else. I don't even remember his name."

Maitland was writing on his knee, on the back of an old envelope. "I am trying, you see, to account for the newspaper cuttings which Dakins had in his possession. They must have come from somewhere, and I can't imagine any friend of Kellaway's treasuring them all these years."

"I should certainly never have dreamed of doing so."

"Keith Lindsay was in Penhaven at the time, wasn't he?"

"He was. He told me he felt responsible . . . that he should have noticed how Beth felt. But I think myself it was very natural, because he had just met Geraldine." He hesitated, and this time Maitland was pretty sure his emotion was genuine. "I should not like you to ask him about this . . . of course, if it were a question of helping Jon, but I cannot see that his opinion could be of the slightest use."

No point in telling him the matter had already been discussed with Keith. "Did Lindsay think his cousin was to blame for Beth's suicide?"

"I'm sure he didn't. The circumstances," said Father William firmly, "were unfortunate."

"Have you ever heard of Fred Bassett, Mr. Webster?" It occurred to Maitland as he spoke that the question perhaps violated the terms of his agreement with Halloran; but Halloran, no doubt, if the connection between the two cases had been suggested to him, would have repudiated it as firmly as Sykes had done.

If the old man was surprised, he didn't show it. "Bassett? That has a familiar sound, but no, I don't think—"

"In the newspapers, quite recently."

"The incorruptible juror!" said Father William triumphantly. "And—if I'm not mistaken, Mr. Maitland—your own name mentioned in some connection or other."

"Yes."

"But what can that have to do with Jon's affairs?" The mild blue eyes had a calculating look. "Or with me?" he added gently.

"If I were in prison," said Maitland, studiedly casual, "or even out on bail with a charge of embracery hanging over me, I couldn't do much about investigating Dakins's death."

"I'm afraid I don't understand you. That would surely be a disadvantage to Jon, and therefore to me." Before he could go on the doorbell chimed. "That will be Keith, I told him you would be here. I think he keeps hoping," he added as he went across the room, "that you will have some good news about Jon."

"So far," said Antony, when briefly he was alone with Farrell, "I haven't given him much cause for hope." He looked at

Roger inquiringly. "Father William took that very calmly, don't you think?"

"What did you expect him to do?"

"Leap about a bit . . . tear his hair—" Antony was at his vaguest, but he broke off as Mr. Webster came back into the room with Keith Lindsay behind him. The clock in the passage that led to the bedrooms was striking ten, he hadn't realized it was so late.

"You know Mr. Maitland, Keith. Mr. Farrell, this is—" The introduction got no further. That was when the screaming started.

For a moment they froze, all four of them. The screams seemed to be all round them, wave after wave of terror. Then Keith said, "Gerry!" and started across the room to the other door. Antony was only just behind him when he reached the bedroom.

Geraldine Lindsay was sitting upright, her eyes were wide, and she was still screaming. The noise was somehow even more shocking now that they could see her. They went one to each side of the bed, and Keith put a hand on her shoulder and said "Gerry!" again; and when she did not heed him he spoke more sharply, and finally slapped her face. The last screams died away in a sob, and gradually her eyes came into focus and the wild, staring look faded. Antony wondered afterward what she made of her attendants, particularly of Roger who must have been the last person she expected to see staring at her anxiously from the foot of the bed. For the moment, however, he had no time to worry about that.

Geraldine was clutching his hands; he thought that her recoil from the slap had been purely instinctive. Her hair was disheveled, and her eyes—perfectly intelligent now—had an imploring look. He said, as calmly as he could, "What is it? What frightened you?" And Keith said, "Gerry, wake up! You're dreaming."

"It wasn't a dream." Her hands were shaking now, her whole body was shaking. Keith bent down and put an arm round her shoulders, and after a moment she released Antony's hands and turned to him. Lindsay sat down awkwardly on the edge of the bed and pulled her head onto his shoulder; his eyes met Maitland's in a long, speculative look.

Father William said, "You must have been dreaming, my dear."

"Oh, no, it wasn't a dream." Her voice sounded stronger, but she did not raise her head.

"Is there any other way into the flat?"

"Only the front door, Mr. Maitland, and that leads only to the sitting-room . . . as you saw."

"A fire-escape?"

"I'll look," Roger volunteered. And the old man called after him, "Outside the kitchen window." He was absent no more than a minute or two, and came back shaking his head.

"All secure."

Geraldine's face was buried against Lindsay's shoulder. "There was somebody," she said, and shuddered.

"Did you see him?" asked Maitland in a matter of fact way.

"No . . . no. He spoke to me." Her voice was drowsy, her eyes looked as if she could hardly keep them open.

"Tell us, then, Gerry; when you've done that you can forget it."

"He sounded so cold, so angry. I never saw him, Keith, I only heard his voice." She turned her head until her eyes met Maitland's, and he thought that she spoke directly to him. "He said 'you'll believe me now, won't you? I can kill you any time I like.'" She drew a deep, gasping breath. "I must have been dreaming . . . of course I must. It couldn't have been Jon."

7

"It couldn't, you know," said Roger a little later, when they were standing by the car. Antony hunched an impatient shoulder.

"And it couldn't have been Lindsay doing a ventriloquist act, because for one thing his voice isn't anything like Kellaway's, and for another I don't think anybody could project their voice through two closed doors." He smiled suddenly. "And what did Aunt Ethel make of *that?*"

"Interesting," said Roger, non-committally. But then he added, knowing perfectly well what Maitland meant, "If you mean the way she clung to him and asked him to stay with her, I think it was touching, too."

Only Roger, of all his friends, could have made a remark like that with complete simplicity. "I suppose," said Antony, pursuing his own train of thought, "you couldn't call anyone 'Geraldine' in bed."

"I don't see what that has to do with it."

"Nothing whatever. Ana says he's a wolf."

"Her vocabulary's a bit out of date, isn't it?"

"Yes, but is she right?"

"Lindsay? I shouldn't be surprised."

Antony thought about that for a moment. "Oh, well, tomorrow is also a good day, as no doubt Ana would tell us. Must you really go straight to the theater?"

"I think I should. I can easily drop you."

"No, I need a walk." He waited a moment, but there didn't seem to be anything else to say. He was still thinking of Keith and Geraldine when he started on his way home.

But he might have done better to devote his attention to Father William's parting words. "If you'll take a word of warning from an old man, Mr. Maitland," he had said, stopping Antony with a hand on his arm, when Roger was already halfway down the corridor toward the lift, "I should advise you to be very careful."

At the time Antony, with the newspaper stories in mind, had thought it was natural enough.

THURSDAY, 25th MARCH

1

The morning papers had the picture, too . . . the one that had been taken at Barnet without his knowledge. A good enough likeness, with B. HUDSON, Greengrocer, clear over the shop door, and no more of Roger visible than his shoulder.

With this reminder of his promise to Halloran, Maitland phoned Paul Collingwood as soon as he arrived in chambers. "I shan't be able to keep the appointment with Swaine . . . no, don't bother at the moment, I've put you to enough trouble . . . I'll let you know."

Collingwood was unconcerned. "You know your own business best," he said cheerfully. And then, unconvincingly casual, "Did you see Albert last night?"

"No. I . . . I changed my mind," Antony told him, and realized as he did so that his reason for not mentioning Falkner's limp to the police was no longer valid. He thought perhaps he would tell Sykes, because just at the moment he didn't quite relish Inspector Watkins's brand of humor.

"He isn't in yet." Collingwood's voice brought him back to more immediate problems. "Come to think of it, I can't think why not, because if ever a chap was incurably punctual—" He was still curious, and his next words did nothing to conceal the fact. "I could give him a message if you like."

"Good of you. But there's no need now."

He had no sooner replaced the receiver than the phone rang again, and there was Inspector Watkins at the other end of the line; for all the world, thought Antony gloomily, as if I'd conjured up the devil, just by thinking about him. But the detective's voice, with its faint, rasping huskiness, was as friendly as ever. "I was wondering, Mr. Maitland, if you could find time to come round and see me."

"Is that a request, Inspector, or is it an order?"

"Now, you know, sir, that isn't the way we do things," said Watkins in mild reproach.

"Then if I say I'm too busy—"

"That would be a pity, Mr. Maitland, seeing as the car's already on its way. It'll be waiting for you in Fleet Street by the time you can get there, I shouldn't wonder." His tone was gently persuasive; Antony had no doubt at all what he meant.

He remembered to stop in the clerk's office on his way out, to tell Mr. Mallory about sending back the Swaine brief. The breach of contract case, he was relieved to hear, had been postponed because the plaintiff had had his appendix out.

The police car was waiting as Watkins had predicted and the journey was accomplished only too quickly. For the first time in several days the sun was shining, but it did nothing to lighten Antony's mood; and when they arrived at New Scotland Yard and he was escorted to Chief-Superintendent Briggs's room that didn't cheer him either. He felt himself stiffen defensively as he crossed the threshold.

The chief-superintendent was a big man, a little stouter now than he had been at the time of their first meeting, his reddish hair growing even farther back from a high-domed forehead. His cold blue eyes would have given a stranger no hint at all of his choleric disposition. He got up from his chair behind the desk as Antony went in, so evidently the interview was to be conducted with some semblance, at least, of the usual courtesies. Inspector Watkins, who had been standing by the window, turned and surveyed the two men with interest and some amusement. He knew as well as anyone in the C.I.D. that this wasn't their first encounter.

Briggs would have denied that there was anything in the least irrational about his feelings: quite simply, he distrusted Maitland, and his dislike was therefore completely logical. There were, of course, any number of other causes for irritation, but he would not have admitted to being swayed by them. Maitland's casual air, the look of amusement which all too often crept into his eyes, his habit of persuading the court —sometimes against all Briggs's dearest convictions—that his client was in the right.

Antony, for his part, knew his own antagonism toward the other man to be instinctive, and therefore unreasonable. He did not find this helped him to master it at all.

Briggs was saying, "So glad you could manage to come." (Ordinary courtesy? He had been wrong about that, it seemed. The detective's tone was heavily sarcastic.)

"We'll play this straight, Superintendent, if you don't mind. I didn't understand that I had any choice in the matter."

Watkins came forward then, with a gesture that seemed to deprecate this lack of finesse. "If you were to sit down, Mr. Maitland, we could all be more comfortable." Antony took the chair that was indicated, and let his eyes move deliberately round the room. "Such splendor," he remarked, after a moment. "Is it intended to lull the malefactor into a sense of security?"

Briggs had sunk back into his chair again, but now he leaned forward. "There is nothing funny about the reason you were asked to come here," he said.

"Tell me, then," Antony invited. "I can't begin *not* to laugh until I know." His tone was flippant, but Watkins thought the strain was there all right.

"There are a few questions first, Mr. Maitland," he said. "To begin with, your movements last night."

It was the last thing Antony had expected . . . unless, of course, they knew of his second visit to Father William. But even so . . .

"You don't like that question, do you?" said Briggs. Those cold eyes saw too much.

"Not particularly. But you haven't told me why I should be asked to explain—"

"Let me point out, Mr. Maitland, we are still waiting for the explanation."

"Well, I don't think you're going to get it, you know." He contrived to sound apologetic. "Not unless you tell me the reason."

Briggs's color was rising. Inspector Watkins coughed to attract their attention. "Will you take my word for it, Mr. Maitland, that it's a serious matter."

"Willingly." His eyes left Briggs's face almost with regret, and met the inspector's quizzical regard. "You haven't thought it necessary to caution me," he said.

"That, you see, sir, depends on whether you can give us a satisfactory account of what you were doing."

"Nor have you asked me if I should like to see my solicitor."

"Well now, that never occurred to me," said Watkins, as though he was taken aback. "Not in your case, Mr. Maitland." He sounded solemn enough, but there was a lurking twinkle in his eye. Antony gave a reluctant laugh.

"You know all the answers, Inspector."

"Now that's just where you're wrong." Watkins sounded rueful now. "But I'm still hoping you can give us some of them."

Antony did not answer this directly. "I asked Mr. Horton to join me here." He did not add that Geoffrey had been with a client, and would be unable to get away for a while. "You should be grateful to me for thinking of the proprieties."

Briggs's voice cut harshly across the silence that followed. "It seems then that you are not quite so ignorant of our purpose as you would have us believe."

"In view of Inspector Watkins's previous questions, I imagine I have a very good idea. I admit I was not exactly overjoyed to receive your summons, but I'm not altogether without experience in these matters, you know."

"I know that very well," said Briggs with meaning.

"Still it would do no harm for you to tell us where you were." Watkins's tone successfully ignored the tension that was building up between his companions. "I mean, you're the only one that knows that, not this solicitor of yours, nor anyone else." He looked at Antony as hopefully as a dog will look at a bone; and indeed his brown eyes were reminiscent of one of the larger and gentler breeds . . . a St. Bernard, perhaps.

"If you must have it," said Antony, exasperated, "I was visiting *Señorita* Ana's flat. I suppose she has a surname, but I don't know it. She's a dancer."

For some reason, Watkins was shaking his head over the information. Briggs said sourly, "I thought better of your ingenuity." And added, with a contempt that left Maitland momentarily puzzled, "The oldest alibi in the world!"

124

"You'll be telling us next she's willing to corroborate your statement," said Watkins in a disappointed way.

"Don't be d-daft!" Antony's temper flared for a moment. "She w-wasn't there."

That produced another silence. Watkins said tentatively, "Do you usually—"

"I said I went to her flat . . . not, on this occasion, to see her." He paused, but what was the use of fencing, after all? If he couldn't look after himself it was unlikely that Geoffrey could help him. "If you want corroboration, there is my friend, Roger Farrell, who accompanied me. And Keith Lindsay, and Mrs. Geraldine Lindsay. It was Mr. William Webster I went to see . . . when I want to arrange a perjured statement I always make sure there are plenty of witnesses."

The two detectives exchanged a look. "Now, you know, Mr. Maitland," said Watkins, "the Kellaway case is nothing to do with me."

Antony was aware of a sense of anti-climax, of having braced himself against a danger that did not exist. It did not immediately occur to him that the import of the questions might indicate something even more serious. "I don't know what you want with me then," he said in a flat voice.

"Where would this apartment be, now . . . the one you were visiting?"

"Maddox Court. In Edward Street."

There was the merest flicker of expression in Watkins's eyes . . . regret . . . satisfaction? Antony didn't know. "What time did you leave?" the detective asked.

"I should say . . . just before ten-thirty. Mr. Farrell might know."

"And what did you do then?"

"We talked for a short time. He had his car, but I wanted to walk." He hesitated again, remembering the impression that had come to him gradually, that someone had been following him.

Briggs's eyes were fixed on Maitland's face, his look hard and skeptical. Watkins said, with a persistence that belied his casual air, "Which way did you go?"

125

"Along Edward Street, across Savile Row, into Clifford's Mews—"

This time there was no mistaking the quality of the look the two detectives exchanged. Briggs had a triumphant, I-told-you-so air; Watkins was definitely startled. But for all that the inspector spoke quickly, before Antony could continue.

"From that end it looks like a cul-de-sac."

"That's why I went that way. It's quiet, very few people use it."

"Was there anyone about?"

"I didn't *see* anybody."

He didn't realize that he had stressed the word until he saw Briggs scowling at him and heard Watkins say, "That sounds rather evasive, Mr. Maitland. What exactly do you mean?"

"No more than I say." (I couldn't be sure I saw anybody, but when I looked round I thought for a moment that someone whisked into a doorway out of sight. But then I forgot all about it because there was certainly nobody trailing me after that.) "Do you want me to go on?"

"Did you meet anyone on your way home?"

"A hundred people, I dare say. No one I knew."

"Can you tell me what time you arrived in Kempenfeldt Square?"

"No, I can't." (Why should I have noticed a thing like that? I went in, and Jenny had just made up the fire, and she mixed me a drink, and I told her about Geraldine's nightmare.) He turned from Watkins to look at the chief-superintendent. "You're going to have to tell me, you know; this doesn't make any sense at all." But he was worried now; and if the atmosphere in the room was anything to go on, he was right to be worried.

"Very well." The words sounded like a threat, or was that more imagination? "Do you know a man called Albert Falkner?"

"Yes, of course. For one thing—"

"He was found dead in a doorway half-way down Clifford's Mews last night at approximately ten forty-five," said Briggs. "There is no doubt at all, the doctor tells us, that he had been murdered."

For a moment, in the light of his own knowledge, it seemed to Maitland completely logical that the police should link his name with Falkner's. Then he realized that there was no apparent connection, it depended on his own tentative identification of the limping man. He said in a voice that sounded strange in his own ears, "I can't see why that should have led you to question me."

Briggs made no attempt to enlighten him, it was left to Watkins to say, "But then, you haven't had the privilege of looking through the poor fellow's papers."

"At his office? Collingwood didn't know—" He let the sentence trail away inconclusively; on the whole it didn't seem worth the bother of finishing it.

"I meant his private papers, Mr. Maitland." The inspector did not so much as glance at his superior officer, as most men would have done before embarking upon an explanation which might not be approved. "There was a collection of newspaper stories covering a variety of criminal trials in different parts of the country. Somewhere the prisoner had been sent down, and in each case a short paragraph of later date was stapled on, recording the suicide of Mr. So-and-so, who had been worried recently over a spell of jury duty; others where the jury, 'after a lengthy absence,' had found the accused Not Guilty."

"Had Falkner had his throat cut?" asked Maitland suddenly.

"One thing at a time," Watkins told him. "We've a lot of checking to do, but what with one thing and another there's some of us that find all this . . . suggestive. Then we came across a notebook with entries of cash received and payments made. Nothing but initials, it'll need a bit of study, as I say, but it doesn't seem to have anything to do with his bank account or his regular salary checks, and the dates of the payments coincide roughly with the dates of the trials. He used initials in his diary, too; he went to see 'F.B.' on the 18th March, for instance." He paused, and smiled at Antony in his friendly way. "Do you remember my telling you that when we found the go-between we might be half-way to finding his principal?"

"I remember."

"Well, now, it seems likely—doesn't it?—that Falkner is the man who called on Fred Bassett, especially as Mrs. Bassett mentioned that he dragged his left foot slightly." His voice was as mild as ever, his expression remained guileless, but he didn't miss a trick. "That doesn't surprise you," he said.

"I've talked to Hudson. He told me."

"Did he? I'm not an imaginative man, Mr. Maitland," Watkins went on, "but someone who was . . . well, they might think—"

"I've listened to all this very p-patiently, Inspector," said Maitland, and the slight, angry stammer gave him the lie. "You may be right about Falkner's complicity in the bribery . . . plot . . . racket . . . whatever you like to call it. But there's nothing to connect me with it, or with him, and you know that perfectly well."

"Except Hudson's statement. His rather detailed statement," Watkins pointed out. "And now Falkner's dead, and when we ask you where you were . . . there's some people don't like coincidences, Mr. Maitland."

"You said he was m-murdered. How did he die?"

Briggs had been out of the picture long enough. "You're here to answer questions," he said curtly.

"To listen to your questions, and answer, or refuse to answer, as I choose."

"I am obliged to you for the correction." If Briggs was grateful he hid it well enough; his appearance rather suggested an incipient apoplexy. "How far can you lift your right arm?" he asked.

There was a silence. Watkins, who had strolled back to the window again, looked round curiously, and saw Maitland's face completely devoid of expression.

"I d-don't really think I w-want to answer that, Superintendent."

"It might save a good deal of trouble, one way or another," said Watkins, apparently addressing the remark to a point on the ceiling above Antony's head.

"Is that a threat, Inspector?"

"How could it be?" Watkins wondered. "I only said *might* . . . I can give you no guarantee."

"Do you really think you have enough evidence for an arrest at this stage, if I refuse to talk?" His tone conveyed nothing but the vaguest interest. Watkins did not reply directly, but his eyes shifted away from Maitland's to rest for an expressive moment on the top of Briggs's head. The implication was as clear as if he had spoken it aloud . . . don't count on *him* being reasonable. But all he said was:

"Some people might think you're asking too many questions."

"Well, if you m-must know,"—Maitland accepted the necessity of answering with as good a grace as possible—"almost to s-shoulder level." He did not add, "painfully, and with difficulty." The words stuck in his throat.

It was Briggs who seemed unwilling to let the subject die. "What exactly is the nature of the injury?"

"That, at l-least, is nothing to do with you." It gave him some small satisfaction to say it, but he was a little surprised when the detective accepted the rebuff . . . until he saw that Briggs was looking at him in a calculating way.

"Falkner was five foot six—" he said.

"Careful, Superintendent! Aren't you in d-danger of giving information to the enemy?"

Briggs was too preoccupied even to notice the gibe. "—and you, I should say, are quite six inches taller." His eyes were frankly appraising.

"You're not measuring me for my c-coffin yet," said Antony tartly. But his tone was ragged, and Briggs had a satisfied look.

"I am willing to give you this much information: Falkner died of cerebral anoxia—"

"What the devil does that mean?" asked Maitland, but he wasn't surprised when the question was ignored.

"—his assailant would need both hands at his throat, but no great strength."

"I see." That made sense . . . too much sense. Quiet, and quick, and easy. And this was the point where Geoffrey, if he were here, would certainly tell him to keep his mouth shut. "You mean he was strangled, don't you?"

"But no sign of a cord being used, or anything like that," said Inspector Watkins helpfully. And added in a ruminative way, "Someone who knew just how to set about it."

"If he was killed by pressure on the—the artery—"

"The carotid artery."

"—I shouldn't have thought that was very easy to prove."

"Unfortunately," Watkins told him blandly, "there was a certain amount of bruising." His pause was really extraordinarily expressive. "On the right side of his throat."

"Which suggests," said Briggs, rubbing the point well in, "that the murderer may not have been too sure of his right hand, so that he used more pressure than was needed with his left by way of compensation."

"A s-sort of trademark," said Antony sardonically, and watched the superintendent's color rise with a pleasure that was almost dispassionate. "Are you arresting me?" he wondered.

"I'm warning you, Maitland—"

That might be taken, perhaps, as a denial. "Then, where do we go from here?" he asked. "You've established my presence at the scene of the crime within a short time of Falkner's death. You think you know I'm physically capable of having killed him. Is there anything else you want of me?"

For the first time Briggs smiled openly. "Quite a lot," he said. "Quite a lot." He glanced at his subordinate, and the smile still lingered when his eyes came back to Maitland's face. "We'll start with your visit to Barnet yesterday afternoon," he decided, "and work back from there."

Antony had a sudden sensation that he was being suffocated, that the walls of the room were closing in. Briggs was bland now, pleased with himself and the situation; Watkins was no less dangerous for the mild friendliness of his manner. He looked from one of them to the other, but he knew the choice was already made. If he didn't answer . . .

"Don't be afraid to take your time," said Inspector Watkins kindly. "We've got all day."

It was at this point that Geoffrey Horton arrived.

Watkins had over-estimated the superintendent's patience. At twelve forty-five they came out onto the Embankment, leaving Briggs unmistakably dissatisfied, and his colleague amiable as ever. Antony was walking aimlessly, while Geoffrey deliberately gave him his head. After several minutes had gone by, "What a mess; what a bloody, unadulterated mess," Maitland said. And then, with a poor attempt at a smile, "Who will you brief to defend me?"

"It won't come to that."

"Don't be too sure." There was an exhausted note in his voice that Horton did not like. "If once they can establish a *prima facie* case I'm finished, whatever the verdict. Unless, of course, the newspapers have finished me already." He did not speak of the deeper fear that was in his mind.

Geoffrey said roughly, "You need a drink," and began to look around for a cab. Antony made no comment when he was conducted to a pub in the West End; it was crowded, of course, but there was nobody who knew them. That would have been the last straw, and he was grateful to Geoffrey for realizing it. They drank in silence, and he made no protest when Horton said, "We can eat downstairs," and led the way, and chose the table, and ordered the meal without further reference to his companion. When the soup was before them he said firmly, "Now we can talk."

Antony picked up his spoon. "I'm hoarse already."

"Never mind that." Geoffrey had evidently given him as much rope as he felt was reasonable. "How did you get into this?"

"Would you believe me if I said it blew up of its own accord?"

"Is that what you think?"

"Not quite." The soup burned his tongue, but on the whole it was worth it. "First there was Hudson's story; but that would have meant nothing by itself, if the police hadn't been predisposed to believe it."

"And now Falkner is dead. I suppose there's no doubt he was part of the bribery set-up."

"No doubt at all, to my mind. And by the time the police

get through with his effects they'll probably be able to prove it. What I don't think"—he was warming to his subject now, and the alcohol and the hot food were having their effect—"is that he organized it, or that he dealt personally with the recalcitrant jurymen."

"I don't see why anyone wanted to kill them at all," Geoffrey grumbled.

"It isn't difficult really," said Maitland encouragingly. "You want to augment your income, so you decide that corrupting jurors would be a profitable occupation."

Horton had grinned at the schoolmasterish tone, partly from relief; but he had no intention of letting his companion down lightly. "Why that in particular?"

"Why does anyone become a sanitary inspector, or an accountant, or a midden-man? The law of supply and demand, I suppose. You find a field that isn't overcrowded—"

"There's been a good deal of bribery going on, you've only to read the papers," Geoffrey objected.

"Yes, but those are individual cases, a gang protecting its own. You're cashing in on the solitary worker, who has no one to turn to in his distress."

"Full of the crusading spirit, I suppose," said Geoffrey dourly, and was surprised to see Antony frown. "Have you thought of something?" he asked, forgetting his determination to keep the other man to the point.

"I . . . no." Maitland sounded vague, and there was an uneasy silence while he traced a pattern on the check tablecloth with his fork. "Do you know anything about the works of John Gay?"

"The Beggar's Opera?"

"That isn't the only thing he wrote. I must look it up." He raised his eyes to meet Horton's anxious look and smiled at him. "Bear with me, Geoffrey. It was only an idea."

"I haven't much choice, have I?"

"You could abandon ship," said Antony seriously. "You've threatened to often enough when you didn't agree with my goings on."

"That was when . . . that was different."

"I know. To get back to the bribery, it's obvious that somebody connected with the law would be a good ally; he could

132

provide you, for one thing, with a ready-made clientele. I don't know how you hit on Falkner, perhaps you know him already. However it may be, a bargain is made. Collingwood always goes to court himself, Falkner used to attend to the office side of things; so there was no danger in using him as an intermediary."

"What about this tale of Bassett having seen him talking to you?"

"I've thought about that till my head aches. There's nothing very odd about our having a word together if we happened to meet—I'd be all the more likely to stop, you know, because I couldn't stand the sight of him—only I'm sure it never happened recently."

"Who's lying, then? Bassett, or Hudson?"

"I think most likely Hudson." He looked vague again. "I should say—wouldn't you?—that he was bribed too."

"This brings us to deliberate malice," said Geoffrey. His tone conveyed neither acceptance nor disbelief.

"Yes, I think so. But we still haven't finished with the jurors. You've the promise of a fee from the defendant; you look the jury over, pick your man. If he's unwilling to accept a bribe, threaten him. Ten to one you can scare him into keeping quiet, a lot of chaps think they'll be blamed if they say anything, they're shy of the law. But that's not to say some of them won't jib at giving a wrong verdict and vote guilty with the rest. And when that happens—" He finished with a graphic gesture, drawing his hand across his throat, and considerably startling the waiter who had just arrived with two helpings of steak and kidney pie. Geoffrey waited until the man had retired, and then asked stubbornly:

"Why?"

"Because the next chap will be that much easier to scare." When Geoffrey hesitated he added urgently, "Imagine you've never opened a law book in your life, never been in court, think of the police as someone out to get you." He paused a moment, while Geoffrey wrestled with this unfamiliar concept, and then said persuasively, "I'm right, you know."

"I'll take your word for it. Yes, I mean it," he went on, as Antony seemed about to embark on a further dissertation.

"You'd better eat that before we go any further. And then you can tell me what the hell you think you were doing, going to see Father William on your own."

"I took Roger with me. He'd have been a perfectly good witness to the purity of my motives if they tried to say I was suborning Father William." He picked up his knife and fork and gave Geoffrey an absent smile. "I must say, I'd like to have a go at it. But I can't help feeling he'd end up corrupting me."

Horton ignored this, as perhaps it deserved. "But if you had to see him again—"

"Geoffrey, I'm sorry. You might not have liked the questions I wanted to ask him. Not that I ever got the chance." He hesitated, but there was no way that he could see of avoiding the explanation. "It was Roger's suggestion—you may not like this either—that Hudson made his statement after I was known to be interested in Kellaway's defense."

"You mean, someone was afraid of your meddling. *That* makes sense," said Horton grimly. But he left Antony in peace after that, until they had finished their meal.

They talked over the coffee cups. They talked at length. "I see your idea about Father William," Geoffrey said at last, grudgingly. "Does that mean you agree with me now that Kellaway killed Dakins?"

"I don't know. All I can say is, I think Father William would be ready to protect him if he did . . . up to a point."

"There's another possibility." Geoffrey stirred his coffee diligently and added without looking up, "Paul Collingwood." His tone was defiant, and Antony put back his head and laughed. Perhaps it was fortunate that most of their fellow lunchers had already hurried back to their office desks. "It isn't funny," said Horton in a huff.

"Not a bit. I'm sorry. Besides, there's something I forgot to tell you: Collingwood knew I wanted to talk to Falkner last night."

"Well then! He wanted to prevent you from doing so."

"The trouble is, it doesn't explain why he should want to frame me."

"Expediency," said Horton promptly.

"Even so, why did Hudson spin the police that fairy tale?"

Geoffrey thought about that. "There are loose ends which-ever way you look at it," he said at last, reasonably. And then he glanced at his watch. "I've arranged to see Kellaway at four o'clock," he said. "Do you want to come?"

"You realize, don't you, that I'm not in a position to act for him, or anybody else, at the moment."

"I believe I have a reasonably good grasp of the situation."

"Don't be pompous, Geoffrey." He drank the last of his coffee, and grimaced because it was nearly cold. "I'd like to come with you, but why do you want to see him, anyway?"

"The tenant of the other apartment on Kellaway's floor has made a statement."

"I suppose you mean something unpleasant. These neigh-bors!"

"It needs explaining," said Horton seriously. "He says he heard a quarrel between Kellaway and Dakins, and one of the things said was 'It's all a question of what made her do it.' And Kellaway said 'You've got it wrong,' and then he said 'I can't explain.' There's more to it, of course, but the point is he's quite definite that they were angry. And the way it was told it does sound as if it might have been Beth Kellaway they meant."

"If he'd heard them discussing the fat stock prices," said An-tony gloomily, "he'd be just as convinced *now* that there'd been a disagreement."

"I know that. You know that. I dare say Counsel for the Crown will know it, too, though I doubt if he'll admit as much. But can you expect the jury to be equally cynical?" Geoffrey argued.

"Never expect anything of a jury; as Jenny would say, that's the first rule in the book. I can see it's got to be explained, however." He began to fumble for his wallet. "I'll pay for the lunch and you can pay for the taxi," he said. "I ought to have asked Jenny to go to the bank."

3

The interview with Jon Kellaway was not reassuring. The actor looked more hag-ridden than ever, though he was obviously taking pains to conceal his nervousness. He laughed angrily when Horton repeated to him the fragment of conversation his neighbor had overheard. "We were discussing a play," he said.

"Quarreling over it?" That was Geoffrey's clients' voice, which carefully did not display his skepticism.

"Of course not. Arguing, certainly. Dakins was a great theater-goer, but he had the oddest opinions. This time he'd been to see *A Doll's House,* and then he read everything the critics had to say about the new production and didn't agree with any of them." He broke off and gave a helpless shrug. "That's all," he said.

"You'll have to be prepared to go into greater detail when you're asked about it at the trial."

"No difficulty about that."

"Without sounding as if you thought Dakins was a wrong-headed bastard who deserved to be killed," said Antony gently.

Kellaway turned to look at him; so far his attention had been concentrated on his solicitor. "I thought you understood, I *liked* him," he protested.

"Just so long as you convey that to the jury. Which reminds me . . . was Dakins himself ever on jury duty?"

"I don't . . . what an extraordinary question to ask."

"You don't know the answer." Maitland sounded discouraged.

"Of course I do. He was on that case where two men coshed a night-watchman and—"

"When was this, and what was the verdict?" Antony was alert on the instant, and Jon Kellaway moved uneasily as though the fact disturbed him.

"They were found guilty. Dakins was worried about that, I don't know why. He said himself it was obvious, I don't know why he should have felt sorry for them. And if you mean, when was the trial? . . . just the week before he died. At least, I don't think they reached a verdict until the Monday."

"I see." He glanced at Geoffrey. "The doctors said there was rather a lot of blood."

136

"Nothing makes sense!" said Horton crossly, and scowled when Maitland asked:

"Oh, don't you think so?" in a cryptic tone.

Kellaway was looking bewildered. "I suppose it's no use asking you to explain," he said, and made a sudden, rather violent gesture which graphically conveyed his discontent.

"It would take too long. Besides, there are other things . . . was Dakins left-handed by any chance?"

The question did nothing to decrease Jon's perplexity. He was frowning as he answered. "Well, yes, he was, but—" He broke off there, but Maitland made no immediate use of the silence. He seemed to be thinking.

"Did you ever do anything to make Geraldine Lindsay afraid of you?" he said at last.

"Good God, man, I want to marry her."

"Why do you think she refused you?"

"Certainly not because . . . well, I suppose I was—angry, that night, but she can't have thought I would hurt her." He paused, and seemed to be making a heroic attempt to subdue his excitement. "Why do you ask?"

"She's been having nightmares," said Maitland unemotionally.

"Is she all right?"

"She's worried." He hoped the half-truth might convey some kind of reassurance. "Why were she and Lindsay divorced?"

"Not because of me, if that's what you mean." (Funnily enough, this had never occurred to Antony.) "It was quite— quite amicable, you know. I think they just decided . . . well, I'm not saying Keith was a saint, which of us is for that matter? I don't know, how can I know? And I don't know why I'm telling you all this."

"Because I asked you," said Maitland, and smiled at him. (And because anything, even the most indiscreet of confidences, is better than the intolerable loneliness of your own particular hell.) "Will you answer another question, if I assure you it is impertinent only in one sense of the word?"

"If—if I can."

"Does Mrs. Lindsay know . . . what happened to Beth?"

"Of course she does! She was there; in Penhaven, I mean. It was only a week or so before her wedding." He started to rise, recollected himself, and sat down again. "Do you think she remembered . . . all this time?"

"She could hardly have forgotten," said Maitland. He sounded oddly detached, but his eyes were intent.

"Then that's why—" Kellaway was staring in front of him, seeing nothing. "There were times I was sure she cared for me, and then all at once there was a barrier, something I couldn't surmount." Geoffrey Horton moved uneasily, and perhaps it was this that brought Jonathan back to earth again; his eyes came to rest thoughtfully on Maitland's face, but he seemed quite unembarrassed as he went on. "Do you think people change?"

"Basically, very little. They develop, I suppose," said Antony seriously. Geoffrey glanced at him in an exasperated way.

"So a cruel man could only hope to grow more cruel with the years."

"I didn't say that, you know. Unless he was completely cruel, no redeeming features at all." Maitland seemed to be giving the question an extraordinary degree of consideration. "If he was just the usual mixture he might go either way, the years might make him kinder."

"I wonder if you're right."

This time Horton's movement was deliberate, and he added a cough for good measure. Antony said, without looking at him, "You're quite right, of course. This is beside the point."

"I'm not so sure it isn't the whole point," said Jon emphatically, and ran a hand through his hair. "You've given me something to think about, at least."

"*He's* given *you*—?" said Geoffrey. "Oh, I give it up!" This time neither of his companions took the slightest notice.

"There's another thing that interests me." Maitland was frowning in his concentration. "Do you think Mr. Webster is sufficiently fond of you to perjure himself for your sake?"

"I don't think an oath more or less would mean much to him," said Kellaway thoughtfully. And then, as the import of the question struck him, his eyes flew, startled, to Maitland's face. "You think he might—might go back on what he's said?"

138

"Well, you see," said Antony gently, "I don't really know him very well."

"I always thought—" He broke off there, and glanced at Horton before he went on. "If you're fond of someone, if you're grateful to them, you have to take them as they are."

"Would you say Keith Lindsay felt like that?"

"About Father William? I'm sure he does," said Jon firmly.

"Do you ever see your brother-in-law now?"

"My . . . oh, you mean Charlie. No, I haven't seen him for years."

"Could he have known Dakins? I'm wondering, you see, if he could have given him the newspaper report of Mrs. Kellaway's death."

"I suppose it's possible," said Jon, obviously doubtful. "He came up to Penhaven for the inquest, and he was bitter enough. I couldn't blame him. But I've no reason to think—"

"The cuttings came from somewhere," Maitland pointed out. "Now . . . something you can answer. Do you know anyone called Collingwood, Paul Collingwood?"

"No . . . no."

"Or Albert Falkner?"

"No." This time the denial came with less hesitation. Antony smiled at him and came to his feet, and was appalled by Kellaway's suddenly despairing look.

"What about Butler's evidence?" he said.

"What about it?"

"He seems very sure . . . he saw me quite clearly." (Horton coughed again, warningly.) "Yes, I know, I've thought about this a good deal. It's a question of who they believe, and I don't want Father William to—to get himself into difficulties on my behalf. You could explain to him, couldn't you? It isn't that I'm not grateful—"

"I'm not quite sure," said Horton slowly, "what it is that we are to explain."

"I want to tell you what really happened. I did go home, as I told you at first; that was all true, except that I went into the house for a few minutes, and I dare say Butler was right about the time I came out."

"How long were you there?"

"Five minutes perhaps. Not more."

"Did you see anything, or hear anything? You'd better tell me exactly what happened."

"But there was nothing!" Jon's voice rose despairingly. "That's why I thought it didn't matter—"

"Exactly what happened, Mr. Kellaway," Geoffrey repeated.

"Well, I—I let myself in with my key. The hall was quiet, I went upstairs without seeing anybody. And it was just the same when I went down again, no sound at all, no smell of burning, if that's what you're getting at. Nothing!"

"I see. Why did you go in, if you'd already made up your mind to go for a walk?"

"To leave a parcel Father William had had sent round to the theater for me." He paused, but went on reluctantly when he met Geoffrey's eye. "If you must know there were five rings, each in its own box. Not bulky, but I didn't want to be carrying them round with me."

"Were you able to retrieve them later? After the fire."

"Yes, I—I could have stayed in my room, it wasn't damaged. I just couldn't stand the smell."

"Had you asked Father William for the rings?" said Maitland. When Jon turned to him he had his vague look, as though he didn't really expect an answer, or even desire one very much.

"No, I hadn't. There was a note, I suppose you could say it explained."

"What did it say?"

"Just, *Choose which you like–or the one she likes–with my blessing.*"

"Did that surprise you?"

"Not a bit. It's just the sort of thing Father William would do if he thought—"

"If he thought you needed a push in the right direction?"

"Yes. So I wondered, you see, if Geraldine . . . she knows him very well . . . she might have said something."

"Indicating a change of heart?"

"That's what I thought. That's why I—" He broke off, and sat for a moment looking down at his hands, which were

140

tightly clasped together on the table in front of him. "I think perhaps I understand the position better now."

"I'm not at all sure that you do," said Antony, and Geoffrey glanced at him quickly, surprised by the hardness of his tone. Jon looked up, too.

"But you said—"

"Never mind that. Have you told us all the truth now?"

"All of it."

"You're not going to remember later that you went round by the garage and—"

"I've told you, no!"

"We'll leave it there, then. Unless . . . Horton?"

Geoffrey shook his head and got up in his turn. "Nothing else," he said. "I shall be seeing you again in a few days, Mr. Kellaway."

Jon was still seated at the table, staring at nothing, when the warder let them out.

4

"What's in your mind?" asked Geoffrey urgently, as they came into the dusty, sunlit street.

"I'd like to know what makes Geraldine Lindsay tick."

"I'd gathered that much." Horton's tone was dry.

"And I'd like to ask *her* if she knows about Father William's *extra curricular* activities."

"I'm surprised you don't then." Geoffrey was still disgruntled. "After the questions you've been asking Kellaway I shouldn't think you'd scruple at a little thing like that."

"Well, you see, I wanted to know," said Maitland apologetically. "But it wouldn't be fair to give Father William away, if she hasn't an idea what he's up to."

"Fair!" For some reason the word seemed to set the seal on Geoffrey's displeasure. "Now, look here, Antony—"

"I also think our friend, Kellaway, has a very trusting nature."

"An innocent bystander, in fact."

"I don't know." He reduced his pace a little to match his companion's shorter stride, and looked at Geoffrey for a moment with a singularly blank expression. "He's going slowly mad in there," he said. "Do you realize that?"

"I never knew such a chap for exaggerating things," Geoffrey grumbled. He wasn't quite sure what it was about Antony's tone that made him so uneasy.

5

Meg was surprised to see him. "Roger isn't home yet, darling," she said, backing away from the door. And then, as she saw his face more clearly, she added without any trace of affectation, "Antony, what's the matter?"

He pushed the door to behind him with his foot, and leaned against it until he heard the lock click and knew it was firmly closed. "Is it so obvious?" he asked.

"Yes . . . to me."

"I—I haven't time to go into details, Meg." But he had to tell her, of course. "The police think I've added murder to . . . the other things they suspect me of."

Something in his face stopped her from making the routine protest. "But you couldn't have killed Bassett."

He accepted the reminder without comment. "I could have done this. Roger told you about Albert Falkner, didn't he?"

"Mr. Collingwood's clerk."

"That's right. He was killed last night."

"Darling, I'm so sorry."

He wasn't in any doubt of her meaning. "I came because there's a question I want to ask you, Meg. Why did you recommend Jon Kellaway for that part in *A Kind of Praise?*"

"Because . . . well, because I thought he was suitable, I suppose."

"Particularly suitable for that particular part?" he insisted.

"I think . . . I don't really understand," said Meg helplessly.

"You said it was a difficult one to play."

"Well, Jon's a good actor. I just knew he could do it. And I don't see why it matters, now."

"Perhaps it doesn't." He sounded unconvinced.

"Darling, Jon couldn't have killed this man Falkner."

"No, but . . . never mind, Meg."

But he was thinking, when he hailed a cab at the end of the street five minutes later, that that was just about the only thing he could be sure of.

6

This evening the papers were more guarded. There was the report of Albert Falkner's death; a paragraph reminding the reader of his connection with the Bassett case . . . a rather tenuous connection, it might be thought; and some mention of the activities of Scotland Yard. All completely harmless to anyone who hadn't seen a newspaper for a day or two. But taken in conjunction with what had gone before . . .

Jenny had handed him the *Evening Chronicle* when he went in, and watched his face while he read. "Roger phoned a couple of times," she said after a while. "He'd tried to get you in chambers but they didn't know where you were."

"I was at Scotland Yard, and then Geoffrey took me to see Jon Kellaway." Antony was folding the newspaper with unnatural precision. "I ought to have phoned you, love, but I thought, you see . . . bad news will wait."

"It didn't wait, exactly." She wasn't looking at him now. "There were two policemen . . . well, they were in plain clothes. They had a search warrant."

"When was this?"

"This afternoon. They wanted to go everywhere . . . downstairs too . . . and I had to go with them because Gibbs was being very cold and distant, and pretending they weren't really there."

He was surprised at the violence of his reaction, though part of his anger was directed at his own blindness. "I n-never thought—" he said, and broke off, because what was the good of excuses. After a moment he put out his left hand and tilted her chin so that she had no choice but to meet his eyes. "B-believe me, Jenny,"—he had almost mastered the stammer, but the bitterness of his voice was equally revealing—"if I'd known what was going to happen I'd have kept you out of it somehow."

"Do you think I care about that?" she asked him furiously.

The extravagance of her anger, no less than its unexpectedness, silenced him. When he spoke again it was to say, awkwardly, "I thought perhaps it had made you feel . . . ashamed."

"I wouldn't mind if there had been a hundred of them," she said, still with the same vehemence. But then she was speaking more quickly, and in a lower tone. "It was just . . . I still don't know what it was about, Antony, but it must be something serious, and no one knew where you were. So I thought, perhaps . . . you weren't . . . coming back."

"Here I am, you see." She was very near to tears, and he tried for a lighter tone. "It explains one thing anyway."

"What—what was that?"

"Why Gibbs waylaid me in the hall and scolded me as if I was thirteen again. I couldn't make any sense at all of what he was saying, except that he intended to inform Sir Nicholas on his return." His mimicry of the old butler was absent-minded, but wickedly accurate; Jenny's answering smile was so watery that he took the handkerchief out of his breast pocket and gave it to her. "Come to the fire, love, it's cold out here."

When he had finished his tale she was calm again, but thoughtful. "They couldn't prove anything," she said. But it had the effect of an unfinished statement, so that he wondered what was really in her mind.

"Proof is a—a delicate balance," he told her. "I think we've got to face it, they're going to have a damned good try." But when she started to speak again he made a sudden movement, silencing her. "Did you notice what time I got home last night?"

Jenny's eyes were troubled. "I couldn't truthfully say I did."

"Bless you, love, I don't want you to start inventing things. I'm confused enough without that."

"And it's no use asking Gibbs, because—do you think he really goes to bed at ten o'clock every night, Antony?"

"He retires, anyway." He got up and started drifting across the room, stopping a moment to touch her cheek as he passed; he wasn't sure which of them was the more in need of comfort.

"I ought to ring Mallory," he said, "in case they were there too."

The conversation was rather one-sided. All Jenny could hear was a sort of clucking noise from the telephone, but she watched the look of strain deepen on Antony's face as he listened. At last he said, "All right. I'm sorry. I'll see you in the morning," and replaced the receiver and added, without looking round, "They were there. I wonder if Dr. Prescott's in. I want a word with him." It wasn't until Jenny got up quietly and went out that he realized she thought it was his shoulder he wanted to talk about. Now he came to think of it, it was hurting like hell. . . .

Dr. Prescott listened in silence to what he had to say. "The thing is, you see, I was there," Antony concluded. "The police think they can prove a connection between me and Falkner over this bribery business. The medical evidence says he was killed by someone stronger in the left hand than the right. Could I have done it?" He paused a moment and added, as though the exact phrasing were somehow important, "Could I have done it now?"

There was a short, uneasy silence. "I'm bound to say, I think you could," said Dr. Prescott unwillingly. "You don't want me to wrap it up for you, do you? But your shoulder would play you up like the dickens afterward."

"I rather thought it would be like that."

"Well, looking at you won't tell me anything. How has the pain been today?"

He didn't make the mistake of thinking the question indicated any distrust. "No worse than usual," he said; and then, "Not much worse, anyway." Obscurely, he felt he owed the doctor so much accuracy, because he never used their long acquaintance as an excuse for asking awkward questions. "You see, I'm familiar with the results of pressure on the carotid arteries, but I don't think many people are."

"Most people would use more violence to obtain the same effect," Dr. Prescott agreed.

"Anyway, it's no use worrying. Tell me, what makes people have nightmares?"

If things had been normal, the doctor at this point would

have told him brusquely, "Stop eating cheese at bedtime, and don't waste my time with silly questions." The fact that he seemed to be giving the matter serious consideration was strangely depressing. "Any one of a hundred reasons—"

"I'd better explain." After all, it was a relief to talk about Jon Kellaway and Geraldine. "I thought myself it meant she believed he was guilty," he said when he had finished, in a tone which conveyed clearly enough his own doubt.

"I'm not a psychiatrist, Antony."

"Still, I'd like your opinion." He did not add, I'd trust it more than most; perhaps his confidence was implicit in the question.

"Well, then, it *sounds* like that," said Dr. Prescott cautiously. "Or the whole thing might have a purely sexual basis; I suppose that would be the popular view today."

"I suppose it would," said Maitland, thinking of Ana as he spoke.

"I don't really know why you're interested."

"Because I don't understand. Never mind. As usual, Doctor, I'm in your debt."

"Don't you start taking that formal tone with me. I won't have it." This was said in a very good imitation of his usual manner. "And don't ring off yet, because I've just thought of something," he added.

"What about?"

"Not about the interpretation of dreams, if that's what you're thinking," said Dr. Prescott scornfully. "The way this man Falkner was killed—"

"Yes?"

"You said not many people would know how, but there was a case reported not very long ago. A hypnotist at a private party—not a very experienced hypnotist, I'm afraid—who killed a man like that."

"But why on earth—?"

"Someone said at the inquest it's a trick they use sometimes with a difficult subject. Not reputable hypnotists, of course. I didn't read all the mumbo jumbo, but apparently if you take a man to the edge of unconsciousness . . . but that isn't the point," said the doctor, interrupting himself in as severe a tone as if Antony had been responsible for the digression. "The point is, he didn't stop in time, and there was quite a detailed report in the papers which anyone could have read." There was a silence when he had finished speaking, so that he added testily, "Are you there? Are you there?"

"Yes, I'm still here."

"Then why don't you say something?"

"I was thinking."

"What has Nicholas to say about all this?"

"He's in New York." There was no doubt that the predominant note in his voice was one of relief, and he had to move the receiver quickly from his ear, or the doctor's booming laugh would have deafened him.

"You're thinking that's a safe distance," he asserted, when he had stopped laughing. "All the same, he ought to be here."

"It may all blow over," said Maitland in a tone that abruptly banished Dr. Prescott's amusement.

"You don't believe that," he said accusingly. "Why don't you send your uncle a cable?"

"What do you propose I should say to him? 'Return at once, am about to be arrested.' "

"I see your problem," Dr. Prescott admitted. But he could recognize a raw nerve as well as the next man, and he did not try to probe any further.

7

Roger arrived while they were washing up after dinner, and came and stood in the kitchen, aimlessly, and very much in the way. After a while he said, "Could you put me straight on this tale Meg says you told her?" and Antony recounted the day's events for the third time. When he had finished Roger picked up a pile of clean plates and put them away in the wrong place in the cupboard.

"Dakins had been on jury duty not long before he died," he said.

"It seems so."

"That means there is a tie-in . . . it must mean that. Between Bassett and Falkner on the one hand, and Dakins on the other. And one man behind the whole thing." But it wasn't the confirmation of his theory that interested him. "If Meg had never asked you to see Kellaway—"

"Oh, for h-heaven's sake!"

Roger gave him a considering look. "This chap Briggs—"

"They have a case already," said Jenny, without looking round. "Not just prejudice, I mean." There was a pause while the two men stared at her, and she added with a touch of irritability, "Isn't that right, Antony?"

"A bit shaky in patches, but yes, it's true enough," he agreed.

"You don't think it's accidental, either of you. You think it's a frame-up. Even to the—the way Falkner died?"

"Even to that . . . I think."

She reached out for the towel and turned away from the sink, drying her hands carefully, but for the moment she did not raise her eyes. "And you said, Roger, 'one man behind it all.' So why should you suppose he'll leave it there? Besides, there's another thing; you're pretty sure Jon Kellaway's alibi is a fake. But how you know it isn't a trap . . . for you?"

"You mean, Father William might go back on his story?" An echo of his own thought when he'd been talking to Kellaway that afternoon, so why did he feel impelled to argue? "He'd be convicting himself of perjury."

"He hasn't sworn it yet. No, listen, Antony, please listen. He could say you suggested it, before ever he got in touch with Geoffrey—"

"I didn't even know he existed."

"But you were alone with Jon Kellaway before he was arrested, he could have told you then. And Father William could say he was tempted, because of his great affection for Jon . . . everyone would be sorry for him, no one would blame him at all. He might even wait until the trial—"

Antony's look was both amused and understanding. "Proper little ray of sunshine, aren't you, love?" He dried the last fork and threw it into the drawer with a clatter. Jenny took off her apron and hung it behind the door.

"The important thing is," said Roger when the two men were back by the fire again, "who killed Falkner? And—I suppose—why?"

"It's a question I can't answer," said Antony irritably. And then, in quick apology, "I'm sorry, Roger. I know it's got to be faced." He knew that Jenny had left them alone deliberately; her absence at once relieved him and made him uneasy.

"Do you think he was following you?"

"I think he must have been. If Collingwood had told him I wanted to see him . . . but then, how did he know where I was?"

"He could have followed us when we left here. I wasn't hurrying," he added, when Antony looked incredulous.

"Well, say that's what happened. It fits, in a way, because if Falkner told his principal, *he* might have been keen to see we didn't get together."

"Collingwood would have known without Falkner telling him."

"So he would," Antony agreed; all the more cordially because he didn't really like being reminded that this was his own fault.

"And it must have been someone who knew a good deal about you." This was dangerous ground, and Farrell took it steadily. "He abandoned his knife—"

"In favor of a method of killing I could very well have used. As a matter of fact"—he glanced round him uncomfortably, as though the big room was no longer friendly and familiar—"he doesn't know how well he chose. If anyone were to go back to the type of training we had during the war . . . let's hope they won't think of it."

"Have you ever . . . I forget what I was going to say," said Roger hastily. Antony smiled at him, but there was no amusement in his eyes.

"I think we'd both better forget it; though I can't somehow see myself confiding in Inspector Watkins," he added thoughtfully. "Tell me something, Roger. It's pretty obvious, isn't it? My shoulder . . . and all that."

"Sometimes more than others. Anyone who was much with you—"

"That's what I thought."

"Collingwood could certainly have known."

"Yes, but I was wondering about Keith Lindsay and Father William."

"Anyone interested enough to try and frame you would certainly study you pretty carefully," Roger pointed out. "But if Falkner was killed within a few minutes of your walking through Clifford's Mews—"

"Yes, there are difficulties about either of those two. What about the fire-escape?"

"Outside the kitchen window, which was shut when I saw it, but could quite easily have been opened from the inside, of course."

"Keith Lindsay had his hands full with Geraldine. I'll ask her, but I can't really imagine he left her very quickly. As for Father William—"

"He's agile enough," said Farrell. "We weren't talking downstairs for long, but I should think he could have made it."

"And been back again before Lindsay came out of the bedroom. I wonder if either of those two heard anything."

"They may have heard, but I'd bet they didn't *notice*."

Jenny came back then, with a bottle held carefully in front of her. Seeing it, Antony got up and went over to the cupboard for glasses. "Uncle Nick's?" he asked.

"I abstracted it," said Jenny proudly, "under Gibbs's nose." She glanced from one of them to the other and added, "I thought we needed it." And then, "After all, he'll be living it up in New York."

"My dearest love, where did you learn that phrase? Anyway, it will only be half past five there, so I hope . . . I wonder how he got on last night."

They speculated in a determined way on the content and reception of Sir Nicholas's address for quite five minutes; after that they went back to the subject of Falkner's death, not quite so outspokenly as before, but just as inconclusively.

8

Antony went downstairs to see Roger out, and stood on the top step to watch the Jensen move away. After the fine day it had turned cold again, and he was shivering as he went inside; he climbed the stairs slowly.

Jenny had turned out all the lights, except the lamp in the corner near the writing-table, and gone back to her favorite corner of the sofa. The room was still warm, though the fire was dying. Antony came in, leaving the door half-open, and stood on the hearth-rug looking down at her. It might have been any other evening, until he saw her eyes flicker away from his for an instant before they were steady again, watching him, a little too intent.

"Go on, love, say it."

She was on the defensive in a moment. "Say what?" she demanded.

His glance followed the direction hers had taken, back to the open door. "How many years is it since I last did that?"

"Left the door open deliberately? Fifteen or sixteen," she told him, and saw in his eyes that her promptness had betrayed her. "It was longer before you stopped having a thing about keys," she went on steadily, because having gone so far she might as well go all the way.

"I've given myself away to you," he said, "over and over again." He raised his hands in a sudden, helpless gesture. "So now you know what I'm really afraid of." After a moment he added, as if it was important to get the distinction clear, "It isn't claustrophobia. At least, I don't think it is. I mean, that's something you can't help, something you're born with."

"But, Antony—"

"Jon Kellaway has a touch of it," he said, ignoring the interruption. "I've watched him since he was arrested . . . because you see, I know how he feels. Even if he did kill Dakins—"

"You don't blame *him*," said Jenny flatly. But she wasn't even thinking about the murder.

"No, because . . . don't you think after all this time I should have got over it? Have learned, at least, to control my feelings, even if I can't altogether forget—" He broke off there, and turned to look down at the remains of the fire, but in his mind the sentence completed itself. "—even if I can't forget what happened to me in Paris during the occupation, what it's like to hear a bolt shoot into its socket, or a key turn in a lock, and know you can't get out." He looked up and his eyes met

Jenny's, and suddenly it seemed important to make her understand. "It's a poor sort of memory that only works backwards," he said, and paused a moment to wonder from what depths of memory the unexpected, absurd phrase had come.

"It's stupid to—to torture yourself."

"I suppose now you're feeling sorry for me." His tone was almost sulky, but he went and sat beside her on the sofa and put out a hand to find hers.

"No, why should I be?" She sounded very cool, very positive. "You think that's going to happen to you, don't you? That you'll be arrested."

"Yes, I do. I know I ought to be lying to you," he said with a kind of desperation, "telling you not to worry."

Jenny stiffened. "That's something I'd *never* forgive you," she told him forcefully; and suddenly the tension was broken and he was laughing at her.

"Jenny, love, don't disown me."

It was a moment before she could relax, too, and smile at him. But when she spoke again, after the silence had lengthened until it seemed almost unbearable, there was a note of uncertainty in her voice. "Don't you think, Antony, that perhaps we ought to tell Uncle Nick?"

"Heaven forbid!"

The flippancy of his tone sparked her to anger again. "Do you think you—you respect him enough?"

He grinned at that, with something like genuine amusement. "When first I came to live here I thought the world would come to an end if I annoyed him. And sometimes," he added thoughtfully, "I wished it would. But I grew out of that quite a long time ago."

"That's obvious. Just because you don't want to admit—"

"I don't, of course, but that isn't really the point." He was serious enough now, and there was a hint of stubbornness in his voice.

"He's got to know sooner or later. And the thing is, Antony, if you don't tell him he'll be so hurt."

"He'll be furious," he amended, and she felt his grip on her hand tighten. But he took time to think about what she had said. "I suppose you mean, that's why," he said then, "and for

all I know, you may be right. All right then . . . give me time
to think what to say, and I'll cable him in the morning." He
got up and wandered over to the bookshelves. "Someone's
moved the *Dictionary of Quotations*," he complained.

"I was dusting," said Jenny, sounding as guilty as if she had
been admitting to holding an orgy, or inviting a witches' coven
to meet in the living-room. "You'd better turn the light on,
Antony. I think it's at the end near the door."

He came back with the book in his hand. *"Praise,"* he said.
"Envy is a kind of. 160b. I knew it was John Gay."

"What on earth—?"

"Fables: The Hound and the Huntsman. How very appropriate,"
said Antony. *"Fools may our scorn, not envy raise. For envy is a kind of
praise,"* he read, in a singsong tone that reduced the words to
doggerel. "That's what the play was about, do you remember?"

"Of course I remember."

"It means something." He snapped the book shut, and stood
looking at her and through her. "I feel it in my bones."

"I don't see what your bones have got to do with it." Jenny
was getting ruffled again. "Unless you mean boneheaded.
That's apt enough, I suppose."

The vague look vanished, there was no doubt now that he
could see her. "Come to bed, love. It's been a long day."

"You've thought of something," she told him, as if it was an
accusation.

"Not so as you'd notice it." He tossed the book down on the
sofa and held out a hand to her. "The night *may* bring counsel," he said, "but I shouldn't count on it if I were you."

FRIDAY, 26th MARCH

1

The morning started badly with an overnight cable from Sir Nicholas which was delivered before the first cup of coffee had had its strengthening effect. Antony went to the telephone to take the message, and Jenny heard him say sharply, "From Reykjavik?" And then, after the briefest pause, "All right then, go on." After that he was writing steadily for a while. "Thank you, yes. Yes, that's quite clear," he said at last, and replaced the receiver, and sat looking down at the pad.

"What is it, Antony?"

"From Uncle Nick," he told her. "My good resolutions were wasted."

"But what's he doing in Reykjavik of all places?"

"God knows, I don't. Nor do I know," he added bitterly, "why he's apparently on his way to Luxembourg."

"You'd better tell me what he says," suggested Jenny practically.

"MEET PLANE FROM LUXEMBOURG EIGHT TEN P.M. TWENTY-SIXTH STOP CAN'T REMEMBER FLIGHT NUMBER BUT EXPECT YOU CAN FIND OUT STOP," he read in a flat voice that was, in its way, expressive enough.

"Well, at least he isn't in a hurry," said Jenny. "Perhaps he just wants to get home." Antony gave a laugh that could only be regarded as disbelieving, and she added defensively, "I know he likes New York when he gets there, but—"

"He can't have heard about Falkner," said Maitland thoughtfully. "I'd say he'd found out somehow that I'd been to see Hudson."

"It may not be that at all."

"I think it is. You see, love, there's another sentence: SUCH

AN EXCESS OF STUPIDITY IS NOT IN NATURE. I don't somehow think he's referring to his own forgetfulness."

"Oh, dear!" said Jenny, staring at him unhappily. Antony came back to the table and sat down and began to stir his coffee. "I wonder if Halloran double-crossed me," he said, but he wasn't really interested in the question. The *Courier* lay at his elbow, as yet unfolded.

After a while, of course, it had to be faced; Falkner's death had made the front page, half-way down. MURDER IN CLIFFORD'S MEWS—ARREST IMMINENT SAY PO-LICE. "They always say that," said Maitland, running his eye down the column, but there was nothing he did not already know. The connection between Paul Collingwood's managing clerk and "the bribery case" was taken for granted; a passer-by had been interviewed at some length by the police; Chief-Superintendent Briggs, in charge of the case, was con-fident . . .

Before they had finished breakfast there had been three tele-phone calls from different newspapers, asking him with vary-ing degrees of suavity whether he had observed anything help-ful to the inquiry during his walk on Wednesday evening. After he had slammed back the receiver for the third time he took it off again. "Better leave it like that, love. If I want to phone you I can give a message to Gibbs." (He didn't know it then, but Gibbs was having troubles of his own.)

"Are you going into chambers, Antony?"

"I must see Mallory. It's only fair. And I want to see Col-lingwood, that's why I'm not hurrying. Of course, he may get to the office earlier now Falkner isn't there." He broke off and smiled at her. "I'm talking for the sake of it, Jenny. The thing is, I don't know how much time I've got."

"But you have an idea—?"

"I always have ideas." He came back to the table again, and stood looking down at her. "If I had just one it would be simple."

"I don't believe you. I think you know."

"I *think* I do, but what's the use of that. There's no proof."

"What are you going to do then?"

"Find some." He was brisk suddenly. Jenny got up and fol-

lowed him to the door. "I'm glad Uncle Nick's coming back
. . . really, love!" He took his coat, and kissed her quickly,
and was gone.

Jenny went back into the living-room and replaced the telephone receiver. On the whole, she thought she would rather
know what was going on. Then she picked up the pad and
read Sir Nicholas's message again, and wondered if, by any
chance, Antony had been right in what he said last night.

2

Paul Collingwood was sorting an unusually large pile of
mail. He looked up, unsmiling, when Maitland was shown
into his room, and though his voice was still hearty there was a
noticeable lack of cordiality in his greeting.

Antony said awkwardly, "I'm sorry about Falkner."

"So am I." The harassed look he gave his correspondence
seemed to argue that his grief was not altogether divorced
from self-interest. "Is that all you came for, Maitland, because
if so—"

Antony stood his ground. (He'd known it would be difficult,
hadn't he?) "I know you're busy, but I wanted to ask you . . .
about this bribery business."

"I can't understand it!" He glowered at his visitor for a moment and then said abruptly, "You'd better sit down."

"Thank you."

"There might be more point, though, in my asking what *you*
know about it."

Considering the bluntness of this remark, Antony reacted
with surprising mildness. "I suppose that does seem reasonable. The police had already questioned me, you know, with regard to Hudson's statement."

"The greengrocer? So I gathered. I may as well tell you,
Maitland, there was a chap called Watkins here yesterday—"

"Asking you about Falkner?" (It occurred to him then that
if there was any justice in the world Collingwood ought to be
grateful to him. If their attention had not already been directed elsewhere, the police could hardly have failed to take
an interest in Falkner's employer.)

"Well, yes, but I was going to tell you . . . he wanted to know about our conversation in the morning. I told him, of course. I also told him that you'd been looking for Falkner the night before."

"I see."

"Well, you couldn't expect me to lie to him," said Collingwood defensively.

"Don't worry. I didn't. Will you tell me something else, though? On Wednesday evening, did you tell Falkner that I wanted to see him?"

"As a matter of fact, I did. I phoned him at home." He met Antony's eye with a certain belligerence. "I was curious, if you want to know."

"That seems very reasonable." His tone had still that unnatural mildness. "I suppose the police told you that they believe Falkner was connected not only with the attempt to bribe Bassett, but with several other cases too."

"They told me that all right," said Collingwood discontentedly.

"Could you throw any light on the matter?"

"Now, look here, Maitland, if you're suggesting—"

"Only that, looking back in the light of your new knowledge, something might have struck you."

"Oh, well, that's different. I can't say it did, though."

"Nothing that he ever did or said that seems strange to you?"

"No." He thought a moment. "No," he said, more positively.

"His friends, then. What about his friends?"

"Nothing at all."

"Do you know Keith Lindsay? He's a reporter on the *Courier*."

"I think I've met him. I don't connect him with Albert, though."

"Or William Webster?"

Collingwood grinned. "Oh, yes, I know him. From time to time he's taken an interest in one of my clients."

"In a purely benevolent way?"

"That's what he *said*."

"Yes, well, we mustn't slander him, must we? Falkner would know him too?"

"In the same way I did myself." He added in rather a resentful tone, "I can't see how this helps you."

"All the same, I'm grateful." He got up as he spoke. "There is one other thing, though. Did Inspector Watkins ask to see Swaine?"

Collingwood looked more uncomfortable than ever. "Of course he did. We went out to the prison yesterday afternoon."

"I see. Does Swaine still deny all knowledge of the approach to Bassett?"

"In the circumstances, I felt I could only advise him to be frank with the police."

"And was he?"

"Up to a point. He admitted having made a deal with Falkner, but denied—of course—all knowledge of another man behind the scenes."

"Of course. Do you suppose Watkins believed him?"

"I should think it very unlikely," said Collingwood spitefully. "I didn't myself." He seemed to have forgotten the waiting correspondence. "Was it you the police interviewed yesterday?"

"It was."

"Oh! Oh, I see." Now he had got the answer he didn't seem very pleased with it. "Swaine always liked you," he said.

"Enough to damn anybody," Maitland agreed.

"Eh? Oh, well, I didn't mean . . . I dare say it will all blow over," said Collingwood unconvincingly.

For the first time that morning, Antony was conscious of amusement. "Did you also explain to the inspector that there was really no need for Swaine to have me to represent him? My junior could have done the job equally well alone."

"Well, you must admit, Maitland, that's perfectly true. If he hadn't been so insistent—"

But Antony seemed to have lost interest. "He doesn't like change," he said indifferently, "and it must be the third or fourth time I've defended him."

"It was different," said Collingwood flatly, "when you were a junior yourself."

And, of course, when you came to think about it, it was.
Quite different.

3

There was a hush in chambers again today, enough to give
a chap the creeps. His talk with Mr. Mallory was quite as
painful as he had expected; the old man's normal acidity he
could cope with, but today he was upset and only slightly con-
soled when he heard that Sir Nicholas was on his way home.
"I always knew how it would be," he said, rather obscurely;
and went away, shaking his head, to put as good a face as possible on the return of several sets of papers.

Maitland phoned the *Courier* office then, but Keith Lindsay
was out on an assignment. "Can't tell you when he'll be back,"
said the helpful voice at the other end of the line. "Can I give
him a message?"

"I'll try again," said Antony. He had better luck with his
next call, which was to New Scotland Yard.

Sykes's voice sharpened a little when he heard who the
caller was. "Mr. Maitland! What can I do for you?"

"There's something I want to ask you."

"What is it?" Some of the eagerness had gone. "I don't
mind telling you," he said heavily, "I was hoping you'd come
to your senses."

"I—" But it was useless, wasn't it, trying to explain? "I was
hoping you'd help me."

"What is it?" asked Sykes again.

"You'll know about the newspaper cuttings found among
Falkner's belongings." The detective's grunt might have
meant anything, he chose to take it as agreement. "Did they
cover the same cases you were investigating . . . the jurors
who were supposed to have committed suicide?"

There was a pause while Sykes examined the question from
all angles. "Yes, they did," he said at last cautiously. "And put
me on to two more besides."

"Did they now!"

Sykes obviously interpreted the exclamation correctly.
"Over a period of four and a half years, and in different parts

159

of the country, and all written off as suicide. It's no wonder the similarity wasn't noticed."

"Well, I can give you another instance, if you're interested. Did you know Dakins had been on a jury a few days before he died?"

"Dakins?"

"Murder and arson. Gilcliffe Gardens."

"How did you know that?" The question came explosively, in something quite different from Sykes's normal manner. Antony grimaced at the telephone and said succinctly:

"Jon K-Kellaway told me."

"Why?"

"B-because I asked him. You may remember I m-mentioned Kellaway when I saw you the other day."

"I remember," said Sykes. The undercurrent of amusement that was usually so noticeable was altogether absent from his voice today. "You were trying to connect the two cases, but don't you think the joke's gone far enough?"

"When I tell you the truth you won't believe me," Antony complained; and waited while the detective worked that out.

"Dakins didn't commit suicide," he said at last.

"No, but there's no telling whether his throat might not have been cut. The doctor said there was a lot of blood. I dare say he was being professionally reticent, but if you could ask him for an unofficial opinion—"

"If Dakins's throat was cut like the others, why try to hide the fact?"

"I'll tell you something else, Chief-Inspector. He was left-handed."

There was another silence. As he waited, Maitland could hear the other man breathing deeply, as though the effort of cogitation was a strenuous one. "You're suggesting that the murderer knew Dakins, but not very well, and remembered that too late."

"Or he might have been flustered. But it was important— don't you see?—because once it was obvious Dakins had been murdered *that way* it wouldn't be long before the connection with the other cases was made. So he set about trying to hide the fact, and he fetched the petrol—"

"You're making out a very good case against your own client."

"So I am." There was an odd note in his voice that puzzled Sykes for a moment, but he was worried too, and on the whole the worry predominated.

"All this isn't going to help you," he said.

"I know . . . I'm displaying altogether too much knowledge. But I only found this out yesterday."

"They'll say you already knew."

"But your own advice to me—"

"My advice still stands, Mr. Maitland. I could ask you, now, why you asked Mr. Kellaway those questions . . . you're still not being open with me, are you?" This time it was his turn to wait for a reply that was not immediately forthcoming, and after a moment he added less hardly, "I'm saying more than I should, but if I were your solicitor—which thank the good Lord I'm not—I know how I should advise you."

"This fixed idea of yours—"

Now he had got started, Sykes wasn't to be stopped so easily. He ignored the interruption. "If you have any statement to make that will clear things up, make it now, before it's too late."

"I don't know anything about Falkner's death. That's what you mean, isn't it?"

"The background," said Sykes slowly, "is almost as important a part of the case as the murder itself."

"The trouble is, the things I know don't add up to any sort of proof. On the whole, I think I'd better reserve my defense."

"I'll not argue with you, Mr. Maitland." His tone was troubled. As clearly as if they had been together Antony could imagine him sitting at his desk and shaking his head sadly over this wrong-headedness. "It's a pity," said Sykes. "A great pity."

"I think so too." He sat quite still for a long time after the connection had been cut, before he pulled open the drawer of his desk and saw for the first time the evidence of yesterday's search. They had left everything tidy . . . too tidy. He wondered idly what they had made of the clutter in his uncle's room. He slammed the drawer shut and pulled the telephone toward him again.

Roger's call came through before he could lift the receiver. "I thought I'd tell you Inspector Watkins turned up at breakfast time, Antony."

"I hope you didn't let your porridge get cold."

"Porridge? What porridge?" asked Roger blankly.

"Meg said—"

"You're driveling. And anyway, the less said about Meg the better," said Roger, but his voice softened as he spoke. "I know it's her fault—"

"Roger, don't keep on and on."

"Well . . . all right. I was telling you about Watkins. He was asking about Wednesday night, of course, but I couldn't help him about times. All that carry-on put everything else out of my head; and though I know exactly when I got to the theater—three minutes before the final curtain—it doesn't really help."

"Never mind."

"Is there anything I can do?"

"Not at the moment."

"You're not holding out on me?"

"No." Suddenly his voice was amused. "I'm not trying to spare you anything, or keep your name out of things. There are one or two people I want to see, but it's too late to worry about appearances now. Afterwards . . . you can keep an eye on Jenny."

"Of course, but—"

"I've been talking to Sykes, and what he didn't say was illuminating," Antony told him. "I rather think Jenny was right, they've more evidence than I've heard so far."

"*Faked* evidence, you mean?"

"As I didn't kill Falkner it would have to be, wouldn't it?" He was touchy again, and Roger pulled himself up on the brink of an apology.

"I'll see you tonight, shall I?"

"We'll expect you."

After that he felt he'd had enough of the telephone, and went round to see Geoffrey Horton instead; and then wished

162

he hadn't, because the clerks in the outer office stared at him.

Geoffrey was in an astringent mood, which was probably beneficial, though rather difficult to appreciate at the time. "I've nothing yet on a possible connection between Kellaway and Dakins, if that's what you're after," he said, looking Maitland up and down and wondering whether he'd had any sleep at all.

"I'm afraid I'd forgotten . . . no, I wanted to tell you the police were at Kempenfeldt Square yesterday, with a search warrant. *And* they went to chambers."

"I . . . see." He waved a hand, and Maitland sat down, with unaccustomed propriety, in the visitors' chair, ignoring the implied invitation to perch on the desk. "Poor Jenny," Horton added, reflectively. And then, "What are you doing, Antony?"

"Consulting my solicitor," said Maitland tartly.

"In that case—"

"And don't tell me everything's going to be all right."

"I was about to say that I agree with Halloran—"

"You would!"

"—you'd do best to keep out of things now."

Antony made no comment on that; perhaps he was regretting his rudeness. "Have you got a copy of Beth's letter?" he asked.

Geoffrey sighed. "I suppose it's no use talking to you."

"Not a bit. Beth's letter," he insisted.

"All right, I'll find it." He put out a hand to the house phone, glanced at his friend, changed his mind, and went on the errand himself. When he came back he held out several stiff sheets covered with a sprawling hand. "This is an actual photostat. The Coroner's Office must have been persuaded to disgorge the original."

"I can't read that," said Maitland, recoiling.

"I suppose you want me to read it to you."

"Yes, please. I mean, I expect you've deciphered it once."

Geoffrey cleared his throat. "*My dearest, I love you so very much, and now that I know you don't care about me any more I don't feel I can go on any longer.* I don't know what good you think this is doing,

Antony," he went on without any change of tone. "It's all pretty much the same."

"I want to hear it," said Maitland stubbornly. "Besides,"—he smiled suddenly—"you read with so much *élan*."

Geoffrey made a scornful noise, but he went back to the letter. He was right though; it continued in the same strain, and it didn't get any more informative. Pretty good drivel, thought Antony, and yet—even read aloud in Horton's stiff, embarrassed tones—it had an odd, touching quality. Beth had been in love, and had asked so small a return of affection; she had been lonely, and now her last refuge was closed to her. It was easy to see the effect her words would have had, even in the dry atmosphere of the Coroner's Court. Certainly no one with the least affection for Jon Kellaway would have treasured for twelve years the report of an occasion which he must have found not merely distressing but humiliating as well.

"Was that quoted in the newspaper?" he asked, when Geoffrey had finished.

"Yes, in full." He threw the sheets into the filing basket. "Nice fellow, isn't he? No wonder Mrs. Lindsay can't quite make up her mind."

"I wonder which of them she really cares for," said Maitland, getting up restlessly.

"Does it matter?"

"Perhaps she doesn't love either of them; that's what Aunt Ethel would say." He was thinking of his talk with Roger, and Geoffrey didn't take the allusion. "I'm sure you're right," Maitland added, "it doesn't matter at all." He was moving toward the door, seemingly purposeless, but he turned before he reached it and said "Thank you" politely. "You'll be hearing from me, Geoffrey . . . sooner than either of us likes, I expect," he added. And was gone.

Geoffrey Horton, who was not given to profanity, sat and swore with considerable fluency for several minutes when he found himself alone.

4

Maitland arrived at the shop in Bedford Lane just as William Webster was closing for lunch. The old man unlocked the grille obligingly to let him in. "If you would care to share my meal," he offered, "I have plenty for two. That is, if you can eat sausages."

You had to admit a degree of humor in the situation. "I want to ask you some questions," Antony said, half in apology; but Father William just stood looking at him guilelessly, so after a moment he added, "I am rather hungry as a matter of fact."

Mr. Webster beamed at him. "For that matter, I may have some questions for you myself," he said in his gentle way. The simple statement was oddly like a warning.

Behind the office they had been in before there was a larger room, less crowded but not much more comfortable. There was a divan bed, a bookcase, one easy-chair, and a table with four hard wooden chairs ranged round it. Father William disappeared through a door at the side, but popped his head back a moment later. "Bathroom through there," he said, with an explanatory gesture. "Make yourself at home."

The bathroom was small, and clean, and old-fashioned. Father William rolled his tube of toothpaste neatly from the bottom, used Palmolive soap and large towels which had been white but now were discolored by age and many washings. There was a bottle of expensive after-shave lotion, and a Rolls razor . . . had he really expected to find a cut-throat, and what would it have told him, psychologically, if he had? Cotton wool, aspirins, a small bottle of disinfectant, hair tonic, another bottle labeled THE TABLETS.

He went back into the other room, and occupied himself with the contents of the bookcase until his host reappeared. William Webster seemed to have an incongruous taste for high adventure, both real and fictional. Most of the volumes were elderly and looked to have been well read, but there were a few in bright, new jackets as well, and on the bottom shelf a row of what looked like textbooks. He was stooping to read the titles when Father William came back and called him to the table. "What do my books tell you about me, Mr. Maitland?" he asked with an amused look.

"That you've always regretted you didn't run away to sea."

There was a disconcerting little silence. "I wonder if you're right," said Webster at last. He seemed to be taking a casual remark with surprising seriousness. "Do you know, I believe you *are* right," he added, and sounded as if the discovery pleased him. As for Antony, he was conscious of a vague dissatisfaction. It couldn't have anything to do with the collected works of Joseph Conrad, or C. S. Forrester, or *The Riddle of the Sands*. Or even with *Twenty Years After*, or *Kontiki*, or Captain Joshua Slocum *Sailing Alone Around the World*. All the same . . .

Father William's repast was surprisingly good. From time to time as they ate, Antony considered the impropriety of eating your enemy's salt, but decided that whoever invented the rule in the first place couldn't have been hungry. In any case, he still wasn't sure.

"You seem thoughtful, Mr. Maitland." Father William was pouring coffee; he pushed a cup across the table and glanced at the clock on the wall. "I have just half an hour," he said.

"I was wondering what happened after Farrell and I left Maddox Court on Wednesday evening."

The old man made no attempt to answer that directly. He stirred his coffee, and when he looked up at last his expression had an alertness that was somehow faintly disturbing. "You asked me rather an odd question that night."

"Yes," said Antony, and left it there.

"From reading the newspapers I have since gained the impression that you are, yourself, in—in difficulties, shall we say?" He paused, eyeing his visitor, and now he seemed to feel nothing but a gentle concern. "I am wondering, you see, what possible connection you think I can have with those difficulties. Apart, of course, from an apparent suspicion on the part of the police that there was some collusion between us about Jon's alibi."

"They asked you, did they, why I came to see you?"

"Oh, yes. And now Mr. Horton tells me you will not use that line of defense. Is that the reason?"

"It was Kellaway's decision."

"You will forgive me for saying that I think he is ill-advised. But you haven't answered my previous question."

A moment ago it had all been clear in his mind. "I mentioned Bassett to you; he was one of the jurors on a case where

I led for the defense." He drank some of his coffee, and raised his eyes briefly to meet Father William's. "Did you know that Dakins, too, had just completed a spell of jury duty?"

"Even so—"

"The answer is, I suppose, that I connect Bassett with Dakins, and Dakins with Kellaway, and Kellaway with you."

The old man showed no signs of taking offense. He bowed his head, as though acknowledging the validity of the point that had been made. "But surely it would be simpler to presume that his death was nothing to do with Jonathan . . . or with me."

"If it weren't for the use of his petrol, which a stranger could hardly have known about; and the report of the inquest on Mrs. Kellaway's death, of course."

"Coincidence," suggested Father William, not very hopefully.

"Somehow, I doubt it."

"Poor Beth," said Mr. Webster, and sighed. "Even from the grave—"

This was almost too much for Antony, he interrupted with a deplorable lack of finesse. "Kellaway says you sent him a number of rings that day . . . the day Dakins was killed."

"Dakins died in the early hours of Wednesday morning, as I understand it. You should try to be more accurate, Mr. Maitland." The blue eyes were grave now, and reproving.

"Very well then. I meant on the Tuesday, of course."

"That is correct."

"Will you tell me why?"

"Is this material to Jon's defense?"

"It might be."

"You said something else on Wednesday night, Mr. Maitland. You said you wouldn't be able to do much for him, if you were in prison too."

This was plain speaking indeed, and the benevolent tone didn't make it any easier to take. "You're right, of course, the brief has been returned."

Father William smiled at him. "So long as we understand each other. You are questioning me on your own behalf, not Jon's."

"Does that mean, you won't answer?"

"No. On the whole . . . no. The affair between Jon and Geraldine had dragged on long enough, I thought. I sent Jon the rings in the hope of encouraging him to take some action."

"Had you any particular reason for sending them then?"

"Keith had been speaking of them . . . of Jon and Geraldine. Even after the divorce he had always a great affection for her, and now he seemed to think . . . well, I suppose he was wrong, Mr. Maitland, but we both of us meant well."

"I see. Were you able to tell the police what time I left you on Wednesday evening?"

"I'm sorry, really I'm sorry. I had only the vaguest idea."

"After I left—" He hesitated, groping for the right words. "Did Mrs. Lindsay recover quickly from her nightmare?"

"Keith stayed with her until a few minutes before eleven. He said she was quite calm then. I went in to see her for a moment after he left, and she was already asleep." He paused in his turn, and gave his companion a quizzical look. "I really do not see why you should try to connect me with this man Falkner," he said.

"You never heard of him either," said Antony; his tone both accepted the denial as inevitable and found it depressing.

"Not until I read the report of his death. I was interested, naturally, because Clifford's Mews is so near. And then, of course, the police came, to ask about your movements."

"Of course." He drank the last of his coffee, and his chair slid back on the threadbare carpet as he got to his feet. "At what hospital did Keith Lindsay do his medical training, Mr. Webster?"

"At St. Benedict's." His eyes had a sharpness suddenly, a calculating look. "If you're thinking that the way Falkner died required some special knowledge, you're wrong."

"Am I?"

"In any case . . . ask Geraldine Lindsay, Mr. Maitland. They were together."

"You know when Falkner died?"

"I know at least when he was found. The police told me that."

"And you know how he died. I suppose they told you that,

too. And a great many other people, you think—besides your-self—would have known exactly how to set about it."

"I won't quarrel with that statement, Mr. Maitland."

"I haven't thanked you for your kindness." He gestured as he spoke, but he was looking at Mr. Webster, and he was star-tled to see a distinct twinkle in the old man's eyes.

"These difficulties of yours . . . are they serious?" He sounded genuinely concerned, but there was still that damna-ble look of amusement.

"Serious enough." After a moment he smiled. "It's a little late now to offer me an alibi," he said, and began to move toward the door.

"A pity," agreed Father William, getting up and following him. "But if there is any other way in which I can serve you—"

It would have been so easy to believe him genuine. "I think you have helped me," said Maitland, and watched the inno-cent blue eyes grow chilly with suspicion. "When I saw the books you keep on your bottom shelf. *A Handbook of Clinical and Experimental Psychology . . . Scientific Uses of Hypnosis*—"

"That's enough!"

"Yes, I think so," said Antony gently.

"Enough for knowledge, Mr. Maitland. You're a very clever young man. But where's your proof?"

"That's just what I'm wondering." But there was an uncer-tainty in his voice, and Father William was smiling again.

"Come now, I see we understand each other." But though he accompanied Maitland to the door of the shop, and un-locked the grille, and set it wide in preparation for the after-noon's trade, he responded only in the curtest way to his visi-tor's final civilities.

5

Ana and Geraldine had lunched off rather more sophisti-cated fare, if the trolley that was being wheeled away from the apartment door was anything to go by. And one of them had very little appetite; the waiter from the basement restaurant had a downcast air, as though he were somehow to blame. He caught Antony's eye and went away shaking his head despondently. Ana pulled the door open again. "*Señor* Maitland! Come in."

Once inside the tiny vestibule she hesitated. "It is Geraldine you have come to see?"

"If she is well enough, *señorita.*"

"Well? She is very well." She stepped back a little, so that the light that came through the archway fell more directly on his face. "If we are to talk of being in good health, *señor*—"

"*Es usted muy amable,*" he said. But there was an awareness in her face, a hint almost of satire; she wasn't going to be put off by any such vague courtesy.

"*Verdad que no es cierto?* You did not kill this man."

"Falkner? No."

"*They* have been here," she said, as though he had spoken his inquiry aloud. "Geraldine can tell them nothing, but Keith has said—" She broke off, and gave him a sidelong look, as though gauging his possible reaction to whatever indiscretion she had in mind.

"What did Lindsay say, *señorita?*"

"That Jon was a fool to trust you. That you are in trouble yourself. Bad trouble."

"Would you rather I went away?"

"Is it true, *señor?*"

"That I am in trouble, yes. That Jon can trust me . . . I don't know."

"But Geraldine can help you?"

"I think she can, if she will."

"*Muy bien.* We shall see."

The big room was empty. He should have known that, of course; Ana had made no attempt to lower her voice. She crossed it quickly now, and came back a moment later, pushing Geraldine in front of her. At least, she didn't actually touch her, but the effect was the same.

Against the vivid background, Geraldine seemed paler and more withdrawn than ever. At first glance, Ana looked plain beside her, if it hadn't been for her animation, which had an attraction of its own. As for Geraldine . . . an iceberg, Meg had said, but Roger disagreed with her; and Ana's own opinion seemed to have elements of both.

At least, she was composed enough. She said, "Good afternoon," and sat down on one of the low chairs. He waited for a speculative look, but none came. She seemed unaware of any difference in the situation since the last time they had spoken together; he wondered if she even remembered how she had clutched his hands on that later occasion, when she came out of her dream.

"May I ask you some questions?" he said.

"If you like."

Something in her indifference stung him. He glanced at Ana and received a grave look in return. "Do you remember that I was here on Wednesday, Mrs. Lindsay?"

"Oh, yes. In the evening."

"You had a nightmare."

"It was stupid to be so frightened," she said. "I know that now."

"Do you remember what happened after I left?"

"Of course I remember." Her calm was unbroken, but from her tone she seemed to find the question unreasonable. "Keith was with me."

"He stayed with you, didn't he?"

"Yes." She smiled a little, as though the memory pleased her.

"How long?"

"I suppose . . . half an hour. Quite half an hour," she said.

"Did Father William come in during that time?"

"I didn't see him again that night."

"But you knew he was in the flat. You heard him moving about, I expect."

"No. Well, of course, I know he was there. But I mean, I didn't notice."

"May we go back a little, Mrs. Lindsay? To the time in Penhaven when first you knew your husband."

"Keith isn't my husband." She hesitated. "You want to know about Beth, and Jon."

"If you will tell me."

"There's nothing to tell. Beth was very pretty, very lively. I

171

thought *then* she was sophisticated"—her tone mocked, gently, her own naïvete—"but I was very young."

"You changed your mind in the light of your own experience," he suggested.

"Not . . . exactly. When she died—"

"What made you change your mind?" he prompted when she fell silent.

"Her letter. I didn't realize she loved Jon . . . so much."

"Is that why you won't marry him?"

She looked puzzled. "I don't know."

"Does your husband . . . does Mr. Lindsay know that Kellaway is in love with you?"

Her eyes slid away from his. "I suppose so," she said in a grudging way.

"Is that why you were divorced?"

"How could it be? It's only a year since Jon and I . . . began to take an interest in each other." The coy phrase struck a jarring note. Antony glanced at Ana again, but her face told him nothing.

"And you were divorced five years ago—"

"Four years and five months."

"Did you bring suit?"

"Yes."

"With Lindsay's consent?"

"Yes." He thought she was going to leave it there, but if she was indifferent to his feelings, she showed an equal indifference to her own. "When I told him he said, 'If that's the way you want it.' And he went out, and I didn't see him again."

"Until after the divorce was final?"

"Except in court. After that—" She broke off, and for the first time a trace of awkwardness crept into her manner.

"You saw him regularly, didn't you?" he asked, puzzled in his turn, and no less so when her mood blazed suddenly into anger.

"He wanted me . . . casually . . . just as he wanted all the others."

"I . . . I see."

Ana's voice, cool and decisive, cut into the silence. "*Señor*

Maitland would like to ask you, *querida,* whether you gave him his wish."

Geraldine gasped a protest. "Ana!" and Ana's smile flickered for a second and was gone. "I didn't . . . of course," said Geraldine. But her calm was broken now, she sounded nervous and uncertain.

He wasn't quite sure whether to be grateful for the intervention. "Did Lindsay make any financial arrangement?" he said, and Geraldine turned to him as though eager to escape from a distasteful subject.

"No, he didn't. That's when Father William offered me a job. I hadn't any experience, you know, but I thought . . . well, I thought perhaps Keith was paying my salary. It would have been very like him to go about it in that indirect way, as if anything else would have been an admission that he was in the wrong. But later, when I took over the bookkeeping, I couldn't see that it had ever been done like that."

"Did you notice any other irregularities?"

"I don't quite know what you mean. Father William isn't very worldly, you know." (Ana was smiling to herself, and no wonder.) "There'd be cash gone sometimes I couldn't account for, but there'd always be a good reason; someone he was helping."

Like Mr. O'Keefe, who brought him shamrock for St. Patrick's day. "You were living alone then, after the divorce, in the house you had shared with your husband?"

"For about two years. It was a flat, though . . . not a bit like this one. Then Ana asked me to join her."

"And at first you would not be persuaded," said Ana. "I had been here one year already, and I do not like to live alone. Nor do I wish," she added thoughtfully, "to live with Enrique."

At any other time, Antony would have found this sidetrack irresistibly beguiling. As it was, he was relieved when Geraldine went on, without prompting. "I couldn't seem to make up my mind. It wasn't that I didn't want to come."

"Your husband opposed the move, perhaps."

This time she let the designation pass without comment. "No, Keith never said anything. Father William didn't like it,

he said 'These things never work out.' He was wrong, you see
. . . I think I knew he was wrong. But perhaps that was what
made it so difficult to decide."

Did it matter? Did any of it matter? "You've been very patient with me," he said; and saw with interest that his words
made Geraldine uneasy.

"If you have finished," said Ana, "it will be correct that I
offer you tea."

"That would be nice." Geraldine was on her feet before he
could reply. "I'll make it, shall I?"

"Tell me one thing first, Mrs. Lindsay. One more thing," he
added, and smiled up at her apologetically. "You know your
husband was once a medical student?"

"That was before I knew him."

"But you might know why he discontinued his training?"

"I don't know. It was a pity, wasn't it? Father William once
said he was doing exceptionally well, and might have had a
brilliant future—"

That was clearly not where the sentence had been meant to
end. "But—?" he said, encouraging her.

"Father William said there was a lot of jealousy. I don't
quite know what he meant."

She went away then, and he looked at Ana. "Am I supposed
to be grateful to you, *señorita?*" he asked her, amused.

"You should be," she told him seriously. "And your own
questions, *señor,* were not all the time with tact."

"They weren't, were they?" He was rueful now. "I don't understand why she didn't take offense, or at least question my
motives."

"I do not understand either, but I have noticed that if one
can shake her from this—this dullness she will be more natural
than before."

It seemed in retrospect one of the queerest conversations he
had ever had in his life. "You're right, of course," he said
reflectively. And then, "Do you know, I don't think I'll wait
for that tea."

She got up as he did, but she seemed to be considering the
remark as though it might contain some hidden meaning.
After a moment she shook her head, abandoning the problem.

"There is one thing I do not understand at all, *señor*. When Keith came to see her yesterday she told him she would marry Jon, if ever he was free."

"What did Lindsay say to that?"

"He said, 'If that's the way you want it.' The same thing, you see, *señor*—"

"Yes. An indulgent husband." He was watching her face as he spoke. "Has she seen him again today?"

"She has not said so. He might have been here, for a moment, while I am with the hairdresser."

"A moment?" said Antony. But he, too, was serious.

"It is a regular appointment. Always on Friday. And I need only go downstairs. So I am gone . . . an hour, perhaps, not more."

"And you think that Lindsay may have been here."

"I speak of the possibility only."

"Yes, I see."

"Of things I know, I can tell you only that *Señor* Webster has called on the telephone."

She had her own air of watchfulness; he couldn't flatter himself that his expression was as guarded as hers. "I am grateful, *señorita*," he said formally. "I don't know why you should help me."

"Perhaps because you need help, *señor*—"

"That's true enough."

"—and perhaps because I think you are helping Geraldine."

For all her self-possession, she was shaken by the way he looked at her. "If you only knew," he said; and turned away with an abrupt movement.

She caught up with him when he had his hand already on the door knob. "What is it that I should know?"

"You shouldn't trust me. You should never have trusted me," he told her with angry violence.

"But does not Geraldine, then, need help?"

"More help than I can give her," he said somberly. And thought, but did not say aloud, "even if I were free to try." Ana was clutching his sleeve and he detached her fingers carefully, giving the action all his attention, so that they were enclosed for a moment together in a wholly illusory calm. Then he raised his eyes to meet hers again steadily. "I am in your debt, *señorita*. I can only hope you will find it in your heart to forgive me."

It was several hours later, and he had lost himself pretty thoroughly in Richmond Park, when he remembered the phrase and felt at once amused and ashamed by its flowery quality. But when he thought of Geraldine Lindsay he wasn't even tempted to amusement any longer.

6

The instinct that had taken him into the open air had been a strong one, not altogether accounted for by the need to think things out, nor even by the fact that the day was clear and sunny and there was the smell of spring in the air. Dusk had already overtaken him before he began to think about going home, and by the time he got there he was cold, and tired, and hungry. To complete his discomfort he had forgotten his key, and had to ring for Gibbs to let him in.

At that hour there was more traffic in the square than usual, and he didn't notice the black car until it drew up at the curb. He stood in the doorway, watching the familiar figure of Inspector Watkins emerge on the pavement side, and a younger, taller man on the other.

Gibbs was hovering. "Miss Jenny went out," he said.

"She's gone to the airport, hasn't she?"

"No, Mr. Maitland, I meant . . . she went out at seven o'clock with the fair young lady, the one who was here last week."

"Well, never mind. I expect she'll phone." The two men were at the top of the steps now, he held the door open invitingly. "Come in, Inspector. And your friend, of course."

Gibbs was going away down the hall. Having the police in the house was in his eyes an almost unbearable affront. Jenny had probably picked up the car and gone straight to the airport . . . the only queer thing really was the butler's evident concern. As for the fair young lady, it might be any one of half a dozen of Jenny's friends.

"I think it would be best if we could speak to you alone," Watkins was saying; his eyes were fixed on Gibbs's rigidly retreating back. "This is Detective-Constable Hazlitt," he went on, and gave Maitland his warmest, most friendly smile.

"You'd better come upstairs," said Antony, and added over his shoulder as he led the way, "My wife won't be home just yet." Watkins kept up a gentle flow of comment as they went . . . a fine day, but now you'd almost think there was a touch of frost in the air . . . keeps you fit, I dare say, all these stairs . . . lucky to find you at home . . .

"Now, Inspector," said Maitland, turning to face them when they reached the living-room. "You're not a chap to beat about the bush," he added, gently mocking. "What's on your mind?" But he did not wait for a reply; Jenny hadn't left a note in the usual place on the mantelpiece, but perhaps there was one on the pad by the telephone. He went over to the writing-table, and stood looking down.

Antony, I have gone with Geraldine—

So that was what Gibbs had meant. Unexpected, of course, but nothing to worry about . . . surely. Even if Jenny had scrawled her message, instead of writing it in her usual neat hand. It only meant she was in a hurry.

Why?

"I might ask you the same thing, Mr. Maitland." Watkins's voice interrupted his thoughts. Antony tore the sheet from the pad and crumpled it into a ball, then changed his mind and dropped it back on the table again.

"The same thing?" he said vaguely.

"Well, perhaps it doesn't matter. You'll not be surprised, I expect—you knowing about these things as you do—to know that I've a warrant here for your arrest."

"On what charge, Inspector?"

The constable opened his mouth and closed it again. Watkins glanced at him and said approvingly, "That's right! Mr. Maitland knows the form as well as we do, but you can't be too careful."

"I'm quite willing to take the warning as read," said Antony. "But you haven't told me—"

"Murder of Albert Falkner," said Watkins. Constable

177

Hazlitt had his notebook out now. "You *are* surprised," the inspector went on. "Well now, perhaps I ought to have broken it to you more gently."

Maitland was still standing by the writing-table; the two men facing him both had their backs to the center light, which he had turned on when he came in. Watkins was playing his usual game, of course, but for all that he thought there was a difference, a shrewdness in the usually bovine stare, or perhaps . . . was he worried? "I thought it would take Briggs longer than this to persuade the D.P.P. that you'd got a case," he said carefully.

The inspector spread his hands in a gesture that seemed designed to make light of any difficulties. "As to that, Mr. Maitland, it may be you're not quite up to date. Do you remember Sammy Barber?"

"Ye-es. Yes, I do. I defended him on a charge of breaking and entering. It must have been three years ago, because it was before I left the junior bar."

"You got him off," said Watkins. The thought seemed to sadden him. "He says the jury was rigged. He says you told him—"

"What in heaven's name are you talking about? There wouldn't have been any need to rig the jury. Sammy's 'not guilty' plea was perfectly correct."

"Come now! I'm a credulous man myself—"

"S-so you've already t-told me!" It was the first sign of nerves that he had given, and he clamped his mouth shut on the words, as though to prevent any repetition. Watkins went on, apparently unheeding.

"—but I know Sammy."

"He didn't do that particular job. As a matter of fact"—he was trying rather desperately for a light tone—"I think he was doing one at Clerkenwell that night. So there was no question of anyone being able to prove he was at Balham."

"And that's what you meant when you told him not to worry, everything was under control."

"If I ever said it." He sounded skeptical. "Collingwood was acting for him," he added thoughtfully after a moment.

"Fits together a treat, doesn't it?" said Watkins with simple pleasure. "Sammy says Falkner took fifty quid off him—cheap at the price, he said, because the judge had warned him last time—and, of course, when you spoke so confident—"

"Just a minute, Inspector. Did he volunteer this information?"

"He's a good citizen, Sammy is, whatever his faults," said Watkins sententiously. "So when he saw about Falkner's death in the paper he thought it was his duty to come along."

"I see."

Constable Hazlitt was still writing industriously, but he raised his eyes now and directed a long look at his superior officer. The only thing you could be sure of about Watkins was that he would take his own way, and it wouldn't be an orthodox one. "For h-heaven's sake, Constable, put that notebook away," said Maitland, with sudden irritation. "Unless you have ambitions as an essayist yourself."

"Sir?"

"You know as well as I do that if you're making notes you'll tear them up at the first opportunity."

"Now, Mr. Maitland, we're just having a friendly chat," said Watkins in a voice that may or may not have been intended to be soothing. "Off the record," he agreed.

"Oh, very well!" said Maitland ungraciously. "What next?" Constable Hazlitt still had his pencil at the ready, but he had stopped writing for the moment at least.

"You're quite right, of course," said Watkins cordially, "Sammy's evidence wouldn't mean much by itself. And, of course, your friend Swaine . . . well, I can't really feel he was trying to be helpful. The thing that clinched it, you see—I was all for asking you for an explanation myself, being always ready to listen to reason; but the superintendent said we'd had enough of that—what clinched it, as I was saying, was the lady in Clifford's Mews. Well, when I say *lady,* that's one way of putting it, but—"

"What did she say?"

"She has a flat there, nice little place . . . private . . . very suitable. And she was looking out of the window, and she saw a man walking from the direction of Savile Row. She may not be able to identify you, Mr. Maitland, there's no saying, but the description was very clear, very clear indeed."

"As I've already told you I was there—"

"A bit after half past ten, she says it was; twenty-five to, most likely," said Watkins, in a tone that managed to convey that he took no responsibility for the interpretation that might be put on the facts he was reciting. "She saw Falkner, too . . . at least she saw a shorter man following the first one. I wonder now, how he knew you'd be there?"

"I hadn't arranged to meet him . . . if that's what you mean." (Falkner might have been waiting outside Maddox Court because he'd followed me there, as Roger suggested; or someone who knew of my appointment with Father William might have told him.)

"Hadn't you, Mr. Maitland?" Watkins's tone was politely noncommittal. "Well, after a bit the tall man turned round and began to walk back the way he had come. And when she turned her head—she couldn't keep both of them in sight at the same time, you see—the second man had disappeared. She thinks he must have been about opposite the doorway where Falkner was found, perhaps he was waiting for the first man to join him there. What do you make of *that*, Mr. Maitland?"

"What else did she see . . . or think she saw?"

"Her telephone rang, so she left the window then." He did not repeat his question, but his eye was alert and inquiring.

"Perhaps that was as well. She'd already seen more than there was to see."

"Meaning?"

"That I think it's extremely likely the two men were Falkner and myself. I had a feeling I was being followed, and I did turn round; but I did *not* take even one step back the way I had come. Did she mean *shadowing*, Inspector, or just *walking along in the same direction?*"

"The latter, Mr. Maitland. I don't think the other ever occurred to her." He paused, watching the effect of his words. "Pity, isn't it?" he asked blandly.

"I still wonder how well she'll stand up to cross-examination," said Antony. But when they came into court it was motive that would convict him: Hudson's statement, connecting him with Falkner; Collingwood's evidence; even Sammy Barber. That, and what the pathologists would have to say about the way Falkner died. He caught Watkins's eye, and thought the detective understood very well what was in his mind, and said abruptly, "I suppose this is where you remind me that I'm under arrest."

"Do I need to remind you?"

"Not really." His voice sounded strange in his own ears, he hoped it didn't reflect the panic he felt . . . which had nothing to do with the strength of the case against him, or Briggs's animosity, which would ensure that it was pressed to the utmost, or with anything reasonable at all. It was cold, and blind . . . the final humiliation. "I suppose you won't mind," he said, still in that careful, unrecognizable voice, "if I pack a bag, and leave a note for Jenny."

He never heard what Watkins's reply would have been, because the phone rang then, so unexpectedly that it startled him. He turned automatically and picked up the receiver, and only then thought that the inspector might have objected if he'd taken time to ask.

"Is that you, Mr. Maitland?" It was Geraldine Lindsay's voice; she sounded very calm now, very sure of herself, and she barely waited for his reply before she went on. "Will you come to Maddox Court, please . . . straight away . . . alone."

"I don't think—"

"If you want to see your wife alive again," said Geraldine clearly, incredibly, with no change of expression in her voice at all. And he heard the quiet click that meant the connection had been broken.

He stood with his back to the room, the receiver still to his ear. *Getting a taste for blood* . . . he'd said that to Sykes, hadn't he? And someone had talked about madness, or was that his own idea too? He couldn't remember, but this was too important for panic. He heard himself saying (and certainly it was without conscious thought), "All right, love, I'll see to it right away." And then, after a pause as though he were listening, "I have to go out but I'll leave a note for you."

When he replaced the receiver and turned back to the two waiting men, whatever self-confidence he had displayed seemed to have deserted him. He sounded nervous and uncertain of himself. "It was Jenny," he said. "I—I couldn't tell her."

"I'm sorry, Mr. Maitland." (That was the first time Watkins had sounded human.) "You'd better write a note, as you said."

"Thank you." He made an indecisive movement toward the writing-table, hesitated, and turned to Hazlitt with an apologetic air. "Constable, would you mind very much looking up Geoffrey Horton's phone number for me . . . his home number, I mean. The directories are over there. He's my solicitor, Inspector Watkins knows." Watkins nodded, and the constable moved obligingly toward the bookshelf. "She asked me to turn off the oven," Antony went on, still in the same rather diffident way. "She left me a casserole, and she thinks she forgot to turn down the gas." He was half-way to the door as he spoke, and out into the hall before Watkins made any move to detain him.

They had their own "front door" between hall and landing, at the top of the second flight of stairs. The big old-fashioned key was still in the lock, though he couldn't recall that it had ever been used in all the years since the alterations had been made. He had reached the door in an instant, opened it soundlessly; moving the key delayed him only a moment more, then the door was shut and locked and he was running down the stairs.

Watkins would have followed him, of course, or sent Hazlitt to keep an eye on him. There'd be a brief delay while he identified the kitchen; even when he found it empty and the front door locked it would be a few seconds before he realized what had happened. But at the very best reckoning there wasn't long.

If he'd had time to think about it he would have realized that this was the hour Roger always arrived if he came straight round from leaving Meg at the theater. As it was, the luck seemed unbelievable. Farrell had his foot on the bottom step of the stair when he saw that Antony was on his way down and backed off quickly to avoid a collision. Antony said, "Thank

God," and grabbed his friend's arm. And then, "Have you got the car?"

A silly question. "Of course," said Roger.

"Meet you in Avery Street," Maitland told him, not wasting words, and disappeared through the door at the back of the hall, where he nearly ran over Gibbs who was making his way more sedately to his own quarters after admitting the visitor.

Farrell had seen the police car, he was parked just behind it. He went out of the house with a despondent look, got into the Jensen, backed up, and drove off in the opposite direction to Avery Street. It meant going all round the square before he could make the turn and pick Antony up, but he had a feeling it might be worth it.

"Maddox Court," said Antony, scrambling in. He twisted round with his left arm over the back of the seat and said approvingly, "A smooth getaway." And still through his mind there ran that thread of fear.

Roger consulted the rearview mirror and made a left turn without very much slackening speed. "I don't want to seem curious—" he said after a moment.

"I've just been arrested," said Antony, his eyes still on the road behind.

"Falkner?" said Roger. His voice had sharpened.

"Yes."

"Then what are we doing here?"

Antony told him, and saw Roger's hands tighten on the steering wheel. "I don't know Watkins well enough to be sure how he'd react if I told him," he concluded, "and I daren't risk any delay. Even now—"

"Hold on," Farrell recommended. And then, after he had made the first of the right-hand turns that would take them back to Edward Street, "When we get there, what are we going to do?"

"I'll go straight up . . . after all, I've been invited." He was staring straight ahead of him and his voice was grim. "I've got a feeling the first few minutes are what will count."

"Then I'd better—"

"No!"

Roger let the silence lengthen for a moment. "What shall I do, then, if I'm not to come with you?"

"I'm sorry," said Antony. His controlled tone shrieked his anxiety aloud. "She said 'alone,' you see, and I'm . . . afraid."

"If you could tell me—"

"There's a great deal of intelligence behind what's been happening, but I think there's a touch of madness too. Once you admit that there are no rules any more, anything may happen."

"Well then!"

"I thought . . . the fire-escape, Roger. Do you think you could find the flat?" After his decisiveness a moment before, the suggestion was oddly tentative.

"Yes, of course." The prospect of action lifted his spirits, and he added quickly, sensitive to his companion's alarm, "Don't worry, I'll take care."

"I know that; thank you." Maitland had retreated into himself again; the words were formal, they might have been spoken to a stranger. Roger swore under his breath and made the final turn into Edward Street. Almost before the car stopped Antony was out on the pavement; he disappeared into the building without another word.

It would have suited his mood to take the stairs two or three at a time. The lift was quicker, but seemed to take an age. The clock on the wall said ten past nine, he noted the fact without interest. He'd forgotten Roger already; forgotten that Sir Nicholas would have arrived at London Airport an hour since; forgotten Watkins, and Constable Hazlitt, and everything in the world except Jenny. He did not know that the attendant was watching him covertly, making a mental note there might be trouble; or that he stood directly in the path of a lady who wanted to get out at the second floor. When they stopped at the fourth he went off down the corridor without a backward glance, and put his finger on the bell outside Ana's door, and kept it there.

It was Geraldine who opened the door. She looked cool, and self-possessed, and pleased to see him in a quite impersonal way. "You're alone, Mr. Maitland," she said, as though she was congratulating him.

"As you see."

She stepped back then, and let him go past her, through the archway into the big, low room that was so full of Ana's personality, not her own. He heard the door close behind him, somehow a decisive sound, as though the whole world outside was of no further concern to him. But the thought wasn't a conscious one. He was looking at Jenny . . .

7

Sir Nicholas Harding landed at London Airport from the Luxair flight LG403 a little over twenty-eight hours after he had left New York. He was not therefore in a condition to be further ruffled by the defection of his nephew and niece, though he felt sufficiently bitter to decide against telephoning. If they were on their way, and had been held up by traffic, that was just too bad. He fixed a customs man who was eyeing his suitcase consideringly with a compelling eye, which resulted (against all the rules of elementary justice) in his being passed straight through; and galvanized his porter into obtaining a hired car back to town with scarcely any delay. It was about two minutes to nine when they drew up behind the police car which was still parked outside the Kempenfeldt Square house and he became aware that something very odd indeed was going on.

The window of the Maitlands' living-room, two floors up, was wide open and a man was leaning out dangerously, shouting. Inspector Watkins was a little hampered by the fact that the driver's name was Micklethwaite, which is a difficult name to yell, but he was making a good deal of noise and Sir Nicholas recoiled as the latest blast assailed his eardrums. "Come up here you idiot are you deaf what are you waiting for get going." Micklethwaite, who had been gazing upward as though seeing a vision, suddenly came to life and went up the steps to the front door at a run.

Sir Nicholas paid off his own car and followed in a more leisurely way. "Can I help you?" he asked, setting down his suitcase. The policeman, who had not heard his approach, whirled round and said, " 'Ere!" in a startled way. And then, pulling himself together, "Who are you?" Sir Nicholas looked him over in silence for a moment, and then inserted his key in the lock and pushed open the door.

"I might ask you the same question," he said. "Do you wish to come in?"

"That's my inspector up there a-hollering," said Micklethwaite, who seemed to have lost all grip both on the situation and his grammar. "I did ought to see what he wants."

"Then let us go up together," said Sir Nicholas. "Ah, Gibbs! Do you know what is going on?"

"I regret to say that I do not." He tried to take possession of his employer's suitcase, but was handed Sir Nicholas's hat instead. Holding this he cast a look of loathing at Constable Micklethwaite, who wilted visibly. "It was my understanding that the persons who are creating this disturbance were from the police." His tone was perhaps unnecessarily frigid, but on the whole 'disturbance' was a fair description: from above came the sound of angry shouting, and two pairs of fists hammered futilely on an unyielding door.

Sir Nicholas moved unhurriedly toward the staircase, but turned with his foot on the bottom step. "Where is my nephew?" he inquired.

"Mr. Maitland went out . . . by the back door," said Gibbs distastefully. For the first time Sir Nicholas evinced a slight interest.

"Er—before or after these noisy gentlemen arrived?"

"About twenty minutes after, Sir Nicholas."

"How very rude of him." He began, still leisurely, to climb the stairs. Micklethwaite, behind him, was practically bouncing up and down with an impatience he dared not show. Sir Nicholas paused on the first landing to deposit his suitcase and briefcase outside his bedroom door.

At the top of the next flight the noise was deafening. The key was hanging, drunkenly, half out of the lock, as though someone had tugged at it in a hurry, and then left it when it would not come out smoothly. Sir Nicholas unlocked the door and stepped back. Micklethwaite turned the knob and pushed, without success, and finally, in desperation, said "Inspector!" at the top of his voice; the hammering stopped abruptly, and a moment later the door was dragged open and the two prisoners emerged, breathing fire.

"Seven minutes," said Watkins. "Seven ruddy minutes! He may be half-way across London by now." He broke off, seeing for the first time that they were not alone, and perhaps conscious that his words contained a certain amount of exaggeration. "Sir Nicholas!" he exclaimed. It would have been difficult to tell whether he was more surprised or put out by the encounter.

"My old friend Sergeant—no, it's Inspector now, isn't it?— Inspector Watkins. I didn't recognize you from the street. Now I think"—the sweetness of his tone would have been sufficient warning for anyone who knew him well—"I really think you must tell me exactly what is going on."

"I'm a patient man," said Watkins, breathing deeply, "but when it comes to locking a fellow in—"

"Am I to understand that my nephew did this? How very odd of him," said Sir Nicholas. He let his eyes travel slowly from one stalwart figure to the other. "*Both* of you?" he asked.

"By a ruse or artifice," said Hazlitt suddenly. (Antony might have concluded that he had literary aspirations after all.) "There wasn't no violence used," he added, and his tone was undeniably wistful.

"Really, Inspector—"

"Just a minute, sir." Watkins was recovering his composure. He looked at his subordinates and jerked his head. "Hop it, you two," he commanded tersely. "Report to Central and then take the car and see what you can do." He waited until the men had gone. "Now, Sir Nicholas, I'm at your service."

"Let us go inside, then." He waited until they were in the living-room before he went on. "You still haven't told me what had happened to make my nephew act in this extraordinary way."

"He was under arrest," said Watkins shortly.

"My dear Inspector, this ridiculous charge—"

"Do you know the charge, Sir Nicholas?"

"I presume that it arises from this man Hudson's statement."

"Not directly. Do you know a man called Albert Falkner?"

"Falkner . . . Falkner? A solicitor—come to think of it, I'm not sure whether he's admitted or not—employed by Paul Collingwood as his managing clerk."

"That's right, sir. Only he's dead."

"And my nephew—?"

"Has been charged with his murder."

There was very little change in Sir Nicholas's expression, but Watkins had the impression that he had retreated to a great distance. There was a difficult silence before he said, from this remoteness, "Do you believe that, Inspector?"

"It's not for me to play judge, or jury," said Watkins, with one of his rare moments of complete sincerity. "But I'm bound to say I don't think he had any idea of running away before the phone call."

"Somebody telephoned?"

"He *said* it was Mrs. Maitland."

"You didn't believe him?"

"I did at the time."

"I see. Have you any idea where Mrs. Maitland is?"

"None at all, but I think there was a note from her." Sir Nicholas was already half-way across the room. "On the desk," Watkins added, and he turned his course and a moment later was smoothing out the ball of paper that Antony had thrown down.

Antony, I have gone with Geraldine— "That's my niece's handwriting."

"Does it say where she is?"

The note changed hands. "I don't know of a Geraldine among their friends, but there is a Mrs. Lindsay—"

"Do you think he might have gone to join Mrs. Maitland?" asked Watkins. He was scowling at the note as though in some way it offended him.

"In the circumstances? Not unless it was some sort of emergency."

"This Mrs. Lindsay, now?"

"He met her through the Kellaway case . . . nothing to do with this. Or, is it, Inspector?"

There had been a momentary alertness in Watkins's expression, but now it had resumed its normal stolidity. "I'm not so sure Mr. Maitland didn't think so. That there was a connection I mean. Between Dakins's death and the attempt to bribe Bassett and all the rest."

"Did he tell you that?"

"No." Watkins sounded regretful. "Not that it would have made much difference, I don't suppose. He told a colleague of mine, Chief-Inspector Sykes, and Sykes did his best to persuade the superintendent to hold his hand a bit, but he wasn't having any."

"Briggs?"

"That's right. Guilty knowledge, *he* said, and a deliberate attempt to deceive. Not that I'd put *that* past Mr. Maitland myself, knowing him as I do," he added reflectively.

Sir Nicholas let pass this slur on his nephew's character. "Where does Falkner come in?" he asked.

"He was concerned in the bribery . . . the man who went to see Bassett. That can be proved," he added, as though his companion had attempted to deny it.

Sir Nicholas was leafing through the phone book. "Do you think you can find out where Mrs. Lindsay lives?"

"Yes, of course. But a moment ago you said—"

"If Antony is right and there is a connection between these affairs, I can see two possible reasons for his acting as he did."

"For his tricking me and locking me in," said Watkins, sighing. "I'm not a revengeful man, but I must say I'd like to have that explained."

"One," said Sir Nicholas, ignoring him, "he thought he saw a chance of clearing the whole thing up—"

"If he knew anything that would do that, why didn't he tell me?" inquired the inspector rhetorically.

"—or, two, that Jenny is in some way in danger."

"Do you really think that?" said Watkins, startled out of his pose.

"I should not otherwise have said it. And if that is the case, my friend," said Sir Nicholas, suddenly radiating a quite uncharacteristic energy, "the sooner we set about finding the pair of them the better."

. . . at least, she was alive.

The sofa was long and low, and covered in a loose-woven material that was more or less the color of a half-ripened tomato. Jenny was sitting sideways, rather near the edge of it. Someone had improvised a gag, a handkerchief stuffed in her mouth and kept in place by a brightly-colored scarf that must surely belong to Ana rather than to Geraldine; there was a cord round her ankles, and her hands were behind her back, they must be tied too. He had not realized until that moment how afraid he was . . . or how angry.

He had started across the room when Keith Lindsay spoke. "Not so fast!" said Lindsay; and when Maitland checked his stride and turned to him he gestured with the gun he held. He seemed oddly self-conscious about its possession, and the movement was a slight one but still explanatory enough.

Maitland's lips twisted in a smile that went nowhere near his eyes. "I am going to release my wife," he said softly, spacing the words as though he was speaking to a person of limited intelligence.

"Don't be a fool." This time the gesture was more confident, more peremptory, and Antony's reply came even more softly.

"If you really want to shoot me, I don't see how I can stop you. If you don't, I dare say you'll allow me this much latitude." He reached Jenny's side as he spoke, his back was to Lindsay as he fumbled with the knot in the soft silk behind her head; it loosened, and he pulled the handkerchief away gently from between her teeth. She tried to say something, and choked over the words; her gray eyes looked up at him imploringly.

"Easy, love, easy. Take your time." If Lindsay hadn't shot by now, presumably he wasn't going to . . . yet. He had to sit beside her to reach the cord that tied her hands, his body no longer sheltered her. This knot was more difficult, the cord had been tightened savagely, so that her wrists were cut.

"Antony . . . please . . . please, don't—" Her voice was no more than a whisper.

"Am I hurting you? It won't take long."

"No . . . no. I meant—"

"I know what you meant, love. I'll take care." The knot had loosened, he pulled the cord down over her hands. "You can move your arms now, Jenny, if you're not too stiff." She did so, cautiously, biting her lips as the blood began to circulate. Though the gag had been soft there was a shadow round her mouth as though a bruise was forming. He glanced up for a moment before he knelt to free her ankles, and saw Lindsay standing stiffly not far from the door that led to the bedrooms and the kitchen, and Geraldine just inside the archway looking on with detached interest, as though the scene was a play being staged for her amusement.

Keith said, "I've no objection to your doing that, if it gives you any satisfaction." His voice was a little higher pitched than normal, it had almost a fretful sound. "I didn't mean any harm to Mrs. Maitland, you know. She came here of her own accord."

Maitland was busy with the last knot. "I'm here now, which I suppose is what you wanted," he said. "So why not let her go?"

"You know better than that. Besides, I've changed my plans. I need her here."

The words had a cold sound, though he couldn't even begin to guess their meaning. The cord fell apart, he looked up for a moment at Jenny, and then came to his feet and turned to face Lindsay. No need, at least, to maneuver him into a different position; his back was squarely to the door through which Roger must come. "You're not very happy with that thing, are you?" Antony said with an inflection of sarcasm, and nodded toward the gun: a small-caliber revolver, he thought, probably not of English manufacture. "Wouldn't you feel more at home with a knife in your hand?"

"Father William said you knew it all." Strangely, there was a note of satisfaction about the statement. "And you're quite right, I don't like this at all. I borrowed it, but I don't like it. A knife's a clean weapon"—he lingered over the words almost lovingly—"and there are times, you know, when a little blood-letting is highly beneficial."

"Did Bassett think so?"

"Bassett was a fool."

"Well, the revolver won't be much use to you," said Maitland casually, "unless you do something about the safety catch." He was tensed for action, but Lindsay only laughed and his eyes never wavered.

"I'm not so easily caught," he said. "And I'm beginning to think I over-estimated you . . . just as you under-estimated me."

"Did I?"

"I rather think so. However, I feel safer while you keep your distance, and I know very well how to use this, as you will see."

No use saying, "The police are outside." If he had been right about Lindsay's madness, there was a contradictory and terrifying sanity about his actions too. If I'd told them, thought Antony, they wouldn't have believed me; he's quite clever enough to have counted on that. And if I persuaded him he was wrong he'd shoot without another thought . . . not only me, but Jenny too . . . rather than miss his chance . . .

"I'm quite willing to grant your versatility," said Maitland aloud. "After all, you've demonstrated it already when you killed Falkner. But you've been to some trouble to get me here, and I can't see why you bothered. Your first plan was working very well."

"I thought it might," said Keith complacently.

"Then why not have let the police take care of everything?"

"Believe me, I'd have been glad to do so. You wouldn't have enjoyed it much, would you? The publicity . . . the trial . . . the inevitable verdict. By the time I'd finished with you it would have been inevitable."

"I suppose Sammy Barber's evidence—"

"I have my contacts."

"And the lady"—unconsciously he mimicked the inflection that Inspector Watkins had given the word—"in Clifford's Mews?"

"A good friend of mine."

"With everything so beautifully arranged, why did you change your mind?"

"Because you know too much. Father William warned me what would happen if you were arrested. I don't think you can prove anything, mind you, but why should I give you the chance of blackening my character, as I've no doubt you'd try to do? Besides, there's Gerry . . . I have to dispose of her."

The temptation to let his eyes flicker for a moment to Geraldine's face was almost irresistible. He heard Jenny draw her breath in sharply, but Geraldine made no movement that he could tell. "That's odd," he said. (How long would Roger be?) "I thought you were rather fond of her."

"Fond?" Keith might have been considering the truth of this, or he might have been sneering at the inadequacy of the word. "I suppose I was . . . fond of her. Why shouldn't I be, she's my wife, isn't she?"

"Your divorced wife."

"In the eyes of the law," said Lindsay. The words seemed to please him, and he repeated them slowly. "That was clever, I rather think. She'd become a damned nuisance, you know. Once the divorce had gone through there'd be no more scenes . . . a man must have his distractions, after all. And no chance of her finding out about my business arrangements with Falkner either. But whenever I wanted her—"

Geraldine still hadn't moved. There was something horrible about this, the self-satisfied voice sickened him. He said, interrupting desperately, "I suppose it's quite easy to hypnotize someone who is fond of you."

"It's never easy." Keith sounded offended now. "What do you know about hypnotism, anyway?"

"Enough to realize what was wrong with Geraldine when I saw the books on Father William's shelf," said Antony carefully.

"Then you'll appreciate my plan . . . my new plan." Lindsay was cordial again. "I meant to shoot you when you came in, you know . . . you and Gerry. Not that I approve of guns, but you're not a man I'd care to tackle at close quarters."

"Why didn't you then?"

"Because now that Mrs. Maitland's here I shan't even need the alibi I arranged. And I'd like you to know . . . you love her, don't you?" In an odd way, he sounded almost friendly.

For some reason it seemed that the admission might make them—both of them—more vulnerable, but he couldn't find words for a denial. Antony was sure he hadn't spoken, but

Lindsay nodded in a satisfied way and said, "I thought so."

"What difference does it make?" Perhaps he didn't want to hear the answer, perhaps he was only playing for time; he added quickly, "What has Geraldine done to you?"

"She fell in love with Jon. Not that I minded that, I knew she'd come whenever I called and it wouldn't be the first time I'd made a fool of him."

"Beth Kellaway killed herself because you were going to be married, didn't she?"

"Yes, of course." The recollection seemed to be a pleasing one. "She was a pretty little nitwit, you know, but I gave her more fun than ever she had with Jon. Now Gerry . . . she may look a bit cold," he said in a considering way, "but that's only on the surface. She—"

"Why did it matter then, who she fell in love with?" (It was stupid to interrupt—wasn't it?—so long as Lindsay was willing to talk.)

"She was turning against me. She was turning to you in her efforts to help Jon, and you were playing up to her, you can't deny that. So now it's only fair . . . it's a pity about your wife, of course"—his voice was petulant again—"but I didn't ask her to interfere."

His mouth was dry. It was an effort to speak, impossible to be silent. "What are you going to do?"

"Arrange a tableau." He considered the word, and again was pleased with it. "Then, when you're dead . . . don't move, Mrs. Maitland. While there's life there's hope, you know; or would you like me to shoot him straight away?"

Jenny froze again. Antony said, "When I'm dead . . . what then?" There wasn't a sound from the corridor, but that oughtn't to worry him, he could trust Roger to be careful. If he'd found the right window, and wasn't in someone else's flat by now, trying to explain himself.

"I shall have almost three hours in which to persuade Mrs. Maitland to co-operate with me. If you want it spelled out"— Keith's voice was petulant again—"to hypnotize her."

"Can you, against her will?" He wondered as he spoke how his voice could be so steady. But the scene was taking on all

194

the more unpleasant aspects of a nightmare; perhaps he didn't really believe . . .

"I admit, she hasn't been exactly helpful," said Lindsay. "I didn't tie her up just to be melodramatic, you know. I may have to use more drastic methods, but one way or another—"

He thought he had never been angry in his life before. "The way you k-killed Falkner?"

"I should stop short of that. I need her, you see."

"You're mad," Maitland told him, and saw Lindsay frown.

"Do you think so?" Then he looked relieved. "Of course I'm not. If I were I'd have cut her throat already . . . after all, she's very much in the way. Or was, until I thought how to use her." His eyes never left Antony's face, but he spoke past him again to Jenny. "You've seen how easy it is for me to make Gerry do what I want."

"Yes."

"Tell him, then!"

There was a silence. Maitland turned his head, regardless for the moment of danger. "Jenny—" He didn't know whether he was asking for a denial, or for reassurance.

"It isn't just that she does what he says"—Jenny's voice was carefully controlled, and her eyes met Antony's steadily—"she *thinks* what he tells her to . . . that's the worst thing of all."

"I don't know why you should say that, it's perfectly natural. That's how it will be, anyway: when she's under my control I shall tell her what has happened, and when she awakes she will remember, and believe it."

Maitland turned back reluctantly. "W-what will you t-tell her?"

"That you and Geraldine had fallen in love with each other, and were going away together. I'm sorry to sound like a novelette, but these things do happen, you know. Gerry told her when she got here, and then you arrived. I expect she'll be a little vague about the time. After that you had rather a violent quarrel. When she saw you were determined to leave her she shot you both."

"But that's"—he sought for the word as if it were important —"that's nonsense."

"Do you think so? I'm telling you what she will think happened, and I dare say she'll deny that part when she sees her solicitor; or is she too honest for that? And nobody will be surprised if she can't remember all the details, after all the whole thing came as a shock to her. And the jury may even take a lenient view, because you treated her rather roughly—"

"Did you have to hit her?"

"She bit me," said Keith simply, "before I could get the gag in place. However, it all fits in nicely, so we needn't worry about that."

"Even with that . . . corroborative detail . . . no one will believe it."

"Why shouldn't they? Whether she admits it or not, she'll believe it herself, and things like that are happening every day."

Rather too sweeping a statement, but it had an element of truth all the same. He didn't even know if he was as crazy as Lindsay, thinking the idea might work. "Besides," said Keith, for some reason bent on convincing him, "Gerry believes it too. She won't be there to say so, of course, but she's left a letter for Ana explaining why she's going away. And then, you're desperate, aren't you? The police are closing in. Just the state of mind where a man seizes any distraction—" He broke off, and his expression hardened. "That amuses you?" he said.

"I was wondering about this alibi you talked of. I can't help feeling Father William's intervention is being a little overplayed."

"I don't mean Father William. And he won't give me away."

"Can you be so sure about that?" Maitland asked, but Keith wasn't listening.

"Gerry!" he said. But he did not turn to look at her as he spoke; eyes and gun were steady.

"Yes, Keith?"

"Go over to Mr. Maitland, Gerry. That's right, close to him, put your hands on his shoulders. Don't move, Maitland!" he added, with a sudden change of tone. "Otherwise I might change my mind, and shoot your wife."

He was quite deliberately, quite cold-bloodedly, setting up his target. There would even be a ghoulish kind of humor in the situation, if only you were looking at it from the other side. Geraldine had hold of Antony's shoulders, tugging gently, trying to make him face her; when he looked down she was smiling at him, warmly affectionate. He could feel the warmth of her body, and the little tremor that might have been excitement that ran through her. In a moment, win or lose, he'd have to make a move; but the nose of the revolver had turned now, if Keith shot blindly it was Jenny he would hit. If not . . . would she watch this, and forget it, and never know—?

"A pretty picture," said Lindsay. A smile quirked the corners of his mouth. He looked poised, and very handsome, and he was as dangerous as a mad dog. "Closer, Gerry, closer. *I* know how you feel, but you must make him understand—" Behind him the door began to open slowly, inch by inch.

And now Antony saw it only with sick apprehension. If he could keep Lindsay's attention . . . but at the slightest sound from the newcomer it was Jenny who would die. "Aren't you forgetting something?" he asked.

"It would look better, of course, if you'd put your arms around her, but I expect that's too much to ask." He was amused again, his tone unbearably patronizing. "And I'm sorry to resort to such barbarous methods, but you do see I've no alternative, don't you? And I'm told it's quite quick—"

If he was right about that it was just as well. The door was open wide now, and he died as he spoke. . . .

9

The noise of the shot was deafening in the low-ceilinged room. Maitland saw Keith Lindsay's body jerk with the impact of the bullet, and his stupefied expression in the instant before he fell. Then he looked up and noted, without awareness of surprise, that it was Father William who stood in the doorway.

Geraldine's grip had tightened convulsively on his shoulders, but she made no resistance when he pushed her gently aside. Jenny was on her feet, her hands to her face, her eyes wide with horror. But if Keith's finger had tightened on the trigger as he fell the sound had been lost in that of the heavier-caliber weapon that Father William held.

It didn't matter . . . nothing mattered . . . if Jenny was safe.

The tableau dissolved into action. Father William came a few paces into the room, and Maitland saw for the first time that Roger was behind him. Jenny moved, too, and went down on her knees beside Keith Lindsay. . . .

"What should we do, Antony?" she said after a moment. "I'm afraid he's dead." But Antony was staring at Father William helplessly.

The old man expelled his breath in a long sigh. He said, "It had to be done," and the echo of Lindsay's words gave Maitland an uncanny feeling, as though time were running backward. "I met Mr. Farrell outside," William Webster added. "He told me you were here . . . and Mrs. Maitland."

"Did you come here to kill Lindsay?"

"I thought . . . I was afraid—" All his gentle self-possession seemed to have vanished. He had a stricken look. "I was kinder to him than he meant to be to you, Mr. Maitland. I spared him the disgrace."

While they were speaking Roger had come forward and held out a hand to Jenny to pull her to her feet. "Are you all right?" he asked, and put an arm round her shoulders. Then he looked at Antony. "I didn't know what he was going to do, of course, but I don't see what else he could have done."

"In the circumstances," said Antony, "nothing." His eyes were on Jenny's face. "If you hadn't been such a bloody little fool as to come here—"

"What *is* all this?" asked Roger, bewildered.

"I don't know how Lindsay meant to get me here, but once he had Jenny it made it easy, of course." He was far too shaken still to be able to think whether his anger was reasonable or not. "And he had this idea . . . he was going to shoot *us* and frame *her*. I don't know if it would have worked—"

"It sounds pretty unlikely to me," said Roger frankly. But Jenny shivered.

"I think . . . it would have worked," she said. And Maitland's anger died on the instant. "But, at least, *I'm* not in a trance," she added, and directed at Geraldine a look so lacking in Christian charity that Antony, who would have taken his oath that she had never had an unkind thought about anyone, fairly reeled in his tracks.

Geraldine had moved away from the group a little; she was sitting on a chair whose violent green upholstery made a singularly inappropriate background, and crying quietly. She raised her head as Jenny spoke, and gave Antony a look of mingled devotion and apology, but he had no time to worry about it then.

"Is *that* what's the matter?" said Roger. "Would you say Lindsay was mad?" His gesture focused attention again on the dead man. "Ought we to call the police, Antony, or would that make things difficult for you?"

"I suppose—" He looked at Father William again. "You saved our lives," he said. "But I'm not sure whether the police are going to thank you for that, or not."

The old man had seated himself, and placed the gun on the table beside him. "With Mr. Farrell's evidence, perhaps all will be well," he said. "If not . . . I must hope you will be willing to use your undoubted talents on my behalf."

"But, I—" He looked at Jenny, remembering she didn't know. "I shan't be able to," he said. "Inspector Watkins arrested me just before I came here. I left him locked in the flat, but it's only a matter of time before he catches up with me."

Jenny had kept her outraged look, but now her expression melted. "Oh, darling!" she said in an exasperated tone. "That was terribly stupid."

"I didn't have much choice, love," he reminded her, but she had turned away and was looking at Father William, taking charge of the situation.

"I'm Jenny Maitland," she said. "I think you must be Mr. Webster." Behind her head Antony and Roger exchanged a long, helpless look.

Father William seemed to find the touch of formality quite natural. "I'm pleased to make your acquaintance, my dear."

"Perhaps you can explain to me. Did you mean"—her eyes wavered a moment to Lindsay's body, lying between them—

"did you mean that *he* had done all the things Antony is accused of?"

"If I understand Mr. Farrell rightly, he has been accused only of murdering a man called Falkner."

"Only!" said Jenny, scandalized. "That would be quite enough, but I know quite well they think he's been bribing people for years, and—"

"All that, I'm afraid, must be put to Keith's account."

"Then—" She broke off, staring at him. "Mr. Webster, I'm sorry. Really, I'm terribly sorry."

"You're quite right, my dear, I had a—a great affection for him."

Jenny put up a hand and rubbed her cheek. "It's just that I'm so worried about Antony," she confided.

"Yes, I understand." He raised his eyes to Maitland's and said with another sigh, "I'm afraid we shall both have a great deal of explaining to do—"

"I'm sure we shall!"

"—but I think I can promise *you* a happy outcome." He paused, and seemed to be looking beyond his companions to something a great distance away. "I warned Keith, you know, after you had been to see me today. I hoped he would go abroad . . . anywhere away from here. That was wrong of me, I know, but I had only just realized . . . and I had no idea of the extent of his activities until I went round to his rooms later, to see if he had taken my advice."

"He thought he was quite safe," said Maitland.

"What I saw convinced me of that. That was why I was on my way here, I thought he might be with Geraldine. Only a megalomaniac . . . but I am trying to tell you, Mr. Maitland, once the police have examined his papers you should be safe."

"I see." He wasn't even aware of relief, he felt drained of all emotion. "I ought—" he began, and broke off at the sound of the chimes from the front door. He turned his head quickly to meet Roger's eyes. "Neighbors? Police?"

"Shall I—?"

"Yes, of course." He smiled suddenly. "There's always the fire-escape." As Roger crossed the room, Antony looked again at Father William. "Whoever's outside, I expect we shall soon know if you were right," he said. He heard the door open, and the murmur of voices, and struggled again with the feeling of inertia.

A moment later Sir Nicholas Harding stalked through the archway with Inspector Watkins at his heels, and stood surveying the scene.

It was Jenny who reacted most quickly to this unexpected arrival. She went straight across the room to him. "Dear Uncle Nick, I'm so glad you've come." Then she drew back a little, studying his face. "You don't have to worry about Antony any more," she told him earnestly. "Father William says he can prove he didn't kill anyone, or—or anything else."

"I am relieved to hear it, of course."

She completely ignored the hint of dryness in his tone. "I wish you'd explain that to the police," she said. "Then we could all go home." Over her head, Sir Nicholas met his nephew's eyes.

Inspector Watkins cleared his throat noisily. "I'm a patient man," he said into the resultant silence, "but will somebody please tell me what has been going on?"

SATURDAY, 27th MARCH

1

They got home at last when the night sky was just beginning to pale toward dawn. By that time Antony was half-asleep, and his uncle considerably the more alert of the pair of them. Sir Nicholas used his latch-key, and switched on the hall light, and stood listening for a moment. The house was quiet, with the utter stillness of early morning. He turned to survey his nephew.

Antony had gone across to the stairs, and sat down on the third step from the bottom. He said, "Well, that's that," in a dead voice, not as though it gave him any satisfaction. And then, "Have you any comments, sir? Because if so I'd as soon hear them now."

"Young Farrell certainly seems to have a head on his shoulders," said Sir Nicholas approvingly.

"That wasn't . . . exactly . . . what I meant."

"No?"

"You know perfectly well," said Antony, rousing himself from his lethargy, "that ever since you decided to come home —and I still don't know why you did—"

"I put two and two together, my dear boy. Knowing you, it wasn't a difficult sum."

"Hudson?"

"Precisely."

"So much has happened since then."

"You still haven't told me what I 'know perfectly well,' " Sir Nicholas reminded him.

"If you didn't come home to read the riot act, why did you come?" said Antony reasonably.

"To try to stop you getting further involved."

"Oh, I see." He leaned his head back against the banisters.

"I was going to get in touch with you yesterday, Uncle Nick, if your cable hadn't got here first."

"I am glad you showed at least so much evidence of good sense," said Sir Nicholas crushingly, and paused a moment to see if any retort was forthcoming. "I can't say I altogether admire your handling of the situation," he added in a thoughtful tone.

"I don't . . . altogether . . . admire it myself, sir," said Antony stiffly; and was taken aback when his uncle, with one of his abrupt changes of mood, gave him a companionable smile.

"If you'd met me off the plane," he said, "I might possibly have done my sentiments justice. As it is, I think you're too tired to benefit from them. Go to bed."

"Yes, but—"

"You don't have to worry any more, you know. Even Superintendent Briggs—"

Antony was on his feet now. "As to that, I doubt it. But that wasn't what I meant." He hesitated. "There's Jenny."

"From what the doctor says she will be none the worse for the experience."

"Damn the doctor!"

"That seems a little harsh. I expect she has had a good night's sleep by now," said Sir Nicholas encouragingly, "and is feeling quite restored."

"I shouldn't have let her get involved. And as if that wasn't bad enough—"

"If it is the first time in all these years that you have felt like swearing at her, I suppose you may consider yourself fortunate," said Sir Nicholas with a complete lack of sympathy.

"*That* doesn't help."

"No? Well, I shouldn't let it worry you." He moved across the hall in his leisurely way to the foot of the stairs, and looked up at his nephew with his blandest smile. "As far as meddling in other people's affairs is concerned," he said gently, "there doesn't seem to be a penny to choose between you."

2

The morning papers had a Stop Press report that a warrant had been issued in the bribery case. The evening papers spread themselves on the subject of Lindsay's death; the implication was unmistakable that the warrant had been for him and that they had known all the time who the guilty party was. The arrest of a "well-known West End jeweler" was also touched upon, more cautiously. "I think Father William's a pet," said Jenny, throwing the *Chronicle* aside. "Do you think they'll send him to prison, Uncle Nick?"

They were having tea in the Maitlands' living-room, and Roger had brought the papers when he arrived with Meg half an hour before. "Over my dead body," said Sir Nicholas lazily, and sipped his tea as though he had nothing more important on his mind. When he found Jenny's eyes fixed on him he roused himself to give her a more complete answer. "If he isn't released after the inquest on Lindsay, the case will be dismissed at the magistrate's court hearing."

Antony said, "You hope," under his breath; but Jenny seemed reassured and said, "That's all right then," on a note of relief.

Meg leaned forward. "Roger will have to give evidence, won't he? But what about Geraldine?"

"Doctor's certificate," said Antony. Roger, who had been answering her questions all day, was slightly more explicit.

"She has to be re-hypnotized, or de-hypnotized, or whatever, and all the—the ideas taken out of her mind."

"Post hypnotic suggestion," said Sir Nicholas, as confidently as if he had made a study of the subject for years.

Meg said, "That explains everything, of course," and gave him a look of exaggerated respect. "What about you, Jenny?"

"I have to be there, but I don't mind . . . really."

"That's what she *says*," said Antony gloomily. However relaxed he might appear it was obvious that there was a certain brittleness about his mood, and Meg brought out her next suggestion cautiously.

"If I'm not going to die of curiosity, darling, you'll have to tell me . . . when Geraldine phoned and you went rushing round to Maddox Court, did you know you'd find Keith Lindsay there?"

"I suppose I did. I knew at least that he'd killed Falkner, and all the rest of it."

"But Geraldine said . . . it's no good, you'll just have to tell me the whole thing from the beginning."

"Meg, I—" He broke off as he caught his uncle's eye.

"It will be good practice for you," said Sir Nicholas. "For the inquest," he explained.

"If you think last night wasn't enough—"

"Last night you were being heckled by a series of unsympathetic policemen."

"Until Inspector Watkins got back from searching Lindsay's rooms."

Sir Nicholas nodded his agreement. "Their methods may be admirable for their own purposes, but they do not produce a connected narrative. And you must remember that I was not privileged to see your final statement," he said.

"Oh, all right, but Roger could tell you just as well."

"Roger will no doubt supply your deficiencies."

"Well," said Antony, and paused long enough for a degree of impatience to manifest itself in his uncle's manner. "At first it never occurred to me that the two things were connected . . . Bassett's death, or suicide, or whatever-it-was, and Dakins's murder. It was Roger who first pointed out the possibility and though his reasons were perfectly valid there was still no certainty about it."

"Knowing your predilection for leaping from conclusion to conclusion, I'm surprised you didn't embrace this one immediately," said Sir Nicholas, and passed his cup to Jenny for a refill.

Antony acknowledged the thrust with an absent-minded smile. "Sykes gave me the first clear picture of what was happening when he told me about the other jurors who had died. Someone was trying to implicate me in the bribery, and I thought about Collingwood, of course, and more than ever when it became obvious that Falkner was involved. It was evident from the beginning that Hudson had been got at; for one thing he wasn't afraid of me, and he ought to have been if he believed one half of what he was saying. And Bassett's supposed questions to the man who went to see him showed a degree of cunning not at all consistent with his character as Inspector Watkins saw it. Still, that didn't get me very far. And then Jon Kellaway told me that Dakins had been on a jury too, just before he died.

"As far as I was concerned, that settled it. The two things were tied together, as Roger had suggested. At the same time, it was a bit of a facer . . . I was less able than ever to see where we went from there. Collingwood was more or less washed out—"

"Why?"

"My dear Meg," said Sir Nicholas, taking up the tale as smoothly as if he had never protested his own confusion, "it would have involved *two* coincidences. Surely you can see that?"

"No," said Meg simply.

"Then Roger must have made his explanations very badly," said Sir Nicholas unfairly. "It would have meant, you see, that Dakins *happened* to have the report of the inquest on Beth Kellaway in his possession; and that he—or someone else connected with the household—*happened* to have brought Kellaway's can of petrol into the house for some reason unknown, so that it lay ready to the murderer's hand."

"Thank you, darling." Meg smiled at him. "That's beautifully clear." Sir Nicholas scowled and said testily to his nephew:

"Go on, Antony, go on."

"Are you sure you wouldn't rather—? Well, anyway, I needn't go into the reasons Dakins's death was camouflaged, we've talked it over often enough. So eliminating Collingwood seemed to leave me with Father William and Keith Lindsay . . . unless some person unknown fulfilled the various conditions equally well, and I couldn't get wind of anyone likely. At first, when I was considering Dakins's murder separately on Jon Kellaway's behalf, I had been interested in Lindsay. There was his likeness to his cousin, for one thing, but when the witness in Gilcliffe Gardens identified Jon positively that seemed like a red herring too."

"It *was* a red herring," said Sir Nicholas, as distastefully as if the offending fish was decomposing under his nose.

"No, sir, not altogether. But we're talking about the time when I realized the Dakins case and the bribery case were one and the same, and Father William was a much more attractive suspect. Made to measure, you might say."

"It seems extremely unlikely. If I were to employ such a metaphor, why should I do so?"

"His secondary occupation, Uncle Nick. The police suspect he's a receiver, but they've never been able to prove it."

"And this is the man," said Sir Nicholas reflectively, "with whose defense you have insisted that I associate myself."

"Have you no gratitude? He saved my life."

"I suppose that is a matter for rejoicing?" He was still thoughtful. Jenny passed him the buttered toast, and looked hopefully at Antony who took the hint and went on:

"Even so, I wasn't altogether happy about it. I wasn't very happy about the attempts to frame me, either, but I suppose they were nothing to be surprised about. But whoever had killed Dakins had tried to lay the blame on Jon Kellaway, deliberately and maliciously. Father William may be an old sinner, but I don't believe he has an ounce of malice in him. If he'd ever seen that newspaper report of the inquest he'd have thrown it on the fire, not hoarded it all these years. All the time there was that sort of mental conflict . . . I felt I ought to concentrate on him, it was the sensible thing to do, but there was something not quite right about it.

"So I began to think about the man who had been organizing the bribery. When Sykes told me about it I said to him, 'He's getting a taste for blood,' and I didn't think anything about it at the time, it was just a casual remark. But then . . . it isn't really natural, you know, to go about cutting people's throats just because they've disobliged you, even as a warning to other people. At first it had only happened in widely separated parts of the country, but now there'd been two cases in the London area in the space of a few weeks.

"What was I looking for then? A man malicious enough to want to injure John Kellaway . . . not just to protect himself, but in the most hurtful way; a man, perhaps, with a grudge against society . . . I say that because, though it's natural to want to make money, the precise way he was doing it wouldn't have been everyone's choice; a man mad enough to enjoy bloody murder—"

" 'I wants to make your flesh creep,' " said Meg.

"Yes, well, I didn't much like the ideas I was getting myself. This man also had to be dexterous enough—or strong enough—to commit his crimes and make them look like suicide. I didn't think that last applied to Falkner, which was one reason why I didn't think he was in it alone. And then I thought about *A Kind of Praise*."

"Now that's just nonsense, darling. It hadn't anything to do—"

"I don't understand this myself," said Roger. "Can't you get on with it, Antony, without making a speech?"

"I'm trying to convey a state of mind," said Maitland with dignity.

"If you mean you were confused," said his uncle cordially, "you have succeeded admirably in what you set out to do."

"I thought about *A Kind of Praise*. You've all seen the play, but I will just remind you: it's about a man so eaten up with envy that it destroys his whole life, and finally destroys him. A form of insanity. Jon played the part to perfection, everyone agreed on that. And, consciously or unconsciously, it was a straight take-off of Keith Lindsay every inch of the way."

"You know, darling," said Meg slowly, "I do believe you're right."

"Of course I'm right. Think about Jon, as himself . . . he's never still a minute. Lindsay is . . . was . . . so self-controlled it was hardly believable."

"If that means anything, which I doubt—"

Antony turned eagerly to his uncle. "I can't possibly convey it to you, sir, when you've never seen Keith alive, and Jon only on the stage. It was"—he gesticulated—"a thousand little things."

"More guess-work," said Sir Nicholas, resigned.

"Well, never mind. It made me think very seriously about Lindsay, but there was still the problem of Geraldine. If she'd fallen in love with Jon, why wouldn't she marry him? Why did she take that overdose of sleeping stuff? By accident, she said; Ana wouldn't believe that, and Ana knows her very well, but somehow I thought Geraldine was trying to tell the truth. And why did she wake up screaming the night we were at Maddox

Court, Roger, with a tale of a mysterious voice that sounded like Jon's? Even when I talked to Dr. Prescott about the way Falkner had been murdered, and he mentioned a report in the Press that an amateur hypnotist had once killed a man that way, I only thought that the same method could have been used to quieten the other victims—the ones who had their throats cut—and I wouldn't be surprised if I was right about that. But I never thought of hypnotism in connection with Geraldine until I saw the books on Father William's shelf. *Scientific Uses of Hypnosis.* That made me think."

"At this point," said Sir Nicholas, "I think I had better tell you what Mr. Webster said when I saw him today. I have his permission to do so."

"I wish you would, sir. I gather he got the wind up after he talked to me—"

"He did not put it quite like that. He said—I am not quoting him verbatim, of course—he said that he had begun to realize that something was radically wrong. He had always known that Keith was resentful of Jon in some way, but he had hidden it well enough until Kellaway's recent success."

"That was another thing," said Antony. "Lindsay was always protesting his belief in his cousin, but he made sure I knew he thought the alibi was a fake."

"Webster had the advantage over you when it came to Mrs. Lindsay, because he remembered Keith's interest in hypnotism when he was a student. Even so, he couldn't quite bring himself to believe what was happening. But the trend of your questions made him doubly anxious, and when he saw you looking at his bookshelves—"

"Why did he have Keith's books, sir?"

"Lindsay left them with him when he went to Penhaven, and never reclaimed them. But I was saying: after you left Mr. Webster on Friday he went round to see Keith and warned him . . . you must remember he did not know the full extent of what had been going on."

"He knew about Dakins, and Falkner, and he must have suspected that Keith had killed Bassett too."

"I think he tried to persuade himself that Falkner was responsible for the first two deaths, and if Lindsay went right away, somewhere where he was safe, he'd be out of temptation. But he did ask him about Mrs. Lindsay . . . this sounds a little melodramatic," Sir Nicholas added apologetically. "He asked him to 'set her free.' "

"And what did Keith have to say to that?"

"He told Mr. Webster for the first time why he had left the hospital in the middle of his medical studies. It is interesting, though not precisely relevant. It seems that his preoccupation with hypnotism was well known, and he had been warned of the dangers of what he was doing; but he went on experimenting with his fellow-students—you can imagine the fascination the subject had for a group of young men, he had no lack of volunteers—until one of them killed himself. I'm afraid neither Mr. Webster nor I know the correct scientific terms for what had happened . . . something to do with not removing satisfactorily a suggestion made in the hypnotic state. In short, the boy believed he had lost his ability to attract women; there is the delight in cruelty present even then, you see. And too many people knew Lindsay was responsible, there was no hushing it up, he had to leave the hospital. Mr. Webster said that when Lindsay told him this it was the first time he had realized the depth of his bitterness . . . as you said, Antony, against society. And it was when he thought this over that he decided that he might have been wrong to warn him, and he went round to Maddox Court to make sure Mrs. Lindsay was safe."

"He must have seen me sneaking down the alley," said Roger. "He caught up with me at the bottom of the fire-escape. There are three along the back of the building, you know; that's why we took such a time . . . I'd got it into my head it was the middle one, and he didn't know any better. But when we got up we found it led onto the landing, much farther on."

"Beth Kellaway killed herself," said Jenny suddenly.

"Yes, but I think she really did," Antony told her. "The letter she left just started 'My dearest' and everyone thought it was meant for Jon; but Keith admitted he'd been amusing himself with her, so I suppose it was his engagement to Geraldine that caused the trouble. But he kept the record of the coroner's remarks about Kellaway. Don't you think it was his character that made him choose that way of making money . . . paying the world back for what he thought it had done to him by—by subverting justice?"

"He worked as a crime reporter," Sir Nicholas reminded him. "That must have put him in touch with the kind of people—"

" 'Envy's a stronger spur than pay,' " said Antony stubbornly; but grinned and added, "I got that from John Gay too," when his uncle glared at him.

Meg had been thinking along her own lines. "But darling, they were all such silly things he did to Geraldine."

"Not really. As far as I understand it, hypnotism is easiest if there's a degree of rapport between the two people concerned, and I expect Geraldine was quite happy to co-operate in his experiments, especially when they were first married. And once she'd done so he'd got her where he wanted her . . . for good."

"I don't quite understand that," said Jenny.

"Well, it might take hours to hypnotize someone the first time—"

"Not invariably," said Sir Nicholas. "On the other hand, with some people it's altogether impossible."

"Yes, well after that . . . once you'd got them hypnotized . . . you could suggest to them that they'd go off again at a given signal, which makes everything easy, of course . . . for the hypnotist. You could also suggest . . . a certain course of action, for instance; at a signal, or even at a certain time—"

"The clock had just struck when she started screaming," said Roger in a pleased tone, as though the point had been worrying him.

"So it had. I expect it was the same thing that woke her up when she thought she hadn't taken her sleeping pills. I don't think he wanted to kill her . . . then; but he wanted to frighten and confuse her, and make her more and more dependent on him. Her confusion was very evident the first time she came to see me. There was this business of not being able to make up her mind, even about things she wanted to do; or changing it when she had succeeded in reaching a decision.

That must have bewildered her, and undermined her self-confidence to a quite fantastic extent. And if you think he didn't make good use of his power, Meg, you must remember he used it to give himself an alibi when Falkner was killed."

"Could he do that?"

"Nothing easier. He'd only to suggest to Geraldine that he'd been with her for at least half an hour."

Meg shivered. "I don't like the sound of that."

"There's something else," said Jenny suddenly. "Geraldine came here yesterday evening saying she wanted to see you, it was terribly important, she said. And then she jumped up—it was just seven o'clock—and said she had to go, even though I'd told her I was expecting you any minute. She was so strange . . . that's why I went with her. I didn't think she ought to be alone."

"Do you mean to tell me," Meg demanded, glaring at Antony as if he were in some way to blame, "that he could make her come to him, even from a distance?"

"Not exactly. But it certainly sounds as if—some time when they were together—he had implanted the idea that wherever she happened to be she should go home not later than seven o'clock."

"Do you think that makes it any better? I don't."

"And I never found out," said Jenny, following her own train of thought, "why she wanted to see you."

"Perhaps I can help you there," said Sir Nicholas. He looked at his nephew. "I went to see your friend *Señorita* Ana after I left Mr. Webster. She said Mrs. Lindsay was worried after you had left them, because she had told you a lie."

(For no reason at all he heard Ana's voice saying, "*Señor* Maitland would like to ask you, *querida*, if you gave Keith his way," and Geraldine's indignant denial.) "I can't think what it could have been," he said, and met his uncle's skeptical look with one unnaturally innocent.

"Yes, I thought there were a few reservations when you were talking to the police," Sir Nicholas observed.

"I hope you made my apologies to Ana," said Antony in a hurry.

"She was a little put out that you had allowed Lindsay to

bleed quite so freely on her carpet." Sir Nicholas smiled in a pensive way, and Antony met Jenny's eye and shrugged his shoulders expressively. "I think she forgave you, however. I—er—promised her my help in preparing a claim on her insurance company."

"But what will you say?" asked Meg.

"The exact truth. They may even believe it."

"Do you suppose," said Jenny, "that Geraldine will marry Jon now?"

"My dear child, that is surely out of our province." But after a moment he relented. "*Señorita* Ana is of the opinion that he should sweep her off her feet"—Jenny gave a little gurgle of laughter, quickly suppressed—"when Geoffrey has succeeded in removing Kellaway from the clutches of the police, of course, which I gather will not be until Monday; and when Mrs. Lindsay is out of the doctor's care. Why are you looking so prim, Meg?" he added, almost without a pause.

"Because she has a very good idea what Ana really said," Antony told him. "And while we're on the subject of your doings, Uncle Nick, I've always heard that Icelandic Airlines are comfortable, but why on earth didn't you come a quicker way?"

It was immediately obvious that the question had been a mistake. "When I was faced with the necessity of coming home in a hurry," said Sir Nicholas awfully, "it was impossible to get a seat on any of the more direct flights."

"But you stayed in Reykjavik overnight."

"Because I had been assured that it might be possible to proceed on the connecting flight, leaving there soon after midnight and arriving in Luxembourg at 6 a.m."

There was a silence while they all contemplated this frightful possibility. After a while Jenny said tentatively, "But there wasn't a cancellation?"

"There was not. The hotel," said Sir Nicholas, in a reminiscent tone which didn't deceive any of his hearers for a moment, "was extremely comfortable. The staff were obliging, not to say enthusiastic. If only I had come a little later in the year I could have been given a flight over a volcano, they said, and waved aside the suggestion that this might be, perhaps, foolhardy. At least I could have no objection to seeing a whale—er—dismembered . . . I forget the term they used. They appeared both hurt and incredulous when I assured them that I should find the sight distasteful. There were so many things, they said, to make a short delay worthwhile. And if you think it is in any way funny, Antony, I can assure you—"

It took Sir Nicholas precisely eleven minutes to make his point clear to them beyond any reasonable doubt.

THURSDAY, 1st APRIL

Mr. Watterson must recently have discovered Astroff's; he was coming out of the bar as they went in. "There you are, Maitland," he said, with too much enthusiasm; and Antony wondered with a sort of vague amusement how long it would be before any of his acquaintances who had studied the newspapers during the last two weeks would encounter him without embarrassment, or meet his eye without yielding to the temptation to let their own slide away uncertainly. Watterson, it seemed, had decided to focus on Meg . . . an entirely reasonable thing to do. "I have had the pleasure of seeing you here before with—ah—your charming wife," he said.

"Oh, I'm not *really* his wife," Meg told him artlessly. Antony, who was feeling at peace with the world, found himself quite unable to resist the look of determined tolerance that the solicitor immediately assumed. He said awkwardly:

"Well, that's how it is," and tugged at his collar.

"He already has one wife, you see," said Meg, going one better. Obviously Mr. Watterson was not a theater-goer; he didn't recognize the look of starry-eyed and uncritical devotion which Margaret Hamilton was directing at her escort.

"Don't you think you've said enough?" said Antony, in a vicious but audible aside.

"And I must say, he's much kinder to her than he is to me," Meg went on, wilting gracefully.

"Yes, I see." Mr. Watterson seemed to be losing all grip on the situation. "Yes, indeed." He turned with an air of relief as a waiter came up, and asked sharply, "Well? What is it?"

"A message, sir, for Mr. Maitland. Mrs. Maitland asked me to tell you, sir, that you'd find her in the dining-room."

"Thank you." He took Meg's arm. "Come along, *darling.* Why not join us, Watterson, if you haven't lunched yet?"

Mr. Watterson murmured something about sandwiches in the office, and made his escape.

"It's just as well he didn't take you at your word," said Meg as they crossed the dining-room. "Because when you see Jenny closely she still looks a bit battered, poor darling, and he'd have been bound to think—"

"That's just about enough from you. Your wife," he added, as Roger got up and pulled out a chair for Meg, "has just been convincing one of the more respectable of my solicitor clients that *she* is a fallen woman and *I* maintain a *ménage à trois.*"

"You needn't be so cross," Meg protested. "You taught me to do that."

"I did . . . what?"

"You taught me to tell the *exact* truth so that it seems to mean something quite different. You did, you know." He regarded her speechlessly for a moment. "*And* you played up to me so that the poor man didn't know what to think."

"And then Jenny's message came." He turned to look at her—as he had found himself doing rather frequently in the last few days—and saw the shadowy bruises round her mouth that the powder couldn't quite conceal. His own lips tightened momentarily, but then he saw also that she had again her serene look, and was content. "I *wish* you could have seen his face, love," he told her.